I0674043

THE CRUISE

LISE GOLD

suddenly realized she was half naked, and closed her robe, looking for something to tie it with.

"Here, take this," the girl said, tugging at the scarf around her neck.

Cara shook her head, knowing she would have to give it back, and that meant having another conversation with the strange creature in the doorway. *Who on earth still wears scarves these days?* "It's okay; I'll find something."

"Alright. Well, sorry for the intrusion." She waved awkwardly and closed the door, leaving Cara with the pounding noise of the drill. *I wonder where Dan picked her up.* It had been a while since her best friend had brought a woman home, and this particular one was an unusual choice.

Cara searched her drawers, but the tie for her robe seemed to have disappeared into thin air, so she tied a long-sleeved T-shirt around it, and went in search of coffee. The mystery girl turned around when Cara entered the kitchen, desperately trying to ignore her.

"Here, let me make you a nice, strong cup of tea. You look like you could use one," she said happily, stirring two cups of tea and reaching for another mug. "I'm Billie by the way. And you must be Cara, Dan's friend?"

Her enthusiasm bordered on mania and Cara winced at the sound of the spoon, scraping against the bottom of the mug. She nodded. "Yep. That's me. But I'll pass on the tea. I need coffee in the morning." Cara regarded the girl through sleepy eyes and suddenly felt self-conscious about the state she was in. Billie didn't look like a Billie. She looked more like a Marjory or a Bettina. Billie's cotton vintage floral skirt and her yellow twinset were crisp and clean and gave the impression that she loved to indulge in household chores. Her eyes were big and blue, and her long, blonde hair was immaculately straightened, like a golden helmet. Cara imagined she could take it off any time when in need of a party trick. Billie was petite but carried herself with confidence, and that made her look taller than she really was.

Cara looked down at her unshaven legs and pulled her robe over her knees in an attempt to cover them. She hadn't had a shower in three days. Her black bob and fringe were tangled and greasy. Although she hadn't looked in the mirror for a while, she guessed her skin would be a greyish kind of pale, the shade that junkies often carry. Billie didn't seem to mind. She smiled and handed her a coffee.

"Milk and sugar are on the table. But you know that of course."

"Thanks." Cara accepted the coffee and sat down at the table, staring at the milk and sugar until she remembered that she drank her morning coffee black. "I don't think I've seen you here before. Have you known Dan for long?"

Billie shook her head and took a seat opposite Cara. "Not long. We only met last month. I've never been here before, though. It's..."

Cara could see her searching for words to describe the apartment without sounding judgmental. "No need to be polite," she interrupted her. "It's a mess. We'll get to it at some point, just not today." There was an awkward silence, but Cara had no intention of filling it. If Billie felt the need to invade her personal space and make conversation, it was up to her.

Billie pointed at the second cup of tea in front of her. "Dan likes his tea in bed, but I bet you know that too."

Cara lit a cigarette from Dan's pack next to the flowerpot that functioned as an ashtray and shot Billie a curious look. "No offense, but you don't seem like Dan's type. Or maybe Dan doesn't seem like your type; it's too early in the day for me to think straight. I mean, he's a mess. Like me, basically. But you..." She gave Billie another good glance-over. "You seem very well put together. You take care of yourself, and you're well-spoken, not to mention the fact that you're wide awake and dressed."

"Well, I have a lot to do today," Billie said matter-of-factly. "My sister's pregnant, and I've promised to go shopping with her. We're decorating the nursery this weekend. And as far as Dan's concerned, I just happen to like him. He's mysterious and artistic and funny, very different from other people I've dated. Other than that, I haven't given it much thought." She tilted her head in Cara's direction. "And you? Any plans for today?"

Cara raised an eyebrow, blowing smoke out in Billie's face. She deserved it for being perfect and asking all the wrong questions. "Me? Nothing. My plan was to sleep all day until those fuckers woke me up." She pointed in the direction of the neighbours and stood up, stubbing out her cigarette. "But I'm still going to try. See you later, Billie."

2

"Cara?" Dan sounded like he'd had a rough night.

"Yeah?" Cara called back from her own bedroom.

"I'm hungry." There was a pause. "Any chance you could put a pizza in the oven for me?"

Cara sighed and got up. She walked into Dan's room, grimacing at the smell, and sat down next to him on the edge of the bed. Dan was lying on top of the bedsheets in his boxers. He had an iPad in one hand, and a cigarette in the other. His dark hair was tied in a bun on top of his head with one of Cara's scrunchies. The beard that urgently needed a trim almost reached his Adam's apple now.

"Gross, Dan. You really need to open your window from time to time. No wonder that chick left so early."

Dan laughed. "Who? Billie?"

"Yeah of course I mean Billie, who else was in your room last night? The one who looks like a Stepford wife. You know. Billie Billie, cheerful and silly. Her floral frock all nice and frilly." She gave him a teasing smile. "And she likes

Dan's tiny willy. Even smaller when it's chilly." Dan pushed her off the bed, and Cara landed on his pile of dirty laundry.

"You're just jealous cause she's gorgeous," he said, laughing. "And the dress can come off so don't you worry about that. There's a banging body underneath it." He picked up a leaflet from the floor and handed it to Cara. "Are you coming to my performance next week?"

Cara stood up and shook her head with a grin. "Not if I can help it."

"Oh, come on. It's not like you have plans." Dan rolled his eyes. "I need at least two people in the audience, or I won't be able to class it as a performance."

"How do you know I don't have plans?" Cara cocked her head, ready to go into defence mode. She knew Dan was right, but it still hurt to hear what a total loser she was. She hadn't met up with friends or old colleagues since she'd moved in with him.

"Don't get upset, Cara. I need to say this, and I need you to listen to me." Dan tried to poke her, but Cara took a step back. "You can't keep lying in that bed forever, feeling sorry for yourself. I'm worried about you." His expression was serious now, a rare occurrence for the always cheerful Dan. "I don't think you're well. Maybe you should see a doctor. Have you considered you might be suffering from depression?"

Cara shot him an annoyed glance. "Depression? Have you lost your mind? What, so you think it's okay to diagnose me because I'm having a bad time? I've had four job rejections this week, Dan. Four. And you have no idea what that feels like because you've never applied for a job in your life."

Dan frowned at Cara's sudden hostility. "But Cara, you sleep all day. You never want to go anywhere or do anything these days, and it's getting worse. When was the last time you went outside? Huh? And when was the last time you spoke to someone other than me?"

Cara rolled her eyes and shook her head. "Mind your own damn business," she sneered, marching back to her room.

The truth was, maybe she was depressed. But then maybe she wasn't. Who cared? It wasn't like a diagnosis was going to change her situation. She had been out of a job for almost a year now after she'd been made redundant in a restructure at The Times. Cara had been the last one to join the team, and the first one to be let go. She had tried so hard to get interviews for jobs in journalism, but no one was hiring. If only she could get her foot in the door somewhere, she'd be alright. In her desperation, she'd even sent open application letters to an old-timer car magazine, an online magazine for cheese enthusiasts and an international blog for new mums, but nothing had paid off. After three months, her hopes had started to recede, and shortly after, her girlfriend of two years had left her, complaining that Cara was too miserable to be around. Within another three months, Cara had made the difficult decision to move out of her Notting Hill apartment, because she couldn't afford the rent anymore.

It had been a terrible year, to say the least. That had left her with only one option, to move in with Dan, her best friend. His apartment was by far the smallest and ugliest she had ever seen. The neighbourhood was questionable and the location far from ideal, but the rent was low, and she could probably stretch her savings for another two to three months. After that, she would have to accept whatever job the agencies could offer her. The gap in her CV would grow bigger and bigger, and eventually, she'd be a lost cause, working in a pub until she retired.

Asking her parents for help wasn't an option either. As far as they were aware, Cara was still working for The Times, and besides, moving back in with either of them was at the very top of her not-to-do list before she died. She was grateful to Dan for taking her in, but she didn't like being out of options. It wasn't the first time she had taken her frustration out on him, and she knew it wouldn't be the last.

There was knocking on Cara's door, hard and persistent. Cara shook her head when the corners of her mouth tugged upwards. She tried to keep a straight face but burst into laughter when Dan let himself in.

"Don't mind me; I just need a poo." He had a toilet roll in one hand and a magazine in the other.

It was a terrible joke, but it always worked on her. Cara had sprayed the message on her door after Dan's one-night stands kept walking into her room, thinking it was the bathroom. There was something about the door itself, that reminded people of bathroom doors. It had a tiny frosted glass window at the top, and the fact that it was located at the end of the landing, like most bathrooms, didn't help either.

"Go away." She threw a magazine at him, but he sat down anyway.

"Listen, I don't care if you're angry with me. We're going to finish this conversation. Understood?" Despite her annoyance, Cara was touched by his concern, so she nodded.

"You need to do something Cara, anything. Just stop lying here, wallowing in your own misery. I can't stand looking at you, being so down."

Cara sniffed. "As if you're so busy making a life for yourself."

"I'm an artist," Dan said defensively. "I live for the art. I'm supposed to suffer; you're not." He crossed his arms over his chest in a dramatic manner. "At least I have something to live for. And you need to find something too; whatever that may be."

Cara's eyes widened. "Dan, you can't call yourself an artist. Last week you made a nest out of dirty socks, and you slept in it while filming yourself. Nobody came to watch it. Not even your so-called friends," she said, making air quotes.

Dan frowned. "That's mean. At least I'm working towards the bigger picture here. I'm doing something that makes me happy." He put a hand on her knee. "Look, you wanted to go into journalism because you love to tell a story, right?" Cara nodded. "Well, what's stopping you then? Write. Tell a story. Write depressing poetry and perform in the local library. Start a blog and write about how it feels to be jobless and to do nothing."

"I'm not you, Dan. I can't just switch myself on whenever I feel like it." Cara sighed. "I hate poetry, and as far as writing is concerned, I don't have a story to tell."

Dan threw his hands in the air. "I give up. You are officially the most miserable person I know. Now please get out of bed and start looking for a job before I find you one. They're recruiting at the pub around the corner; I saw a notice in the window."

"The one where the chef got shot last month?" Cara cast him a sceptical look.

"Well he did have it coming, but I see your point." Dan grinned. "Okay, maybe that wasn't the best idea, but it's not the only option. Let me just throw out a wild card here." He produced jazz hands to build up the tension towards his next brilliant idea. "Why don't you talk to Billie? She works on a cruise ship for six months a year, and I think the season is starting in a couple of weeks. They might need staff."

"Billie works on a cruise ship?" Cara laughed. "I'm not sure I believe that. What does she do?"

"Don't be so judgmental." Dan shot her a warning look. "She's a nice girl. I like her." He paused. "I'm not sure what she does. I think she works in entertainment or something."

"Did she not tell you what she does for a living?" Cara let herself fall back into her pillow and stared at the ceiling.

"Of course, she told me," Dan said. "I just can't remember what it was." He raised an eyebrow. "What? Am I supposed to remember everything a girl tells me? Is that what you do? Keep notes? Because I haven't noticed you being very successful with the ladies lately."

Cara hit him playfully on the head. "That's not fair either, asshole." She sighed. "I'm not saying you should store everything she tells you on your tiny little hard drive up there." She pointed at his head. "But the basics might be useful. Like what she does for a living, where she lives. Stuff like that. Do you know she has a sister who is about to have a baby?"

Dan closed one eye as if digging into his recent memory. "She might have told me, but it doesn't ring a bell." He crossed his skinny arms over his chest. "But hey, she likes me for the artist in me, not my listening skills." They both laughed. "Listen. Billie is coming over on Friday night. Why don't you cook for us and we'll have dinner together? You two can get to know each other better, and maybe she could hook you up with a job?"

Cara shrugged. "Okay," she said, surprising herself. "I have no interest in a job, but I suppose I could clear an hour of my busy schedule to cook for you guys. But only if you promise to clean the kitchen and the balcony. It will be dry this week so we can eat outside while we enjoy the magnificent view of the council flats and the building site."

Dan smiled in surprise. "Did you just agree to cook for us? Holy shit." He jumped out of bed and pulled up his tracksuit bottoms, hanging low on his hips. "I'd better start cleaning before you change your mind."

3

"How are you feeling, Helen?" Billie looked down at her younger sister, who was resting on the couch, exhausted from their short shopping trip. Helen had two pillows propped underneath her feet and three behind her back. She looked tired, stroking her enormous baby bump.

"Oh, God, Billie. I don't understand how people can love being pregnant. I feel like I'm dragging two weeks' worth of groceries around with me everywhere I go. I can't walk for longer than half an hour; you saw me at the store today. On top of everything, I look like a whale." She pointed at her ankles. "Look at me. Are those the ankles of a twenty-five-year-old?"

"You don't look like a whale." Billie rooted through her bag and handed her sister a box of chocolates. "Hang in there, Helen. Just eight more weeks to go. It will all be worth it once you're holding the little one in your arms." She sighed. "I wish the timing was better. I won't be here when you give birth, or when she opens her eyes for the first time."

Helen arched an eyebrow. "I don't get why you still work

on that ship. It's been what, almost ten years? Shouldn't you be looking for something more permanent by now? I mean, what kind of life do you have when you're never here long enough to make a home for yourself? And what does that guy think of it? The one you've been seeing?"

"Dan?" Billie laughed. "Dan's not exactly the traditional type, and that suits me just fine. He's not looking to settle down, and neither am I. Besides, we only met a month ago. We're just having a bit of fun while we're both still here. And as for making a home..." She sat down next to Helen on the couch, readjusting the pillows under her feet. "Sure, I know I should probably be buying a house by now. But it would just be an investment. The ship is my home."

"Right." Helen rolled her eyes. "I'm sorry, I sound like a granny. I forget my age sometimes, what with the prospect of having a baby in the near future." She opened the box of chocolates and held it out for Billie.

Billie shook her head. "No, thanks. I'll be in my swimsuit, giving classes soon, and Mum's cooking has almost doubled me in size." She looked around the living room. Boxes were stacked along the back wall, next to carpet samples and paint buckets. The wall behind the TV was stained with different colours of paint. "Have you decided what colour you want in here?"

Helen shrugged. "Don't know," she mumbled through a mouthful of chocolate. "I can't decide on anything nowadays. What do you think?"

Billie frowned and took a step back. She pointed at the square foot of teal. "That one. Just for the feature wall, then do the rest in white. It'll look good with your couch and your dining chairs." She smiled at her sister and picked up a paintbrush. "In fact, let me do this for you now. It will be one less thing for you to worry about. I'll put together the furniture for the baby's room tomorrow."

Helen held up a hand. "No, Billie. I can't let you do that. I'm happy for you to help me with the nursery, but the living room is a lot of work. I'll hire someone to do it next weekend."

Billie shook her head. "Don't waste money, Helen. You're going to need it for nappies soon. And I'm not doing anything at the moment, so I might as well make myself useful while I can."

4

"Right. What have we got here?" Cara rearranged her groceries on the kitchen counter and glanced over the clean surface. "Good job, Dan." He had even scrubbed the hob, which turned out to be silver rather than black. She picked up one of the asparagus and snapped it. It was the perfect sound of great produce. She hadn't really thought about what she was going to cook, but that was how she liked it. Improvising. Cara was grateful for the local market. It was cheap and just around the corner, so leaving the house for the first time in a week hadn't been that daunting.

She rummaged through the drawers looking for a knife when it suddenly dawned on her that she hadn't used the kitchen for anything other than making coffee since the day she moved in, and she didn't have a clue where anything was. Dan didn't have the best set of supplies, but she managed to find a chopping board, a blender, two pans, a roasting tin, a brand-new set of knives and a box of unopened bags of spices, which she guessed Dan's mother must have donated. She chose the biggest knife and weighed it in her hand. It felt good, and she even felt a tiny sparkle of excitement at the prospect of cooking for people again. Even if it was just for Dan and his weird little Miss Perfect. *I'll show you perfect.*

The tomatoes were large and ripe, and the bunch of fresh herbs smelt delicious. Cara checked her phone. She still had four hours, all the time in the world. First things first, though. She opened the windows, put on her favourite playlist, and poured herself a glass of Chablis from the fridge. Instead of downing it in one go the way she'd been doing lately, she took a sip and savoured the crisp freshness of the wine before getting to work with her ingredients.

She couldn't remember the last time she had felt this close to calm. There was something about cooking that always put her in a better mood. She started by roasting the pumpkin before putting it in the blender with vegetable stock, black pepper, and cream. There was also a small piece of bacon left in the fridge, which she chopped into cubes. She pan-fried them until they were crispy and golden and set them aside for later. Soup as a starter was always a good choice. Who didn't like soup, right? Then she chopped the asparagus into thirds, zested two lemons and squeezed out the juice. She mixed it with sour cream and garlic, ready to add to her linguine, grilled asparagus and a handful of broad beans later.

Cara rooted through the rest of her groceries and realized she didn't have anything for dessert. She inspected the cupboards, the fridge, and the freezer but there was nothing to use, apart from some out of date custard. Thankfully, she hadn't been able to resist the fruit in one of the market stalls, which was a rare occurrence. *My body must have craved vitamins.* She unpacked the last paper bag. There was a pineapple, a mango, a box of strawberries, a bunch of mint and some kiwi fruit. A nice mix of colour. She smiled as she took a seat at the kitchen table with the smallest carving knife.

C ara was just getting dressed in the bathroom when she heard the front door open.

"Cara, are you home? You're not in bed, are you? I don't smell any takeaway."

Cara laughed at Dan's mocking tone and checked herself in the mirror. She looked decent after her shower. Her dark hair had been blow-dried and styled as her hairdresser had intended the cut to look. The straight fringe and bob framed her heart-shaped face, making her dark brown eyes look bigger. She had a beauty mark underneath her left eye, just like her mother. Other than that, she looked nothing like her. Cara had her father's slender figure, pale skin, and a broad smile, although she hadn't graced people with it much lately. She forced the corners of her mouth upwards, studying the wrinkles that appeared around her eyes. Apart from the tiny crow's feet, she liked what she saw.

It had been a while since she had gone through the trouble of taking care of herself, and the feeling of accomplishment was surprisingly uplifting. She rolled up the sleeves of the black sweater she had found in one of her suitcases, with the price tag still on it. Her favourite pair of jeans completed her casual look, which was supposed to say: 'Hey, I've got this. No big deal, I cook for people every day.'

"I'll be right down, make yourselves comfortable on the balcony." She gave herself one more glance-over and ran down the stairs to see Dan's surprised gaze, going over her preparations in the kitchen.

"You're actually cooking," he said. "I didn't know you could cook."

"Dan, come and have a look out here, it's lovely," Billie shouted at him from the balcony.

Cara had found fairy lights in a box with old Christmas decorations and filled some empty jars with candles. She had used a clean white bedsheet as a tablecloth, and there were fresh orange roses in the middle of the table, next to a small bowl of black olives and a plate of tomato, garlic and basil crostini. The two heaters, attached to either end of the balustrade, were on full blast, creating a cosy atmosphere. Cara's eyes met Billie's as she followed Dan outside.

"Wow, Cara, you look so... different," Billie said. "I mean, you look nice. Really nice."

"Thank you, Billie." Cara shot Dan a cocky look. "Please sit down and help yourself to a nibble. Wine?" She held up a bottle of cold white wine.

"Oh, yes, please." Billie nodded in delight. "And thank you so much for cooking. These crostini are to die for," she mumbled, wiping olive oil from her chin. "How did you get so much flavour in here?"

"They're good quality ingredients." Cara smiled, filling up their wine glasses. "And great olive oil. That makes all the difference." She turned to Dan. "Don't you dare fry your eggs in that oil, by the way. Now, would you both care for a bowl of homemade pumpkin soup with bacon and fresh pesto?"

Dan ate his soup as if it was his last meal. "The finesse," he said, putting on a posh English accent. "It's so delicate, so smooth. Why do you never cook for me like this?" He held up an index finger. "Wait, let me rephrase that. Why do you never cook?"

Cara shook her head and shrugged. "I used to cook a lot.

Millie and I hosted dinners at least once a week when we were living together." She sighed. "But lately, I haven't felt like doing anything at all. I'm glad I did today, though. It got me out of bed." She chuckled. "At least for now."

Dan grinned. "It's good to see you up and dressed. You know I love you babe, and I hate seeing you miserable."

He turned to Billie. "Cara here is looking for a job." Dan ignored his best friend's foot, kicking him under the table. "I thought there might be some vacancies on the cruise ship."

Billie smiled and raised an eyebrow, turning to Cara. "Really? They're always looking for staff. What type of job are you after?"

"I'm not looking for a job," Cara said. "I mean, I am, but not on a cruise ship." She took a sip of her wine. "I'm a journalist."

"No, you're not," Dan teased. "You're a full-time sleeper. That's what you are."

Billie ignored him. "That's impressive, Cara. What type of journalism? News? Gossip? Travel?"

"Current affairs," Cara said. "But Dan is right. I haven't been able to find a job in a year."

Billie nodded. "Journalism must be a hard field to be in right now. What with all the papers closing down and everything going online." She closed her eyes at the taste of the soup. "Mmm... this is so incredibly good."

"It is." Cara laughed. "I mean, I was referring to finding a job, not my soup. Applying for jobs has become discouraging, and I'm scared I'll never get back into it again if I don't find anything soon."

Billie broke off a piece of bread and dipped it in her soup. "Why not try another line of work in the meantime though? You could still apply for jobs in journalism while you're doing something else?"

"I know." Cara sighed. "It looks like that's what I might have to do if I don't find something in the coming two months."

Dan nudged her. "Then let Billie check for vacancies. It might be fun to get out of that room and see something of the world, right?"

"I don't know." Cara didn't like asking people for help, and she wasn't entirely comfortable with the situation. "What is it that you do, Billie? Dan told me you were in entertainment?"

"Something like that," Billie grinned. "I'm the head of the animation team."

Cara laughed, causing the soup in her mouth to go straight up her nose. She coughed and recovered. "You mean you're one of those annoyingly happy people who try to get adults to dance in a circle like a bunch of monkeys, or do aqua aerobics and shit like that?" She shook her head when she saw Billie's expression go cold. "I'm so sorry, it just came out. I didn't mean to offend you. It's just that, I went on an all-inclusive holiday with my ex-girlfriend once, and they had this animation team and they..."

Billie cracked up with laughter. "I'm just messing with you, Cara. Yes, I'm one of those annoying people, and yes, we have a lot of haters. But guess what? I don't care because most people love it. They leave reviews saying that our team made their holiday fun and that they met friends for life through our silly group activities." She held up a hand. "Okay, it's not for everyone, and I certainly wouldn't hire you as an animator after your reaction, but cruise life can be fun. We're like a family. There are about ninety people that come back each year. The other two-hundred-and-fifty are just looking for a seasonal job, and this is perfect for them because they don't have to commit to more than six months.

We work long days but every now and then, we get to go to amazing places, and we get to experience that together."

Cara thought about it. "Okay, so you get to see something of the world. That doesn't sound too bad." She gathered the bowls and spoons and kept talking through the kitchen window while she drained the pasta and dropped the other ingredients into a pan with butter and olive oil. "So what's the route? Where do you go?" Cara shouted over the noise of the extractor fan.

Billie followed her and started washing the soup bowls while she was working on their next course. "We go everywhere. Africa, South Africa, Australia, Asia... you name it. But most days are at sea, and that's when our guests need to be entertained, as you can probably imagine. A sunset over the ocean can be breathtaking, but it won't impress you forever. People get bored."

Cara handed her a tea towel. She hadn't expected to enjoy Billie's company, but now she was happy with her presence. It was refreshing to talk to someone other than Dan, for once.

"So?" Dan shouted from the balcony. "Will you think about it, Cara? You have to try at least. Imagine all those rich housewives in their bikinis, lounging by the pool, bored with their husbands and looking for a hot cleaning lady to keep them occupied."

Billie giggled. "Why do you assume she'll be a cleaning lady, Dan? It doesn't seem to me that either of you are talented on that front." She lifted her foot up and down, demonstrating the stickiness of the floor.

Cara grimaced, appalled by the sound it made. "Gross. I guess Dan forgot to clean the floor, and I'm so used to it that I haven't even noticed." She laughed. "Let's go outside; the balcony seems to be the cleanest place around here." She mixed the pasta into the sauce, scooped it onto three plates and carried them out to the table.

"Tell me about the two of you," Cara said after they sat back down. She turned to Dan. "Aren't you going to miss Billie when she's away for six months?"

Dan shrugged. "Of course I will. But we haven't known each other for very long, so we shouldn't make a big drama out of it."

"Exactly," Billie backed him up. "Whatever happens, happens. We haven't had the time or the chance to find out if we'd work together. But we'll keep in contact and who knows?" She smiled sweetly at Dan and he blushed like a teenage boy.

Cara nodded, looking from Dan to Billie and back. The two of them together confused her. Dan was dressed in a pair of old jeans and a sweatshirt with holes in the right sleeve. It was clear he hadn't gone to any trouble whatsoever to impress Billie. She, on the other hand, was wearing a black pleated dress with a white blouse underneath, buttoned all the way up to her neck. The pearl necklace matched her earrings, and her hair was pulled back into a ponytail. A hint of lip gloss highlighted her peachy full lips. Billie's skin looked immaculate. She had a natural glow on her cheeks and bright, blue eyes that were stunning in the dim light of the candles. Cara watched Billie put a hand on Dan's knee and decided that their relationship was beyond her brainpower.

"So, did you always want to work in entertainment, Billie?" she asked, trying to keep the conversation going. "Please don't be offended, but when Dan told me you worked on a cruise ship, I was surprised. I kind of took you for a preschool teacher."

Billie laughed. "Spot on, Cara." She slammed her hand

on the table. "I am a qualified preschool teacher. I don't know if I should be offended now. Or maybe I should be ashamed of myself for confirming the stereotype."

"No!" Cara tried to wrangle her way out of her second faux pas of the night. "You don't. I mean, you look lovely. Trustworthy." She rolled her eyes. "Fuck. This isn't going well for me, is it?" They all laughed. "What I mean is, if I were a parent, I would trust you with my kid."

Billie sighed. "Well thank you, I guess. That's nice to hear. I've never worked as a teacher though. I didn't want to give up my job on the ship. My family think I'm crazy. They don't understand how I can live like this, always away at sea. They've tried everything to keep me here permanently. My father even offered to pay the deposit if I buy a house."

"Maybe they just want to keep you close," Cara said, topping up their wine. "Nothing wrong with parents wanting to have their children around, right?"

Billie shook her head. "If only that were true." She chuckled. "Don't get me wrong; I love my parents. But they're both teachers, and they would love nothing more than for me to do the same. Nine to five job, a house, a husband and a couple of kids... They keep bugging me about starting a life, as if I'm not living right now."

Cara regarded Billie with interest as she spoke. "Expectations can be brutal, especially around our age," she said. "I admire you for doing what you love, and I'm sure your parents will understand one day. Have they ever considered doing a cruise holiday on your ship, to get a better understanding of what you do?"

Billie laughed. "Not in a million years, that's way out of their comfort zone. No, my parents have a cottage in Cornwall, and that's as far as they'll ever go. Believe me; they're not the adventurous kind." She stood up to gather their empty plates, but Cara gestured for her to sit back down and said:

"Please, relax. I'll take care of the rest of the dishes tomorrow. Let me go and get the dessert; I'll be back in no time." She giggled as she took the tin foil off the fruit tray from the fridge, before putting it down in the middle of the table, alongside a pile of napkins and three forks.

"What?" Dan stared at the display.

There were two figures carved out of fruit, assembled between mango flowers and mint leaves. They clearly resembled Billie and Dan, and Cara was pretty pleased with how they had turned out. "I look like Jesus," Dan laughed. He pointed at the man with the long hair, who was handing a rose to the girl next to him.

Billie chuckled. "And I look like Dolly Parton. Why did you make my boobs so big?"

Cara looked down at Billie's chest. "Well... they're not small, are they?" She could have sworn Billie was blushing.

"I think you've got the size about right," Dan joked. He picked up his own fruit face and examined it. "You've got some seriously good knife skills, Cara. Where did you learn this?"

"He's right," Billie said, picking at the heart-shaped strawberries. "Joking aside, you've got talent." She smiled. "You know what? I think I might know just the right job for you."

5

"Ready for your boyfriend's big performance?" Cara nudged Billie, who was trying her hardest not to laugh.

Dan was standing centre stage; his eyes closed in utmost concentration. Over his briefs, he was covered with a layer of white clay that was starting to crack at his joints and on his face. Cara was thankful that he had bothered to cover up his private parts. The turnout was unsurprisingly low, but that didn't seem to bother Dan. It wasn't about the audience after all. It was about the art. He knelt down and crawled over the stage, like he was looking for something, sniffing the wooden floorboards like a dog. Now and then, he would look out over the audience.

"I seek the truth, but you keep feeding me lies," he said in a confident tone. There was no music, and the twelve people around the stage, including his mother and one of her friends, exchanged confused looks.

"I'm not sure if I'll ever be ready for this," Billie whispered.

Dan stuck his finger down one of the holes in the floor

and pulled out a piece of red ribbon that he tied around his ankle. "I am a man," he announced, gazing at the people in front of the stage. "But soon I'll be no more." He stood up and started spinning around in circles, winding the ribbon around both his legs, tying them together.

He paused for a moment to look at his mother. "Mother." And then at Billie and Cara. "Lover. Friend." He continued spinning until the ribbon was near its end. "Because you have made me into your slave and I will die by your feet, cracked like a broken pot."

"Oh God, I think I know where this is going. I can't watch it," Cara whispered. "It's ridiculous, he's going to hurt himself."

The ribbon was attached to something underneath the floorboards, and it was now wound tight around Dan's ankles. He jumped and fell flat on his face with his feet together. The clay was spread out over the floor like dust, and although he must have been in pain, Dan didn't move.

His mother shrieked and rushed over with her friend. "Dannyboy, say something. Are you okay?" They had climbed onto the stage and were now leaning over him. "Goodness, Cara. Don't just stand there. Come and help us turn him over."

Cara and Billie climbed onto the stage too and rolled him on his back. Dan was conscious, but his eyes were teary, and his face was covered in blood. It was seeping out of his nose, soaking into the chunks of clay that were still stuck to his neck.

"I'm okay," he whispered. "Get off the stage, mum. I'm not finished yet."

But it was too late. The audience was making its way towards the exit, seemingly relieved that it was over. Only two men of his own age had the courage to pass the stage on their way out, and Cara heard them whisper something about art and sacrifice.

"Stay still, Dan," Cara said, as he lay prone on his bed, back at the apartment. "I can't help you if you keep moving your head."

"But you're hurting me," Dan said in a nasal voice.

Cara dipped a tea towel in hot water and started cleaning Dan's face. The clay had dried again, after being soaked in blood, and she carefully removed it, chunk by chunk. "Stop complaining. You did this to yourself. Now lift your head so I can clean your neck."

Dan grimaced when Cara ran a brush through his beard. "This won't work, it's all stuck." Cara sighed. "You'll have to have a shower."

"I can't stand up. My head hurts." Dan brought his hand to his swollen face and carefully poked the skin around his nose.

"Then take those painkillers and try to get some sleep. You can have a shower when you wake up." She gestured towards the glass of water and the box of paracetamol on his nightstand.

"How is he?" Billie poked her head around the door. "I'm sorry I ran off, I'm not very good with blood." She stared at Dan's face, her eyes wide. "His face is going black. Are you sure we shouldn't call an ambulance?"

Cara shrugged. "He's refusing to see a doctor. He can be so stubborn sometimes. One time he..."

"Hey, stop talking about me like I'm not in the room," Dan interrupted her. "I'm not dying; I've just broken my nose, that's all." He groaned. "Just leave me alone, please. My head hurts so badly, I can't even speak."

"Fine then." Cara stood up and closed the curtains on the window above his bed. "We'll go downstairs. But I'm going to wake you up every half hour, just in case you have a concussion."

Billie followed her into the kitchen with a bottle of wine in her hand. "I went to the night shop," she said. "Thought we could both use a drink after what happened today. Plus, we might have something to celebrate."

Cara shot Billie a curious look as she produced two glasses from the cupboard. "Wine sounds good. But what's there to celebrate? That Dan broke his nose?"

Billie laughed. "No, not that. I asked around for you. For the kitchen job we talked about, remember?" Cara nodded, suddenly feeling nervous. "Well, it turns out they're in desperate need of a fruit carver. The job is yours if you want it. You'll have to do a food hygiene course and some basic health and safety training before you go, but it's only a couple of days."

"Really?" Cara took a minute to process the information as she poured the wine. The prospect of six months away from her life seemed enticing, especially now that she was getting closer to her credit limit. "Thank you, Billie. I didn't think you'd actually go to the trouble of enquiring for me, that's…"

"No need to thank me," Billie said. "It wasn't any trouble at all." She grinned. "I did lie and tell them you had restaurant experience, so we'll have to get our stories straight before we go." She held up her glass. "Cheers to your first season at sea."

6

'*Welcome to Southampton.*' The sign seemed daunting when they passed it. Cara took a sip of her coffee and looked at Dan, who was driving. He was humming along to the music and seemed perfectly happy with both his girlfriend and his best friend leaving him. His nose was still covered by a bandage, but the worst of the swelling had gone down after he'd finally been to the doctor, who had to break it again in order to fix his breathing problems.

The dunes of the coastline came in sight. It was getting real now. Cara could smell the sea and opened the window further to soak up the fresh air, even though the early morning breeze was cold. Billie was in the back, doing some paperwork in preparation for her new starters. She looked up to meet Cara's eyes in the rear-view mirror.

"No turning back now," Billie said as if she could read her thoughts.

Cara sighed. "A couple of weeks ago, this just seemed like a fun idea. Now I'm saying goodbye to the mainland for six months, and I don't even know if I'll get seasick. I've never been on a ship before, and if I hate it, I won't be able to get off." She laughed nervously. "Why do I feel like I'm going to prison?"

Dan slowed down as they came across a long queue of catering trucks, but steered around them when Billie directed him towards the crew entrance.

"Don't be nervous." Billie leaned forward and placed a hand on Cara's shoulder. "You're going to love it."

"I guess this is it," Dan said as he stopped the car, pointing at the customs sign.

Cara got out and looked up at the ship that was towering above her like a giant monster, swallowing the trucks with its gaping mouth. "It's huge."

The clean body was white, with blue accents. The ship's name, 'Pelican', was written on the side in an ornamental script. There were at least a hundred people at the staff entrance, waiting to go through customs. Most of them were saying goodbye to family and loved ones before disappearing through the gates.

Dan unloaded their cases and turned to Billie. Suddenly, he didn't look so at ease anymore. "I'll call you," he said, taking Billie into his arms.

Billie shot him a reassuring smile. "I'll answer. Promise."

Cara looked the other way until they had said their goodbyes. Then she gave Dan a long hug, swallowing her tears. She hated seeing him vulnerable. It didn't happen very often, and she was surprised he was letting his guard down today. She sniffed. "Sorry, this is stupid. I didn't mean to get all emotional. I'm going to miss you, Dan."

He smiled. "Stop sobbing. You'll make me cry, and my nose hurts enough as it is." He laughed off their emotional exchange. "Seriously, I'm going to miss you too, Cara. But I'm also looking forward to turning your bedroom into a microbrewery, so don't worry about me, okay? There will be plenty of beer when you get back." He hesitated before he got back in the car. "And Cara?"

Cara turned. "Yes?"

"Take care of Billie, will you?" Cara nodded and smiled, as she dragged her suitcase towards passport control.

7

Cara followed Billie into their cabin. It was simple but sufficient. A bunk bed, two small closets, and a bathroom that reminded Cara of the Dixi toilets at building sites or festivals. It was bare minimum, but it still made her smile. This would be her home for the coming six months. She would be at sea, traveling the world and leaving her troubles behind. Cara climbed onto the top bunk and bounced up and down on the mattress. She could feel the springs through the thin foam.

"I bet these come from the same factories that make prison beds," she joked. "Although, I suppose this is my prison now."

"True," Billie said. "You might feel like that now and then, but overall, I think you'll enjoy it. Apparently, work and travel are an addictive combination. Very few people who take to the lifestyle don't come back after their first season."

"What makes you think I'll take to the lifestyle?"

Billie shrugged. "Just a feeling. I'm usually right about these things." She climbed up and sat down on the bed next to Cara. "Hey, it's going to be okay. The first day is always awkward, but as soon as you get to work, you won't even have time to think about that. And you've got me, remember?"

"Thanks." Cara smiled. "And thank you for this too." She gestured to their bunk bed. "For letting me stay with you. It's a bit of a risk, sharing a room with someone you barely know. What were your other roommates like?"

Billie smiled. "I've had many over the years. This is the first time I've had a double room. The rule is that women share with women and men share with men. But it's not like anyone's checking. Sometimes people swap after a couple of weeks, after fights, or when friendships are formed. But in general, we don't spend a lot of time down here, apart from when we're sleeping, so it's not really a big deal."

"Have you ever..." Cara hesitated. "Have you ever dated someone you've worked with? On the ship?"

"No, not really. I mean, define dating." Billie rolled her eyes. "We have parties here, and people get drunk. People flirt, and things happen sometimes. It's happened to me a couple of times, the odd hook-up here and there. But I've never dated someone I've worked with or shared a room with. Imagine that. I think I'd get serious cabin fever."

Cara giggled. "I can see that." She leaned back on her elbows. "Are you going to miss him?"

Billie frowned and cocked her head. "Who?"

"What do you mean, who? Dan of course." Cara laughed. "Or have you forgotten about him already?"

Billie laughed along and buried her face in her hands. "Sorry, I wasn't prepared for that leap in the conversation. But since you ask... Sure. I'll miss him. When you know you're going away for a long time though, you treat relationships differently. More casual, I guess. That's why I like Dan so much. He's not looking for a serious relationship either. It's relaxed with him. No promises and no drama. And if we still feel the same way about each other when I'm back, we'll take it from there." She arched an eyebrow. "But I expect Dan to want more than to just sit around, waiting for me. Don't you think?"

"Yeah." Cara paused. "He's not exactly the romantic type, I suppose."

Billie jumped down and held out a hand for Cara. "Come on. Enough with the chit-chat. Let me show you around while we're still in our own clothes."

They left the staff quarters through a maze of narrow corridors and took the elevator up two floors. "Our room is on lower deck minus one," Billie said. "The pantry and the laundry room are on the ground floor. There's not much to see there apart from tons of food in one hall and washing machines and heaps of bed linen and towels in the other. Oh, and there's also a small morgue and a jail cell."

Cara laughed. "You're joking, right?"

Billie shook her head. "No, I'm not. Where do you think they take the bodies when we're at sea for a full week? People die when they die. It's not like they're going to wait until we get to shore. The doctors act as coroners too. Their practice is upstairs, though."

"And what about the police?" Cara asked.

"We have a security team, hired through a private company. Most of the time we're in international waters, you see, so the Captain is the ultimate authority. He makes the arrest in case of a serious crime. It happens now and then, but in general, people tend to behave when there's nowhere to escape."

Cara's eyes widened when they exited the elevator. "Wow, it's so grand." The opulence of the first floor was a stark contrast to the student-like staff quarters below decks. A broad, marble staircase led to the higher decks, spiralling upwards in the centre of the ship. Modern crystal chandeliers were lined up along the corridors and on either side of the staircase, creating an intimate atmosphere, despite the size of the space. They passed a juice bar, a spa, and a gym with exercise bikes facing the windows towards the ocean. There was also a dimly lit indoor pool with daybeds and magazine racks, perfect for relaxing on a rainy day. The whole floor smelt of flowers and coconut.

"This is the only child-free zone, apart from the casino on deck six," Billie said. "It's nice and quiet, but unfortunately, I don't get to work here much, apart from the occasional yoga lesson when I have to fill in for our regular teacher."

"You teach yoga?" Cara studied Billie with interest. She did have toned arms, and although Cara hadn't seen Billie in anything other than her dresses, in today's sportier ensemble, her tiny frame looked like it was being subjected to regular exercise.

"It's not my specialty. But people get sick and sometimes we have to improvise and help each other out. I know what I'm doing, and I have the certificates for it. I'm just not very flexible, so I'd rather leave it to the experts." Billie laughed. "I mostly teach aqua aerobics classes in the outside pool or dance classes on the deck, if I'm not entertaining kids, or playing the magician's assistant. I like working outside in the sun though; it gives me energy." Billie pushed open the sliding doors to a room with fluffy carpet and classic leather couches in front of an electric fireplace. "This is the library."

The light was cosy, and the homely smell of coffee and

freshly baked pastries welcomed them as they walked in. Books covered the shelves on the back walls, and there were magazine racks and iPads attached to a long bar in front of the coffee machine.

"Morning!" Billie smiled at an older lady who was plating cinnamon rolls onto a tray in the back of the room.

"Oh hey, Billie! Glad to see you're back. I've missed you." She came out from behind the bar to greet them. "I'm Margret." She reached out to shake Cara's hand.

"Cara. Nice to meet you."

"Margret has worked on this ship for ten years," Billie said, hugging her. "She's our mother figure. Always full of friendly advice and wisdom, and a great drinking companion too."

Margret laughed, exposing the crow's feet around her eyes. She took a step back and ran a hand through her short, peroxide blonde hair. "Now, now. You're making me blush, Billie."

She turned to Cara. "On this ship, we're all family. We laugh and we fight, but mostly, we laugh. If you ever feel lonely, come and sit here with me after hours. I'm a bit too old to hang at the staff bar with all the youngsters every night." She winked. "Although I do play a mean game of pool when I've had a couple." Margret looked Cara up and down as if trying to figure her out. "So, what will you be doing here, my love?"

"Kitchen," Cara said. "But I wouldn't call myself a chef. I'll be doing the fruit carving to start with."

"Oh, my. That sounds exciting. But you better brace yourself for the boys' club in the kitchen. They can be a rough bunch, those cowboys. Always swearing and chasing women."

Cara laughed. "Thanks for the warning, Margret. I'll make sure to stand my ground."

"Very well. That's the spirit." Margret held up a bag of coffee beans. "Would you two like a coffee? I was just making some for myself."

"That's very kind of you," Billie said sincerely. "But we should get going. Cara's briefing is in three hours, and I want to show her around before the early birds start checking in. But I'll be back soon to catch up, okay?"

"You do that," Margret said, smiling. "Enjoy your first season, Cara. And don't be a stranger."

They took the stairs up to the second floor, where they passed shops, cafés, a tourist information desk and a cinema. The popcorn machine was already set up, spreading a delicious aroma, and the cinema staff were trying on their red and gold uniforms and hats in front of the large screen. Billie knew many of the crew members, and they seemed genuinely happy to see her again. She introduced herself and Cara to people she hadn't met before. Billie was clearly at ease on the ship, striding through the corridors as if she had just come home. The Pelican's interior was elegant, decorated in neutral colours, with dark grey carpet throughout all floors.

"It's much bigger than I expected," Cara said, looking up at the staircase that went up another five floors. "And so luxurious."

"Just wait till you see the rest." Billie beckoned Cara to follow her up to the third floor. There were balcony suites along the outer edge of the ship, and a grand theatre in the middle. Billie pushed open the heavy doors leading to a stage that was covered by a black curtain with gold stars. Around it were rows of red velvet theatre chairs, built up in a semi-circle.

"We've got five hundred seats here. This is where I play the magician's assistant or host talent shows two nights a week." Billie climbed on the stage and pushed the curtain aside before helping Cara up.

"You're brave, Billie. I have to give you that. This is a big stage." Cara looked out over the seats. "I'd be terrified if I had to get up here."

Billie laughed. "Well, I was, the first time. I was shaking so badly I was afraid that the box I had squeezed myself into might start to vibrate. But I got used to it, and I know what I'm doing now, so at least I won't mess up Mr. Lombardi's show."

Cara tried to picture Billie on the stage, but she found it hard. She had noticed though that Billie had swapped her usual immaculate look for a more casual one today. She was wearing black leggings, trainers, and an oversized grey sweatshirt, and it suited her.

"What happened to the heels?" Cara asked.

"My heels?" Billie laughed and looked down at her trainers. "Ah, you mean I look different?" Cara nodded. "It's just not practical here. I can't iron my clothes or hang them anywhere, so this is what I wear when I'm on the ship. Besides, I'm the head of the animation team, so I'm supposed to look sporty, even on my days off. It's an image thing."

"I like it. It suits you," Cara said.

Billie smiled and winked at her. "Thanks. Happy to please my new roomie." She led them out of the theatre and called the lift. "The next two floors are cabins, more balcony suites, and restaurants. That's where they'll be serving your food. But you won't go there very often unless you're on buffet duty." Billie pointed upwards. "You'll get a detailed tour of the gastro floors after your briefing so let's not waste any time there now."

The wind caught them by surprise when Billie opened the heavy doors to the outer deck. "This deck is the ship's pride and joy," she said. "We have one of the largest outdoor recreational areas of all the cruise liners, worldwide." She gestured towards the long pool that split into two arms, following the ship around on both sides. "You can swim around the entire body. It's cool, right?"

Cara was too stunned for words. She had studied the pictures on the website many times, but the ship seemed even bigger now, without guests on board. A staircase led up to a running track, that circled the ship on the upper deck.

"You can use the track before eight in the morning," Billie said. "In case you get cabin fever. We have a gym in the staff quarters too, but sometimes it's good to get some fresh air before spending hours on end in the kitchen." She walked down the stairs leading to the pool. "Come on, this way."

"This is amazing." Cara looked out over hundreds of white sun loungers, each with a large, fluffy towel. They passed a bar and an al fresco restaurant, both still closed. Billie waved at one of the men who were stocking the fridge behind the bar.

"Billie-boo. Good to see you!" he shouted over the music in a heavy Australian accent. Cara regarded him in amusement. He looked like a rugby player. Tall, tanned and muscular, with blonde hair and a neat row of white teeth.

"You too, Arnie. Looking good!" Billie rolled up the sleeve of her T-shirt and flexed her arm, exposing her bicep. "I can see you've been working out, big boy."

Arnie grinned and winked. "Where's my hug, Billie? Come over, I need a hug." Billie took Cara's hand and led them to the bar. She held out her arms and Arnie picked her up and spun her around as if she weighed nothing. "And who's your pretty friend here?" he said, after he had released her from his grip. He looked Cara up and down.

Billie rolled her eyes. "Arnie, meet Cara. We're sharing a room." Billie looked at Cara. "Cara, this is Arnie, self-proclaimed stud of the Pelican."

"Pleasure to meet you." Arnie took Cara's hand and held it longer than necessary.

"Likewise." Cara giggled, taken aback by his directness.

"Okay, time to go." Billie put a protective arm around Cara. "We'll see you later, Arnie. Let's catch up over a drink this week."

"Don't mind him," She said as they walked away. "Arnie's the sleazebag of the ship but he's also my friend of many years. He'll try anything to get new staff members into bed, and I think he's got his eye on you already." She chuckled. "It's best to be straightforward with everyone about your sexuality. I mean, you're hot so the guys will be hitting on you twenty-four seven if you don't tell them to back off. And the girls... well, let's just say you could have a lot of fun here if you wanted to."

Cara raised a teasing eyebrow. "You think I'm hot?"

"I don't think anything. You just are." Billie rolled her eyes and laughed. "Anyone would agree with that." She beckoned Cara to follow her around the left side of the ship and pointed out the recreational areas. "Pool tables are over there, and the dartboards are behind that wall, so people don't get hurt. There's a mini-golf range on the other side arm that runs for a decent length along the ship. It's very popular and usually fully booked." She nodded towards an enormous pink box. "That pink podium is an exercise stage for out of water classes, but it also functions as a stage for evening entertainment."

Cara stopped and looked around to get her bearings. "I'm glad you're here, or I'd be lost already."

Billie grinned. "Oh, just wait. You will get lost, time after time. Especially in the staff quarters; it's a labyrinth down there."

They turned a corner, and Billie gestured to the other pool at the back of the ship. "There's the party pool. They play music here until ten at night, and the bar is open late." Cara stared at the oval-shaped pool with its purple lights and iridescent mosaic tiles. There was a bar in the middle, surrounded by stools that were lined up below the surface of the water. She tried to imagine it full of people, the lucky ones, who could afford a holiday like this.

"Regardless of what it may look like, this isn't really a party ship," Billie said. "Strictly amongst staff, we've divided our customers into three groups: the newlyweds, the overfeds, and the nearly-deads."

Cara laughed. "That's mean."

"Yeah well, imagine entertaining the same people for six months and being stuck with them for sometimes weeks on end when we're at sea. It's impossible not to give them nicknames." She grinned. "The newlyweds are young couples. Sometimes on their honeymoon, as the word suggests, and sometimes in between jobs and looking for a well-deserved rest with their other half. The overfeds," Billie continued, "are here for the unlimited buffets. They're the ones that will drag your margin down if you suddenly decide to put smoked salmon on the menu. Sometimes, the overfeds get heart attacks, but then so do nearly-deads. In general, the pensioners are the ones we worry the least about, though. They tend to be relaxed and easy-going, and they rarely binge-drink." Billie giggled. "Sometimes they get lost on excursions, but ever since we introduced bright blue back stickers, herding them has gotten much easier."

Cara laughed. "Do you ever get close to guests? I mean, I can imagine that you might take a liking to some of them."

"Yeah, sometimes." Billie shrugged. "Most of the guests are really nice. We keep professional boundaries on the ship and don't mingle with them when we're off duty. But sometimes people just grow on you and you can't help it. I'm still in contact with a handful of our former cruisers, and I know that some of the other staff members have made friends over the years too."

They walked around the pool to the back end of the ship, currently facing England's south coast. Cara leaned over the balustrade and watched the last trucks unload on the dock. The drop-off area was now full of people, looking up at the ship the same way Cara had done just a couple of hours ago. It suddenly dawned on her that she really was leaving.

"England looks beautiful from here," she heard herself say.

"It does. You always appreciate what you don't have, isn't that what they say?" Billie shook her head. "Wait till we get to South Africa; you'll have forgotten about the English coastline in no time."

"I'm sure I will." Cara turned and pointed up towards the only place on the ship they hadn't been yet. "What's that circular thing at the top that looks like a spaceship?"

Billie laughed. "I suppose you're right. It does look like a spaceship." She shielded her eyes from the sun as she looked up. "It's a fine dining restaurant with a strict dress code. They serve French cuisine, and it's not cheap. A lot of chefs aspire to work there but take my word for it; it's not for the faint-hearted. It's run like the military."

"So, people have to pay to go there? I thought this was an all-inclusive cruise?"

"It is." Billie pointed at the al fresco restaurants on the deck. "Those are included in the cruise, and so are the buffet restaurants on all decks. But there are some exceptions. *La Mer* is one of them. Also, the à la carte section of Chef Claudio's restaurant, where you'll be working. Your kitchen will prepare the buffets, as well as cook to order. Apart from the buffet restaurants, all coffee, tea, soft drinks, wine, beer and selected spirits are part of the package. If guests want something else, we'll make it, but they'll have to pay."

"And the staff," Cara asked?

Billie laughed. "We have to pay for alcohol, but we get a good discount. Imagine if staff could drink for free, it would be chaos."

"Of course. That makes sense."

They both jumped at a loud beep, followed by the cruise manager's announcement that the ship was ready to board. Billie held up both hands, indicating that the tour was over. "We'll have to go back inside now. I'm going to round up my team, and you'll have to get ready for your briefing. But you've seen the important sites, I'll let you figure out the rest on your own." She winked. "I don't want you to get bored straight away." She nodded towards the coast and nudged Cara. "Say goodbye to home now. It's going to be a while before we're back."

8

"Are you Cara Matthews?" Chef Claudio asked.

Cara nodded while buttoning up her chef's whites. The jacket fitted like it was made for her, and her initials were sewn on in navy letters. "Yes. That's me."

"Great. Come over here. We have a lot of preparation to do before the main service." She followed the tall, skinny chef with the ratty face over to the far end of the kitchen, where boxes of fruit awaited her.

"It's pretty simple," he said. "We do both buffet and à la carte. The buffet dishes are prepared upfront, in the morning, and the à la carte dishes are done to order. But you don't need to worry about any of that. You're good with fruit carving, right?" Cara nodded. "Good. Show me what you can do. We need a centrepiece for the dessert buffet. Anything is fine as long as it's decorative." He handed her a file. "Here's a book with some acceptable examples. Follow the pictures if you're not sure. Nothing rude, do you hear me? No melon tits or banana penises. The last person who tried that was dropped off in Trinidad and had to make his own way home." He opened a drawer underneath the work surface.

"You'll find everything you need in here. If you can't work out the purpose of one of the appliances, ask Eduardo over there." He pointed at a short chubby guy who was running around like a headless chicken, cursing at other staff members who stood in his way.

"I will," Cara said obediently.

"Okay everyone," Chef Claudio shouted. "Five hours till showtime. It's our first night so let's make it a good one. Is everyone clear on what needs to happen?"

"Yes chef," the staff shouted back in unison.

He turned back to Cara. "Oh, and one more thing. If it doesn't look presentable, you'll be doing the dishes until we get to our next port of call." Cara nodded, but he wasn't done speaking. "And it's 'yes Chef.' Loud and clear. Not 'yup' and no nodding. I need to be able to hear you. Understood?"

"Yes, Chef." Sweat was dripping down Cara's spine, and it wasn't from the heat in the kitchen. This guy meant business, and he didn't seem like the forgiving kind. She glanced around at the others and decided she had to do a very, very good job.

At five o'clock on the dot, Chef Claudio was back. Over thirty chefs put their dish in the middle of their workstation, stepped back and straightened their backs as if they were in an army line-up, waiting for inspection. Cara was the last one in line and watched him walk past the dishes, tasting them. She was still fine-tuning the last mango flowers.

"Hey, psst." The chef next to Cara was trying to catch her attention. She looked up at him and read his nametag, which told her his name was Ben. "Put down the knife and step back. It's time."

"Why?" she whispered. "It's just the centrepiece."

"Doesn't matter. Just do it." When Cara didn't move, he kept looking at her sternly until she finally dropped the knife and stepped back.

Chef Claudio went over the starters first, smelling and tasting each dish. He pointed at a plate of deep-fried squid. "What's missing?" he asked one of the chefs, who was sweating profusely and shaking his head in confusion.

"I don't know, Chef. I followed the recipe, and I'm pretty sure all the ingredients are there. The pickled seaweed and the aioli and..."

"Colour!" Chef Claudio shouted. "The colour is what's missing. Do I want to taste that? No. Why? Because it doesn't look appetizing." He gestured to the squid rings in tempura batter. "They are beige. And beige food does not leave this kitchen unless it's mashed potato. Gold. That's the colour I want to see. Do you understand?" The young man nodded. He looked terrified when Chef Claudio stuck his spoon in the aioli to taste it, but he didn't comment on it and walked on, concentrating on the next dish.

"Did you make this consommé?" he asked the man behind the next section. The man nodded. "It's good. Pure flavours, nice and clear. Great job."

Cara could see the man exhale in relief and looked at her own fruit display, suddenly feeling nervous. Although she had never made anything as significant as this before, she had been practicing at home and had watched YouTube videos on peeling and carving techniques. She had approached the project like a flower arrangement, by building height first, and then working outwards. It looked great to her, but now she wasn't sure whether that was good enough.

"Did you use up all the fruit?" Chef Claudio turned the

heavy marble display board around to inspect her work from all sides.

"Yes, Chef." Cara tried to read his face, but apart from the stern frown between his eyebrows, he gave nothing away.

"Looks good. Since you have time left, you can do the cheeseboards too." He turned to the chef next to her. "Ben, show her where the cheeses and figs are, and give her the recipe for the camembert honey coating."

9

"Hey, Cara. Are you awake?"

Cara woke up to find Billie on her tiptoes, looking through the railing next to her mattress. She blinked. Billie was wearing an outrageous sequined dress with a feather headpiece and way too much make up. "I wasn't, but I am now."

"Sorry. Just curious to hear how your first night went."

Cara smiled and sat up in bed, adjusting the pillow behind her back. She was still wearing her chef's whites. "Thanks for waking me up. I should probably have a shower." She yawned. "Just wanted to lie down for a minute."

Billie laughed. "Heavy first night, huh?"

Cara smiled. "Yeah. But it was good. Nothing like what I expected it to be, but I don't think they'll offload me at the next port. Chef Claudio seemed pretty pleased with my dessert arrangements." She frowned. "He's not one for small talk, is he?"

Billie shook her head. "I don't know him very well, but I've done this route nine times with him and we haven't exchanged more than five sentences so no, I don't think he is." She walked over to the mirror and kicked off her heels.

"So, what the hell have you been up to?" Cara asked. "Or is that what you wear to bed?"

Billie chuckled and took off the headpiece, which she carefully placed into a box. "Brazilian-themed welcome night in the theatre. We were trying to get people on the dance floor so they wouldn't drink too much on their first night. People can get pretty carried away when they realize they have six months off work and their drinks are free, so we try to distract them, wear them out." She unzipped her dress, revealing a matching white lingerie set. Then she removed the clip from her hair and shook out her long, blonde locks.

Cara forced herself to look away while she strutted around half naked, looking for something to sleep in. It was nothing short of shocking, seeing prim and proper Billie transform into a sexy vixen, right in front of her eyes. Billie had great legs that never saw the light of day underneath her calf-length skirts, and a curvy, petite frame that was both feminine and athletic.

"Do you want to go first, or can I jump in the shower?" she asked.

"Go ahead," Cara said, trying not to stare. "I'm not sure if my legs will work yet, I've never moved so much in one night." She watched Billie slip into the tiny bathroom and caught a glimpse of her full perky bottom before she closed the door. She shook her head and smiled while removing her jacket and her black trousers. *Damn you, Dan. Good for you.* This was not going to be easy. If only her friends knew she was spending six months in a cabin with a gorgeous straight woman...

10

"Alright, let's get this show on the road." Billie scrolled through the list of names on her iPad, checking if everyone was there. She wiped her forehead and switched on another fan before starting the briefing. "Carol-Anne, this is your third run with us, so you'll look after the trainees this week. Make sure they circulate and know enough to be able to function on their own if we're a man down."

"Of course. I'll make sure they're up to speed in no time."

"Great. Heather, you're doing the yoga classes today. Is that correct?"

"Yeah, that's right. First one is at three pm."

Billie nodded. "Okay. Dorian, Dessi, Aleksandra and Josipa, you'll be on the pool deck. The dancing competition starts at four, and we'll have a quiz at the pool bar straight after. I removed a certain song from your proposed playlist; it didn't seem appropriate for kids. Did you get that memo?"

"Yep. It's gone. I replaced it with Abba." Dorian grinned sheepishly.

"Thank you, Dorian." Billie laughed. "Sinita and Frank, you guys will be on climbing wall duty and Philip, you'll

51

take care of the darts competition. Danielle, you're on the mini-golf course all day. Let me know if it gets busy, and I'll find someone to help you out." Billie raised her voice. "Everyone okay with that?"

Her team muttered agreement. "You'll find the time of your breaks on the schedules I gave you. People who do double shifts get a three-hour break, but no drinking, understood?"

Everyone laughed. They seemed like a nice bunch this year, Billie thought. All full of energy and eager to get to work. "Anything else I should know about?"

Josipa held up a hand. "There's this guy at the pool bar... he's constantly hitting on me. I thought he would give up after two days, but he hasn't yet. I'm not sure how to deal with it."

Billie nodded and shot her a reassuring look. "One of those, huh? Give me a shout when he's up here, and I'll take care of it." She looked around the semi-circle. "Anything else...? No? Okay. Have a good time and don't forget to smile. For those who have a double today, we'll come back here at six to go through the evening schedule."

B illie let out a sigh when she was alone. It felt good to be back. She took off her polo shirt and her shorts, leaving her in a red bathing suit with the Pelican logo on the chest. Then she grabbed the net with floaters, switched on her wireless headset and stepped out into the sun. "Good morning, lovely people! Who's up for some exercise?"

A group of seniors made their way into the pool, cheering and clapping. There was a large turnout of both the young and the old, but it wasn't unusual for the first week. A lot of guests started their cruise with a hopeful promise to themselves to get healthy and fit during their holiday. Of course, they rarely succeeded.

"Can I join in?" said a young woman of Billie's age, standing at the edge of the pool. She wore a sunhat, shades and bright red lipstick. Her frilly bikini didn't seem practical for exercise, but that wasn't Billie's problem.

"Of course. Everyone's welcome." Billie pointed at the woman's head. "Just leave your accessories by the side of the pool, otherwise you're going to lose them." She looked around, greeting the eager faces, smiled and turned up the music.

"Hey. That was a great class. It's Billie, right?"

Billie shielded her eyes from the sun as she regarded the woman she had spoken to earlier. She had put her hat and her shades back on, along with a black kimono.

"Thanks. Yes, it's Billie. And you are...?"

"Gwen," the woman said, reaching out to shake Billie's hand. "I'm Rob Harriss's daughter."

Billie smiled at the familiar name. "Ah, so you're the Captain's daughter? Well, in that case, I'm delighted to meet you, Gwen. He's told me a lot about you. I was wondering when you would join us for a holiday."

Gwen giggled. "Likewise. My father told me you would be the best person to know on this ship. He said you know your way around here."

"I guess I do," Billie answered. "Will you be here for the full six months?"

"No, don't be silly." Gwen shook her head. "I'm just here for the ride. I'm visiting friends in Australia and traveling with my family seemed like the perfect way to get a tan and catch up at the same time." She paused, pushing the shades further down her nose, so their eyes met. "Would you mind showing me around? It's my first time here, and I've been struggling to get the right food to suit my diet. I'm trying to lose some weight before I get to Sydney, you see. I'm sure you know all the right people?"

Billie tried not to stare at her skinny waist. This woman needed more food, not a diet. "Sure. I could show you around. Will you be at the pool today?" Gwen nodded, batting her long eyelashes. "Great. I'll come and get you on my break. Is that okay?"

To her surprise, Gwen kissed her on the cheek. "Thanks, dear. That would be excellent. I think you and I will have a lot of fun together." She winked. "I'll see you later."

11

———

"How was your day?" Cara removed her chef's jacket and draped it over a barstool. It was warm in the communal living room of the staff quarters. They were docked at Las Palmas, and the Canary Islands seemed to be suffering from an unusual heatwave for the time of year. The living room was the only space without air conditioning, so they had to do with the fans that were scattered around the tables and the bar.

Billie shifted on her barstool, trying to get comfortable. "It's been good." She hesitated. "Oh, I don't know. It's been a bit weird, to be honest. The captain's daughter came on board yesterday, and apparently she's my responsibility now." She sighed, looking down at her beer that was still untouched. "I gave her a tour of the ship, but that clearly wasn't enough. When I ran into the captain last night, he asked me to show his darling daughter a good time until we get to Sydney. Sydney, Cara! That's three-and-a-half months from now." Billie shook her head. "She's hard work, you know. She orders things like cucumber juice with chili and superfood salads, and she behaves like a total diva. The staff are scared to tell her no, so they all run around trying to please her, instead of focusing on their jobs. It's not right." She picked up her glass and took a long drink before continuing. "The worst thing is, since we've spent the morning together, she's been acting like we're best friends, clinging to me whenever an opportunity presents itself. It was my morning off, Cara. I was looking forward to reading the papers and relaxing, but instead, I've been dragging Gwen around."

Cara laughed. "Come on, how bad can it be? Maybe she's just lonely?"

Billie frowned. "There's something about her. She's... I don't know... flirty, I guess."

"Are you serious?" Cara's eyes widened in amusement. "The captain's daughter is flirting with you? I don't know what she looks like, but still, that sounds like every lesbian's ultimate fantasy." She scanned the staffroom for the bartender, but he was nowhere to be seen, so she leaned over the bar and pulled herself another pint. "I guess this one is free, then." She slapped Billie on the shoulder. "Why does it bother you so much? Does she make you feel uncomfortable? Are you sure she's flirting with you?"

"As sure as I can be. Trust me, I've been flirted with before."

Cara smiled. "I bet you have."

Billie chuckled, ignoring the comment. "It's the little things," she continued. "The looks she gives me. She keeps commenting on my ass, and she took my hand today as we were walking down the corridor from the restaurant. The whole situation's just too ridiculous for words."

Cara winked and cast her a playful smile. "Well, I can't disagree on that one. You do have a pretty great ass." She watched Billie blush and couldn't help but giggle. "Sorry,

Billie, but she's right. Can't blame a girl for trying, especially with you. Why don't you just tell her that you have a boyfriend? Or that you're not into women?"

Billie took another sip from her beer and licked the foam from her upper lip. "That's dumb. She'll probably laugh in my face and make it seem like I've been imagining things." She turned to Cara and arched an eyebrow. "Anyway, you've got the wrong idea about me. It's not that I'm not into women per se. I've been with a woman before."

"You?" Cara's interest spiked immediately. "You've been with a woman before? Why didn't you tell me?"

Now it was Billie's turn to laugh. "Why would I? So that we can bond over lesbian stuff? Compare experiences? Besides, it was only one woman, and I was pretty drunk, so there's not much to tell. I don't see a need to label myself. I am who I am, and I like who I like. Right now, I'm with Dan, and I don't like Gwen. It's as simple as that." She shook her head and downed her beer before handing her glass to Cara. "Please pull me another one. I've tried a couple of times, but they always turn out half foam."

Cara leaned over the bar again to refill the pint and handed Billie her glass back. "I thought you guys were open to seeing other people?"

Billie rolled her eyes. "Yeah. I suppose so. But it doesn't make sense, does it? I don't like the idea of Dan with another woman, and he wouldn't like the idea of me with another man. I probably shouldn't tell you this because you're his best friend, but maybe we should have just broken up before I left." She closed her eyes and threw her head back in frustration. "I feel like I'm leading him on. It's not like we have anything in common, or a future together. I liked Dan immediately when I first met him. I still like him. We just click, you know. But he's called me every day so far, and he's so sweet on the phone..." Billie shook her head. "He was never that thoughtful before. I guess I didn't expect it to go this way. The right way, I mean." She leaned to the side and rested her head in the palm of her hand. "I don't know what I want anymore. Oh God, I'm a bad person. Are you mad at me?"

"Mad at you?" Cara chuckled. "Why would I be mad at you? I love Dan, but I know better than anyone that he's not exactly boyfriend material." She leaned in closer. "Listen, I don't want you to take this the wrong way, but Dan generally gets over girls faster than you can count to three. He just doesn't work like most people. I'm impressed that he's calling you, to be honest." The alcohol had kicked in, and Cara finally felt her shoulders relax. She rolled them back and forth, relieving them of a hard day's work.

"Okay, I guess you know him best," Billie said. A frown appeared between her brows. "I expected him to start dating other women the moment I left the country. We were just casual, after all. But now he says he doesn't want to. He even told me he missed me last night."

"Wow. Dan said that? He must be pretty smitten with you, then." Cara laughed. "It's going to be fine, Billie. I'm just teasing you. Dan and relationships are not exactly a match made in heaven, no matter what he says. I'm sure he'll get bored of the idea soon enough." She smiled. "Don't worry. I won't tell him he's got fierce competition in the form of the captain's daughter."

Billie nudged her. "Not funny. You need to help me out with Gwen. How do I let her down easy? I don't want to be stuck here with someone holding a grudge against me. She's asked me to join her at the captain's table tomorrow evening."

Cara burst into laughter again, snorting as the beer went

up her nose. "She doesn't waste any time, does she? Are you going? I think you should. I bet not many people can say they've eaten at the captain's table."

Billie chuckled and shook her head. "You couldn't be less helpful if you tried, Cara. Hey, where is everyone?" They looked around the empty living room. The last people to leave had forgotten an old iPod in the dock. It was still playing country music. "I want to show you something," she said. "Unless you're too tired? We can go another time..."

Cara shook her head. "No, what is it? You've made me curious now." Billie stood up, beckoning Cara to follow her. She switched off the music and turned down the lights before rushing after Billie. "Where are we going?" she whispered as they walked through the narrow corridors of the staff quarters. She had no idea why she felt the need to keep her voice down.

"We're going out on the deck." Billie pointed upwards and smiled.

"But we're not supposed to go up there at night. And anyway, it will be closed by now."

"I know." Billie winked. "Just trust me." She led them into the laundry hall, where the nightshift staff was steaming, ironing and folding. The radio was on and they were chatting away in the brightly lit room. A couple of people looked up from their work when Billie and Cara passed.

"Hi guys!" Billie waved and was greeted in return. "You didn't see us, okay?" They laughed and shook their heads.

"As long as you bring us chocolates next time," one of them shouted.

"I will. Promise!" Billie turned around and put a hand on her heart. "This way, Cara." She pointed to an elevator. "The cleaners use this to move the laundry up and down. It leads all the way up to the deck."

Cara followed her and chuckled as they moved up. "You certainly seem to know all the ins and outs here."

"Arnie showed me," Billie said, as they exited the elevator into the towel room on the front deck. "He used to date a girl who worked in the laundry room. Although dating might be an overstatement." She laughed. "You can't tell anyone about this, okay? Needless to say, this area is for cleaners only. I sneak in here to get towels when I've run out. And now, you can too." She winked and opened the door to the deck.

Cara needed some time for her eyes to adjust to the dark. The faint light of the coastline and the sound of the ocean at night were peaceful compared to the afternoons, when the poolside was crowded, and music was playing from the bars.

"Thank you for sharing your secret," she said, closing her eyes at the breeze that finally cooled her down for the first time that day. "It's nice to finally be outside. I tried to sit down in the staff smoking area, but it's kind of grim."

Billie laughed. "Tell me about it. Last time I went there to get some fresh air, I became a victim of verbal abuse by one of the cleaning ladies who claimed I was sitting in her chair." She shrugged. "I also ended up smelling like an ashtray."

"Yeah." Cara laughed. "They're quite territorial about their chairs." She nodded towards the benches at the front, facing the ocean. "But now we have all the seating space in the world." They walked over to the side of the ship and leaned over the railing. "Las Palmas is still awake, I see." She pointed to a building projecting blue laser beams into the sky. A club, she guessed. There were many of them, and now and then, they all projected at the same time, creating a network of coloured lines against the dark night. The view from the deck was great, and they were high enough to see the island's city centre, with its famous party scene.

"It sure is." Billie stared out over the coast and Cara couldn't help but look at her. The wind was sweeping her hair back, making it dance behind her. The faint light highlighted her high cheekbones and her slightly pouted lips. Billie turned and smiled as if she could feel Cara's eyes on her. "If you want to go out, you'll have to find someone else to go with. I'm too tired and I've got an early start. Or you could call Arnie. I think the deck crew is out tonight. I'm sure they'd be delighted with your company."

Cara shook her head. "Not a chance. I'm exhausted too." She stretched her arms up in the air and yawned. "I need to get used to the physical labour after spending months in bed. My muscles feel like I've climbed a mountain."

"Let's go to bed then," Billie hooked her arm into Cara's.

Cara giggled and let Billie lead her back towards the towel room. "It's been a long time since someone said that to me."

12

"Hey, Arnie. Have you seen Chef Andre from the sixth floor?" Cara looked up at him, shielding her face from the sun with her hand. "I'm supposed to get Chinese plum powder from his kitchen, but his chefs don't seem to know what that is. Apparently, he's around here somewhere."

Arnie smiled. "Sure, hot stuff. He's right there on the front deck, talking to the captain. Looks like they're talking business. Do you want to wait behind the bar until he's free? You can't walk around here with a bleeding heart." He pointed at Cara's whites.

Cara looked down at her jacket. There was a red stain from the beetroot she had cut earlier, on the left side of her chest. "Thanks, that would be great." She chuckled, following Arnie around the back door into the pool bar.

"Take a seat, they might be a while. Captain's just ordered two coffees." He pulled out a couple of plastic crates, placed them on top of each other and moved them to the back of the bar, facing the pool deck. Cara sat down and leaned against the wall, cherishing the break from standing all morning.

"God, that feels good." She adjusted the fan on top of the fridge and closed her eyes when the cool breeze hit her face and neck.

"Water?" Arnie handed her a pint glass of water, ice, and lemon. "We're all having drinks in the staff quarters tonight. It's Josipa's birthday." He gestured towards a girl on the stage, leading a children's dance class. "Are you joining us? Be my plus one?"

Cara laughed. "You're barking up the wrong tree there, Arnie, but sure. I'll join you for a drink." She frowned, looking at the sun loungers along the poolside. "Hey, is that Billie over there? Who's that girl she's with?"

Arnie shot her a surprised look. "The one who looks like a model? I thought you knew. That's Gwen, the captain's daughter. Billie's been hanging out with her quite a bit. She told me she's even had dinner at the captain's table. Strategic choice of friends, don't you think?"

Cara didn't answer as she watched Billie closely. She seemed relaxed, cheerful even, as if she was having fun. Gwen was wearing a black bathing suit and a matching sarong. She was showing Billie something on her phone. They were both lying on their side, facing each other as they talked. There was something not right about the two of them together. Cara felt a strange sense of annoyance, but she couldn't look away either. Billie was wearing a blue bikini that showed off her toned body. Her abs were clearly visible as she sat up to tie her blonde hair into a knot.

Arnie was staring at her too. "She's hot," he said, tilting his head as if trying to get a view from all angles. "They both are. Hey, are you not going to wave her over? I thought you guys were friends."

Cara shook her head. "Not now, Arnie. I'm working. God, you're such a perv."

Billie was talking now, and Gwen batted her eyelashes, pretending to be all ears as she handed Billie a bottle of sunscreen and turned around on her sun lounger. Billie untied Gwen's bikini strings and squirted some cream on her tanned back before rubbing it in. Was she enjoying it? It was hard to tell with the shades Billie was wearing, but she did have a smile on her face. It was uncomfortable to watch, and Cara finally looked away, rolling her eyes. "Jesus, is she her personal assistant now?"

Arnie laughed. "What's up with you, woman? Are you jealous?"

"Me? Why would I be jealous?" She tried to laugh it off, but it didn't sound genuine. "It just feels forced, that's all." Cara picked up an orange and threw it over to Arnie. "The captain's daughter comes on board, picks someone that she likes the look of, and that person is put on babysitting duty. It's ridiculous, don't you think?"

Arnie shrugged, throwing the orange back at her. "Don't ask me—I don't mind the sight. Wouldn't mind babysitting Gwen either. Besides, she's not exactly a baby. Have you seen those tits?"

"Hey, are you going to serve me at some point today, or are you too busy gawking at women?" A chubby man with a German accent leaned over the bar, trying to get Arnie's attention. His face was an angry shade of red, and he sounded annoyed.

Cara shot Arnie an amused look. "I should go. Chef Andre looks like he's done with his meeting. I need to catch him before he's gone."

13

.

"Happy birthday!" Cara smiled as she handed Josipa the box with red velvet cake she had taken from the dessert pantry in the kitchen. "You don't know me, but Arnie insisted I come along, so I couldn't come empty handed."

"Thanks! That's so kind of you." Josipa was already slurring her words. "I know who you are, though. You're Billie's friend. She talks about you all the time." She pointed to the far end of the room. "Please join us, we're over there in the corner."

Cara followed her across the room towards the table where Josipa's friends and colleagues had gathered for a late-night celebration. Although it was after midnight, the party had only just started, after the late shifts finished. Most faces were familiar, but Cara introduced herself anyway.

"Shot?" Arnie seemed to have produced a tray with shot glasses from out of nowhere.

Cara grimaced at the sight of the blue mystery liquid. She hadn't had a blue coloured shot since her student days. "No thanks. I'm not very good with that kind of stuff."

"Come on, it's my birthday," Josipa insisted. "Don't be rude. You need to drink at least five."

Cara laughed as she picked one up, already regretting it. "Is Billie not coming?" she asked, after ordering a round of beer.

Arnie shrugged. "I saw her backstage with Gwen, after Mr. Lombardi's show."

"Right." Cara took a long drink from her beer and leaned back. "Do you think there's something going on there?"

"What? Between Billie and Gwen?" Arnie laughed. "Imagine that..." He stared into space with a smile on his face.

Cara nudged him. "That wasn't an answer, Arnie."

"Okay, okay." He held up both hands. "A man can dream, right? And why is it such a concern of yours, anyway? Have you got the hots for Gwen?" His eyes narrowed. "Or is it Billie?"

Cara kicked him under the table. "Don't be such an idiot, Arnie. Billie is my best friend's girlfriend. I'm just making sure no one gets hurt." The words were out before she had thought them over. Was that really the case? Because honestly, Cara didn't think Dan cared enough to concern himself with Billie's whereabouts. Was she really being a good friend? Or was she looking out for herself?

"Alright then. I'll let you off the Billie hook for now," Arnie finally said. "If you have another shot with me."

"Yes, shots!" Josipa yelled. "And cake!" She opened the box on the table and scattered a couple of napkins around. "Help yourselves people. I've already eaten all the icing, but there's plenty left."

"Did someone say cake?" Cara turned to find Billie

standing behind her in a dangerously revealing silver-coloured dress.

"Hey," she stammered. "How long have you been standing there? Are you alone?" She checked the room to make sure Gwen wasn't there.

Billie arched an eyebrow. "I've just arrived. Why, have you got a bad conscience?" She looked from Arnie to Cara and back. They were both staring at her like two deer caught in the headlights. An amused smile played around her mouth. "Never mind. Looks like the two of you have been drinking." She pulled up a chair and sat down in between them. "And I'm going to join in."

The night passed in a haze. Drinks were served, snacks were brought in. Glasses were broken and so was Dessi's ankle. People were singing and dancing. Josipa passed out before anyone else had the chance to.

"Come on, I think it's time to go home," Billie said, when there were only a handful of people left. "Unless you want to stay? It's up to you." She stood up and gathered her things from the table. "Anyway, I'm off to bed. I can't even see straight anymore after that damn blue drink."

"Sure." Cara giggled. "That sounds good. I'll come home with you." She stood up, but a slight tilting of the ship made her fall right back into her chair.

"Here. Take my hand." Billie held out her hand and helped her up. "Hold on to me, I'm used to this."

Cara leaned into Billie as they walked back to their cabin. She felt Billie's steady arm around her waist and inhaled deep as she buried her face in Billie's neck. There was a faint hint of jasmine and vanilla. "You smell so good."

Billie chuckled. "Thank you. So, do you. Now let's get you into bed. At least we never have to go far around here."

Cara dropped down on Billie's bed and fell into a deep sleep before her shoes were even off. Billie sat down next to her and watched her, wondering if she'd be able to climb up into the top bunk. Then she shook her head and draped herself alongside Cara on the mattress.

14

"Hi there. Sorry to bother you all." Billie hopped uncomfortably from one foot to another and waved in the general direction of the kitchen as a matter of greeting. The kitchen staff turned and immediately dropped what they were doing.

"Are you lost? This is the kitchen, half-pint Smurf," one of the sous-chefs laughed. "What the hell do you want?"

Billie shook her head. "I didn't mean to barge in like this." She grimaced. "I know you're all busy but Gwen... she asked me to get her lunch."

Chef Claudio's eyes narrowed as he walked up to her with a large knife in one hand. The frown between his eyebrows had taken on enormous proportions, and if he meant to come across as intimidating, he certainly succeeded. "Are you messing with me, Smurf? There are three restaurants open for lunch at the moment. Why is she sending you down here? We're busy."

Billie nodded. "I know, and I'm so sorry. It's just that she's on a diet and..."

Twelve men and two women burst into laughter. Cara

LISE GOLD

felt sorry for Billie but couldn't repress a grin at the sight of her in her blue Smurf outfit. She was wearing a blonde wig with pigtails, blue tights and a matching blue top underneath her white dress and hat. Her natural petiteness wasn't helping either. She folded her big, blue Smurf hands in front of her while she stared down at her feet, avoiding the mocking gazes.

"I'll take care of it, Chef." Cara looked around the room. "It's for the captain's daughter. We can't really say no to her, right? Besides, I'm almost done here." She pointed at the opulent fruit display in front of her.

Chef Claudio shrugged. "Whatever. Just be quick. We'll need the cooking stations in twenty minutes."

"Thanks, Chef." Cara turned back to Billie, who sighed in relief.

"Thank you," she articulated.

"No problem, Smurf." Cara grinned. "What does she want then? Let me guess, something tasty but without the calories?"

Billie nodded. "Kale and fish. That's what she asked for. If you happen to have any kale lying around. Shall I send someone to pick it up in ten minutes?"

"Make it seven," Cara said. She winked at Billie. "See you later, roomie. And good luck with Gwen. Sounds like she's hard work."

She walked over to the stove with a cod fillet and grabbed a bag of kale from the pantry on her way. "May I?" she asked one of the chefs who was getting ready for his shift, gathering pans and ingredients.

He nodded. "Do you know what you're doing?" He watched Cara throw a generous knob of butter into the pan.

Cara chuckled. "I know exactly what I'm doing." She added olive oil and waited for the base to get steaming hot before dropping the fish in. Then she seasoned the fillet, turned it around and seasoned it again. The colour was perfect, and she smiled as she put the fish aside and started working on the kale. She chopped garlic and added it to the pan with another knob of butter and the kale.

"Is that what you call diet food?" Chef Claudio asked. He seemed genuinely intrigued by Cara's cooking skills and moved closer, leaning over the stove.

Cara laughed and added a dash of cream to the kale in the pan. Then she grated some nutmeg on top. "No, but she won't know the difference. And if she's going to behave like a diva for the coming weeks, I'll make sure she packs on at least another six pounds."

Everyone laughed as they watched Cara plate the food. Kale first, then the fish on top, still dripping from the butter. She finished it off with some roasted vine tomatoes that had already been prepared for the starters. "There," she said. "Two thousand calories worth of fish and kale. In under seven minutes."

Chef Claudio scraped the pan and tasted the kale, seemingly surprised. "Not bad, Cara. Not bad at all."

Cara grinned. "Thank you, Chef."

15

Billie took off her white Smurf hat and threw it in the bag together with the rest of the costume. She hated it. For years, she had managed to get out of Smurf duty, but someone had called in sick today, and no one else was available to take over. It wasn't that she didn't like kids, on the contrary. But the whole acting thing just didn't come naturally to her. She felt uncomfortable with the squeaky voices she had to put on, and with all the hopping around, singing silly songs with the other members of her team. Luckily, the kids on the ship were all young and easily pleased. She put on her red polo shirt and a pair of khaki shorts, cursing when she noticed she had pulled them up back to front. Billie knew very well why she was in a bad mood. Not only did she feel angry with herself for dancing to Gwen's tune the whole afternoon, she also felt embarrassed that Cara had seen her in that stupid outfit. *Why? Why do I care what she thinks?*

Seeing Cara in the kitchen that afternoon had stirred something up inside of Billie. The way she moved through the kitchen as if she owned it, the way she interacted with the other chefs, holding her own in a male dominated room. And the way she looked when she rolled up her sleeves with a knife in her hand…

"Something on your mind, Smurf?" Arnie walked in and helped himself to a bottle of water from the fridge.

"Nothing worth sharing with you. I'm getting dressed. Didn't you see the sign on the door?"

Arnie shrugged. "But you're dressed, so what's the big deal? Besides, I see you in your swimsuit every day. What's the difference between that and underwear?" He grinned. "Unless you're not wearing any…"

"Shut up, Arnie. I'm not in the mood for jokes today." Billie zipped up the bag with the fancy dress outfit and shoved it in the storage cupboard. Then she straightened her back, determined not to let anyone else get to her. "Look, I'm sorry," she said. "You just caught me at the wrong time, that's all."

Arnie smiled and spread out his arms. "Do you want to use me as a punching bag?" He patted his chest. "Go ahead, I'm all muscle, won't feel a thing." Billie finally broke out in a smile and punched him playfully in the abs. "Come on," he said, trying not to flinch. "You can do better than that."

She shook her head. "I don't want to punch you, Arnie. I need a hug."

Arnie laughed. "Ah… come here, Billie-Boo." He took her in his arms and held her. "What's the matter? You can tell me."

Billie shrugged and sighed. "I have no idea."

16

"Are you coming to shore with us next week?" Billie stuck her head around the corner of the bathroom. She was wearing nothing but her underwear and a towel on her head.

Cara pretended to be reading, keeping her eyes fixed on the middle of the page. "I'd love to. Who's coming?"

Billie squirted some lotion into the palm of her hand and started applying it to her legs and arms. "Just me, Arnie and Gwen. She's been bugging me about it all day. You don't mind if she comes, do you? I mean, I couldn't really say no." She handed Cara the bottle of moisturizer. "Would you do my back, please? I can't reach."

Cara let her gaze run over Billie's toned back before she applied the cream with gentle strokes. Billie's skin was smooth and tanned, soft under her fingers. She was surprised how self-conscious she felt, touching her. "No. Why would I?"

Billie shrugged. "Don't know, just checking."

Cara tried to hide her annoyance. She didn't mind Arnie so much. To her surprise, he had grown on her in the past weeks. But why did Gwen have to get involved? "You two seem to get on well, though," she said, trying not to sound accusing. "I saw you at the poolside the other day. Looked pretty cosy to me."

Billie looked over her shoulder. "We were just hanging out."

"Sure, whatever you say." Cara cursed herself for sounding cynical.

"Okay..." A small smile tugged at the corners of Billie's mouth. "Wait a minute. Are you jealous?"

Cara laughed nervously. "Have you lost your mind? Why on earth would I be jealous? If I were looking for a fling, I'd go for the opposite of Gwen. She's not my type. She's got long fingernails and wears way too much make-up. I prefer my women more natural."

"Oh yeah?" Billie turned to her and took the bottle back. "Then who for example? Anyone in the kitchen you fancy? Or anyone from my team?"

Cara shrugged. "I don't know. No one in particular, I guess."

Billie cocked her head. "So, you're telling me that in the three weeks you've been on this ship, you haven't flirted with anyone? I mean, you know you're gorgeous, right?" She pointed at Cara's face, resting a fingertip on her nose. "Someone must have commented on your slender figure or your cool haircut. Or that beauty mark underneath your left eye."

"It's a mole." Cara wanted her to stop, but Billie was on a roll.

"I don't care what it is; I want one. I used to draw them on when I was younger. My mother had to hide the markers from me before I went to school in the mornings. I was desperate to look like Madonna."

"Well, I'd give it to you if I could." Cara stood up and opened her closet. "Have you seen my Rolling Stones T-shirt recently?" she asked, trying to change the subject.

"You mean your pyjamas?" Billie shot her a sheepish grin, before pulling something from underneath her pillow. "I do apologize," she said, pleading guilty. "I've been sleeping in it since last week, when I ran out of clean clothes." She removed her sports bra, leaving her only in her briefs, before pulling the T-shirt over her head.

Cara stood nailed to the ground after catching a glimpse of Billie's breasts. They were full and round and perfect. *Don't look.*

"Do you mind if I wear it for one more night?" Billie stroked the fabric. "It's so soft and comfortable. I couldn't resist when I saw it lying on your bed. I'll wash it tomorrow, promise."

"Of course, you can." Cara tried to pull herself together. "You know what? It looks good on you, and I've got plenty of other T-shirts I can sleep in. Keep it."

"Really?" Billie took two strides towards her, crossing the length of their tiny cabin. "Thank you, Cara. I think I'll accept your offer." She winked and slapped Cara on her bottom before jumping into bed.

That night, Cara was wide awake, staring up at the ceiling. The thought of Billie sleeping in the bunk bed underneath in her T-shirt turned her on, and for that, she was annoyed with herself. Billie was flirty with her, but maybe she was just flirty by nature. The Billie she had met in London couldn't be further from Cara's type, with her fifties housewife outfits and her over-groomed appearance. Billie here, however, was a whole different package. It was almost like she had dropped her facade, relaxing back into an environment that was natural to her. She was spontaneous, fun, witty, and she looked casually sexy in a way Cara never could have imagined. Had she known, she might not have agreed to share a room with Billie, because staring at her best friend's girlfriend at every chance she got, was most definitely a no-no. Cara had also noticed that the guests loved Billie. They all knew her by name and joked with her whenever she passed through the corridors. Surprisingly, Billie knew a lot of their names too, and that made them feel special. She had a way with people. She made them smile and engaged with them, making them happy.

Cara turned on her side, hoping to get some sleep by avoiding the red nightlight on the ceiling, but every time she heard Billie move in the bed below her, she felt an unsettling sense of arousal. *This is not good. Not good at all.*

Something was happening to her, and she hadn't seen it coming. The worst thing was, she was starting to feel jealous now. Seeing Billie by the pool with Gwen had upset her. She couldn't remember ever being jealous when she was with Millie. Not once in their two years together had Cara felt anything close to what she felt when she saw Billie and Gwen laughing together. It made her furious. Why didn't Billie just ignore Gwen? And what about Dan? Was he serious about her? She picked up her phone and scrolled back through the messages he had sent her. None of them indicated he was. He hadn't even asked about her. Cara shook her head. It didn't matter how Dan felt. The fact was, Dan was Cara's best friend, and she shouldn't even be looking at Billie. She closed her eyes tight and pulled a pillow over her head, trying to erase all thoughts from her mind.

17

"Hey guys, can I borrow a pair of scissors?" Josipa dipped her head into the kitchen.

"Sure." Eduardo rooted through his drawers and handed her a pair. "Don't forget to bring them back, or I'll be coming after you." He smiled at her.

Josipa didn't flinch. She took the scissors and disappeared without a word of gratitude. Both Cara and Ben stared at Eduardo in surprise.

"You're awfully nice today," Cara said.

"It's Josipa." Ben chuckled. "He fancies her."

"Shut up." Eduardo cast them a warning look.

"Well, she's pretty hot," Ben continued, ignoring Eduardo's annoyed stare. "Seriously." He turned to Eduardo. "Would you, though?"

Eduardo shrugged, and couldn't seem to suppress a small smile. "Oh yeah, I would. Would you?"

Ben shook his head. "Nah. She's not my type but I can see where you're coming from." He turned to Cara. "What about you, Cara?"

There was a chuckle from the two kitchen porters, listening in on their conversation.

"What?" Cara frowned.

Ben rolled his eyes. "Would you do her?"

"What kind of question is that?" Cara put down her knife and faced him.

"It's the kitchen kind, genius," the only other woman in the kitchen shouted from behind the deep fat fryer. "Get used to it. They're all disgusting, these pigs."

Cara laughed. She didn't know the woman's name. She never really spoke, and although Cara had tried to connect with her, she didn't seem interested in socializing.

"Well?" Ben and Eduardo both looked at Cara, waiting for an answer.

"Right." Cara chuckled and shook her head. "I don't know. I don't think so. She seems a bit young to me. And grumpy, mostly. Anyway, what is this nonsense? It's disrespectful."

"It's entertainment," Ben said matter-of-factly. "We don't get much of that around here so don't ruin the game." He squinted as he thought about his next question. "What about Billie? The hot chick from the animation team? The one who was dressed like a Smurf the other day. You helped her out, remember?"

Cara felt her face flush. "Of course not," she said, a little bit too fast. She didn't mention Billie was her roommate.

"Well you've obviously got no taste." Ben laughed. "I certainly would."

"Me too," someone shouted from the pantry.

"Me too," Chef Claudio mumbled from behind his clipboard, causing startled glances from his staff.

"Yeah, she's banging hot," Eduardo added. "Maybe one of the hottest on the ship, wouldn't you say, Ben?"

Ben nodded. "No doubt about it. That Billie's got some good billies on her." They all laughed.

Cara rolled her eyes. "I'm sure Billie would be delighted to know you're all impressed by her billies." She put away her knife and her chopping board. "But if you don't mind, I'm going to go on my break now, and pretend this conversation never happened."

18

"How's your roomie?" Arnie stubbed out his cigarette and downed his bottle of water. He was sitting opposite Billie, wide legged on a stool. "I like her. But she's always working, right? Must be nice sharing a room with someone who's never there. Are you two getting along?"

Billie stretched her legs out on the sofa, determined to get the most out of her short break. "Yeah, we are. I couldn't have hoped for a better roommate. Cara's funny, I love spending time with her." She smiled. "I just wish she was around more often. Is that weird?"

Arnie laughed. "Yep. That's super weird." He removed his T-shirt and grabbed the fan from the table, waving it in front of his bare chest. "I happen to share a room with three pigs who steal my clothes, throw up on my bed and smell like a sewer. You should see the state of the place."

"In my case, I guess I'm the resident pig." Billie smirked. "I borrowed Cara's T-shirt to sleep in, and I'm still wearing it." She gestured to the wet Rolling Stones top she was wearing over her swimsuit. "I love it. It's so..." There was a knock on the door. "Hide the ashtray," Billie hissed. She waited for Arnie to put the ashtray in the cupboard and opened the door, only to meet Gwen's heavily made-up face, half covered by her enormous shades. "Oh hey, Gwen. I'm just on my break."

Gwen nodded and laughed. "I know, silly! That's why I'm here. Thought we could hang out together."

Billie smiled back, trying her hardest to stay polite. "I can't let anyone in here, Gwen. This is the staffroom. I'll get in trouble for it."

Gwen wasn't having any of it and pushed the door open. "Don't be silly. I'm the captain's daughter. I can go anywhere I want." She sat down on the couch and crossed her legs. "Arnie, darling. How are you?"

Arnie flexed his biceps and produced his most charming smile. "Just chilling with Billie, Gwen. You're looking beautiful as always." He looked her up and down and winked.

"Oh Arnie, stop it." Gwen giggled. She took off her shades and started cleaning them with the sleeve of her kaftan. "Hey, would you mind getting me one of those darling cocktails you made me yesterday? The low-calorie one with the raspberries and the..."

"Arnie's on his break, Gwen," Billie interrupted her. "There's plenty of bar staff out there." She turned to Arnie, but he was already getting dressed.

"Anything for a beautiful lady." He grinned. "You can help me make it if you want? I can teach you."

Gwen shook her head. "Thanks, Arnie. I'll come and pick it up in a couple of minutes. I just need to talk to Billie." She stood up and closed the door behind him, then turned to her new friend. "So, I was thinking...you and I get along great, right?"

Billie wasn't sure how to reply, so she nodded without much enthusiasm.

"Well," Gwen continued, "I happen to have a king size bed in a spacious room with a balcony. At least for the coming three weeks." She batted her eyelashes. "You're in a tiny room with that chef, and it must be terribly cramped and smelly in there."

Billie frowned. "Her name is Cara. She kindly made you food on request twice yesterday."

Gwen waved it off. "Of course she did, and I'm grateful. But that's her job, isn't it? Anyway, I was thinking, why don't you move in with me?" She smiled and put an arm around Billie's shoulder. "Think about it. We could have coffee on the balcony in the mornings, sundowners at night, watch movies together... It will be fun." She leaned in closer and whispered: "I hope you don't mind me sleeping naked."

Billie's eyes widened in shock. It was one thing to suspect that Gwen wanted something more from her, but another to hear her say it. She shook her head. "No, Gwen. That's not going to happen. I think you have the wrong idea of our..." She searched her vocabulary for the right word to describe their one-sided relationship, but nothing sprung to mind. "Friendship?"

Gwen looked at her as if she was speaking an ancient language. "What do you mean, Billie? I don't understand what your problem is. We're both here, both good-looking, both bi-curious. Arnie told me by the way, so please don't be mad at him. Why not have some fun together while we can?"

Billie sighed. How on earth had she gotten herself into this mess? "Gwen, I'm sorry but I can't do that. I never meant to lead you on, if that's what you think I did." She paused. "I have a boyfriend. His name is Dan. He's Cara's best friend." Billie cursed herself for being such a coward. Why was she using Dan as an excuse? Why not just tell Gwen that she wasn't interested in her? That she wanted her breaks and her rare free afternoons to herself?

"Oh." Gwen nodded. "That's great. I didn't know that. You never talk about him."

"I'm sorry if I gave you the wrong impression," Billie said, certain that she hadn't. "You never asked, and I've only known you for a little while."

"Are you two serious?"

"Yeah, we are," Billie lied. "Pretty serious."

"Right." Gwen pulled herself together and smiled, batting her eyelashes. She wasn't going to give up that easily. "Well, my offer still stands, so think about it. Life is a lot more comfortable up there, but I'm sure you're aware of that." She pointed towards the upper decks. "And boyfriends don't have to know everything. I have no doubt he's been keeping secrets from you too since you left. No man can handle that much freedom."

Billie smiled back at her. "I don't think Dan would do such a thing. He's a nice guy, and I'm faithful to him too. But thanks for the invite anyway. It's very generous of you to offer. And hey, no hard feelings, right? Are you still coming to see the flamingos with us tomorrow?"

"Of course." Gwen kissed her on the cheek and squeezed her arm. "I'll see you in the morning." She turned around before she opened the door. "And you know where to find me if you change your mind."

Damn you, Arnie. Billie sat back down on the couch after she'd closed the door, relieved that Gwen was out of sight. Why had he told Gwen about her fling with Sigrid? It was years ago, and Billie hadn't thought about it in months. She had already been drinking at a staff party the night it happened, and Sigrid, the Swedish card dealer from the casino, had invited her over to her cabin for a nightcap. Billie had a crush on Sigrid, back then. She was tall, with short bleached hair and dark eyes. Sigrid had been flirting with her for weeks before the staff party, and she had flirted back.

Billie had always known she was attracted to women, and theoretically considered herself to be bisexual, but she'd never acted on it until that night. She shook her head at the memory of her first experience with a woman. It had also been her last. Not because she hadn't enjoyed it, quite the opposite. But the very next day, Sigrid had her mind set on her next victim, and she had lost all interest in Billie. The meaningless encounter had left Billie scarred and insecure around women for years, and Cara was the first woman she had felt truly comfortable with in a long time. *I wonder if Cara is like Sigrid. If she's a player?* Not that it mattered. She and Cara were just friends. But she couldn't help wondering why Cara's ex-girlfriend had left her. It was hard to believe that someone would leave Cara. She was attractive, she was funny, and she had this sexy air about her...

"Billie, are you there?" She jumped up at the sound of her name. The door opened, and Josipa appeared, looking even more grumpy than usual. "This stupid kid has just thrown all our golf balls overboard and now we have nothing to play with. I've got twelve people booked in, waiting for me. Do you happen to have an extra box lying around somewhere?"

"Sure." Billie sighed. "I think there's a box underneath the stage. Come on, I'll show you where it is."

19

"Dear passengers, welcome to Walvis Bay. We are now ready for you to disembark the ship. Please keep your cruise ID card with you at all times and report to your designated area to avoid crowding at the exits. Our members of staff will meet you outside and take you to your tour bus." The cruise director's voice echoed throughout the ship.

"Namibia," Billie said, yawning. She kicked Cara's bunk bed above her. "Come on; we need to get up."

Cara was awake in no time and jumped out, almost landing on Billie, who was searching for clothes in a pile on the floor. "Thanks for waking me," she said, rubbing her sleepy face. "I can't wait to feel land underneath my feet again. It's been so long now that I've almost forgotten what it feels like." She found a pair of shorts and a navy tank top. "Funny," she remarked. "I've hardly worn any of the clothes I've brought along. Just my chef's whites."

Billie sighed. "Lucky you. At least you don't have to wash your uniform. It's been a nightmare, finding a machine that's free. I waited for two hours last week, and then I gave up because I had to get back to work. And I'm always too tired to do my laundry in the middle of the night." She reached the bottom of the pile, found a yellow sundress and shook out the creases. "This one looks clean enough."

"You're not exactly your prim and proper self here," Cara said with an amused look. "I thought you were a neat freak, from the way you dressed in London." She held up a hand. "Sorry, no offense."

Billie laughed. "Yeah well, there's just no other way, is there?" She bent forward, shook out her hair and tied it into a topknot. "That will do for now."

"I need to change up some money," Cara said, rooting through her bag. "I don't even know what the currency is here. Where are we anyway?" She grinned sheepishly. "Namibia, did you say?"

Billie burst into laughter. "Are you serious? You don't know where you are?" She opened her arms and took Cara into a tight embrace. "Don't worry, hun. I'll take care of you. Yes, we're in Namibia, which is in Africa, in case you were wondering." She ignored Cara's offended gasp. "And Arnie's got dollars so we'll settle it with him. He's found a driver to take us to Sandwich Bay, it's not far."

The driver of the open 4x4 gave Arnie a fist bump. He looked him up and down, then shifted his gaze towards the girls and grinned. "You're the man, dude."

Arnie winked and grinned back at him, before opening the back door to let Cara, Gwen, and Billie climb in.

"Well this is disappointing," Gwen sneered as soon as they drove off.

Cara turned her head away and rolled her eyes. "It's a port, Gwen. Have you ever seen a pretty port?"

"Yes, I have as a matter of fact. St. Tropez is nice."

"St Tropez doesn't have a port." Cara arched an eyebrow. "It's got a harbour."

Gwen ignored her, focusing on Billie instead. "I don't like it here. Wouldn't you rather be by the pool, Billie? It will be nice and quiet now. We can still go back. It just looks so... I don't know. Poor, I guess."

"I'm not going back," Billie said. "I've never been here, and I've been looking forward to seeing the coastline. But we can take you back if you're uncomfortable, it's not too late to turn back."

"No, it's fine." Gwen held on to her designer handbag with a firm grip. "I don't want to cause any inconvenience."

The industrial landscape around the port appeared dry and empty at first. There were only a few abandoned houses outside the city. Most of them were missing parts of the roof or walls. A lonely farmer was herding goats along the road, accompanied by his dog and a child, who was carrying water. Their driver waved and yelled something at them as they passed, and they smiled and waved back.

They turned off the main road, onto a bumpy sandy path that followed the unspoiled coastline, full of birds, nesting on the higher parts of the wetlands. It was raw and untouched. Then the dunes came into sight ahead of them, varying in colour from a sandy yellow to bright red, depending on the angle of the sun. It was beautiful.

Cara and Billie stood up on the back seat and held on tight to the robust framework of the car that was now jumping up and down as it made its way through the sand. It was a mesmerizing sight, seeing the red of the dunes merge with the pure blue colour of the sea and even Arnie, who had been talking to the driver non-stop since he got in the front seat, was suddenly quiet. The colour of the coast-line changed in the far distance, and as they came closer, Cara realized it wasn't the sun's reflection that gave the shore its unusual pink glow. The car came to an abrupt stop when their driver parked it a little further down.

Cara climbed out and felt her feet sink into the loose sand of the dunes. "Wow. This is incredible."

"It sure is." Billie took her hand and led them closer to the shore.

Thousands of flamingos formed a sea of pink. They moved around in flocks, seemingly not in any particular direction, but some of them looked like they were doing the Moonwalk. Their heads bobbed from front to back and from left to right as if they were all listening to the same music. Billie laughed at the comical sight.

"They are choosing their mates this time of year," their driver explained. "Birds interested in each other, call each other in unison." He pointed to one of them. "Look. If a female wants to let a male know that she's interested, she lowers her head and spreads her wings."

Cara, Billie, and Arnie quietly watched the mating ritual. The flamingos didn't even give them a second look, too busy finding their partner for the season.

"These two right there." Their driver gestured to a flamingo who was running away from the group, swiftly followed by another one. "The female has chosen him," he said. "And now she's taking him away to make babies." He laughed. "Look at him. He's a happy man."

Cara moved closer to Billie. "It's fascinating, isn't it? I didn't know what to expect when you said you wanted to see birds, but this has just exceeded my expectations."

Billie nodded. "This makes it worth it, right? All the hard

work?" She put an arm around Cara's waist and rested her head on her shoulder. "I feel so lucky to be here with you guys."

Cara's heart skipped a beat at their closeness. Billie looked strangely attractive today, with her messed up hair and bare legs. She took a deep breath and tried to focus on the flamingos. *Don't be stupid. She's your friend. And your best friend's girlfriend.*

Arnie laughed. "Are you two inspired by the mating ritual, or is my mind just going places it shouldn't?"

Billie rolled her eyes at him. "Pervert. This is the very reason you never have a girlfriend, Arnie. Your mind always goes places it shouldn't."

Gwen kept to herself. She stood on a plastic bag and took selfies on her phone with the birds in the background. "Oh my God, I'm so glad I came," she chirped. "This place is Instagram heaven." She pouted into the camera, looking over the rim of her sunglasses. "Come over here, Billie. Let's take a picture together."

Billie smiled. "Sure, Gwen. How do you want me?"

"How do I want you?" Gwen giggled suggestively and held out a hand for Billie. "Get your cute ass over here and put an arm around me."

Cara's stomach turned when Billie happily complied, smiling into the camera. Gwen zoomed in on the picture and frowned.

"Oh God, I'm fat," she shrieked, looking down at her belly. She took hold of the tiny bit of fat she had above the edge of her jeans and grimaced. "I think I might have put some weight on. How on earth is that possible? I've been on a diet forever. And my face looks big too." Gwen sighed and waved her phone at Cara. "Cara, would you be a darling and take one from further away?"

Cara shot Arnie an annoyed look before she walked over and snatched the phone out of Gwen's hand.

"Higher, Cara," Gwen shouted, shaking her head. "No, I didn't mean for you to walk up the dune, silly. Hold the phone higher and take a picture from above. It's more flattering."

Cara sighed as she took a couple of pictures, trying to catch Gwen with her mouth open from the worst possible angle. "Here." She threw the phone back and rejoined Arnie and their guide, determined to ignore her for the rest of the morning.

"Cara?"

"What?" Cara turned around and gave Gwen a warning look.

"I'm afraid these aren't good enough, babe. Could you try again, please?" Gwen batted her eyelashes. Cara looked to Billie for help, but Billie just shrugged and laughed.

Then, she crossed her arms, inhaled, and let rip. "Seriously, Gwen? Would you like a cocktail with that? Or maybe some kale and fish? Huh? How about a massage?" There was an awkward silence. Both Gwen and Billie were staring at her in shock, and Arnie was cracking up behind her.

"No worries," he jumped in. "I'll do it."

"Traitor," Cara hissed as he passed her. He winked and lowered his voice.

"I'm on to you, Cara." He moved closer to her ear. "But don't worry; your secret is safe with me."

20

Billie pulled a pair of denim shorts over her red swimsuit, slipped into her cowboy boots and put on a hat. She pulled a large box with pink cowboy hats in front of the stage and connected the speakers on either side.

"Okay everyone, please grab a hat and get on the stage with me. We're going to do some line dancing. Y'all got your cowboy boots on?" she joked through the microphone.

Two chubby English ladies in their fifties sprinted to the stage, determined to stand up front. They both had the same red perm and were wearing identical floral kaftans over their swimsuits.

"Good morning, ladies," Billie said, moving in between them. "Are you two sisters? Twins maybe?" She pointed the microphone at the one to her left, but the other one snatched it away and looked into the audience, which consisted of a couple of beer-drinking men by the bar with very little interest in the activities. "No, we're not, Billie," she answered in a deep voice, batting her eyelashes. "We're friends. My name is Patty, and my friend here is Sonya. We're..."

Sonya managed to get hold of the microphone and pulled it back towards her. It was an awkward moment. Billie shot Arnie, who was now crying with laughter behind the bar, a desperate look. To her embarrassment, Cara was standing next to him grinning with her arms crossed.

"We're single and ready to mingle," Sonya shouted through the microphone. Both ladies cracked up laughing, clearly intoxicated. Billie stepped back, taking control of the situation again.

"Well, that's great news for all the single men on this ship, Patty and Sonya." She looked out over the pool area. "Let me remind you all that we have a speed dating event in the casino at eight tonight. Please register with my handsome colleague Arnie over there at the bar if you'd like to participate. And who knows, he might be one of the bachelors..."

The stage was now full of ladies, giggling at the sight of Arnie, covering his face with his hands. "Okay, where are all the men?" Billie smiled at the men by the bar, pointing at the pink cowboy hats.

"I ain't wearing no pink," one of them shouted. His friends laughed and raised their glasses.

"We're real men," a tattoo-covered bald man said. "We'll stick to the beer."

Billie giggled and shrugged. "Very well, just the ladies today, then. Are we ready? Who's up for some dancing?" She looked at the twenty or so women on the stage, who all responded with excited cries. "Okay, we'll start simple, and I'll repeat each routine eight times, so don't worry if you don't get it right the first time around." She searched for 'Achy Breaky Heart' on her iPad and turned up the volume.

. . .

"Why were you two standing back there, laughing at me?" Billie asked Cara after the dance class. She slipped behind the bar and helped herself to a bottle of water.

Cara protested her innocence. "I just came up to bring Gwen some food." She gestured towards Gwen, who was eating her meal on her sun lounger. "A healthy curry. She said she fancied something spicy today, and clearly none of the dishes from our five Asian restaurants were good enough for her, so I had to help the poor soul out. She comes straight to me now. Did you know that?" She failed to mention that she had put three large scoops of ghee into the chicken curry, and finished the rice off with oil and full-fat coconut milk. It was great entertainment for her colleagues in the kitchen, and they had all chipped in with ideas on how to fatten up Gwen. Eduardo had even offered to sacrifice some of his precious weight-gain protein powder for her breakfast pancakes.

"That's very nice of you, Cara." Billie gave her a suspicious look. "But somehow I find it hard to believe that you go through all this trouble to keep Gwen happy."

Cara shrugged. "Hey, what can I say? I'm a people pleaser." Her gaze travelled down to Billie's legs. "You look great in those boots. It's kind of hot."

Billie laughed, shaking her head. "Really? These boots? I feel like a clown. But if you like them, I'll wear them in bed tonight."

Cara winked at Arnie, who was clearly beside himself from their flirty banter. "That's how you do it, Arnie," she said. "Watch and learn."

21

"Look at this, Edward. It's a floral fruit display. So pretty, don't you think?" Cara was just about to head back to the kitchen after placing her fruit display on the dessert buffet, when she heard someone talking about it. The lady in the fuchsia pink dress was scanning the room, assessing the security risk of sneaking one of the flowers onto her plate. "Do you think I could take one of those? It would look so nice in a picture."

Her husband sighed. "Don't be daft, Caroline. They're for decoration. You're not supposed to eat them. Someone spent a lot of time on that, and you just want to put it in your mouth?"

Caroline nodded, the colour going to her cheeks. "Yes. Well, I suppose I should leave it then, shouldn't I?"

Cara walked up to her and smiled. "You can take whatever you like, I make a new one every day."

Caroline beamed, looking strangely star-struck. "You made this? But goodness, you're only young. So talented, isn't she, Edward?" Cara nodded, suddenly feeling proud of her work.

"Certainly," Edward said, mildly embarrassed by his wife's enthusiasm. "Well, you heard her. Go on, take whatever you like, Caro. Now let's go and eat. I've booked the mini golf for eight, and I don't want to be late again."

Caroline winked at Cara as she carefully placed a watermelon rose on top of a generous pile of cakes, before wobbling off to their table. "Thank you, dear. Keep up the good work." She gave Cara a thumbs-up.

Cara laughed and winked back. She didn't have much interaction with the guests, and it was nice to get the occasional compliment.

"Have they let you out of the kitchen?" She turned to find Billie behind her with a clipboard in her hand.

Cara's eyes lit up at the sight. "Not really. We were waiting for someone to take the fruit in, but the front staff seemed to have forgotten about it, so I thought I'd take it myself."

"I see." Billie smiled and held her gaze.

Cara blushed as she tried to think of something to say. Seeing Billie during work was always a bonus. Her enthusiasm was energizing, and it made a long day a little bit easier.

"So, what are you doing here?" she asked.

Billie shrugged. "Just looking for volunteers for the magic show tonight. People feel extra special if you ask them upfront. They also get a fancy cocktail before they go on stage, to calm their nerves, so I'm taking their names and orders." She looked Cara up and down. "You know, you look really good in uniform."

Cara laughed. "What are you talking about? I'm just in the same chef's whites I always work in."

"Hmm." Billie seemed to think about that as she tugged

on Cara's jacket and straightened her collar. "I suppose that's true. But still..."

Their conversation was interrupted as the ship leaned to the side, causing the cutlery to slide off the bar. There were murmurs and a couple of yelps from guests. Cara would have lost her balance if it wasn't for Billie steadying her. She didn't seem fazed by the sudden turn the weather had taken and faced the passengers with a confident smile.

"Please stay calm," Billie shouted over the noise. "We're at sea; this happens sometimes. You're all fine to stay here unless the captain decides otherwise."

Cara watched the diners hold on to their drinks with a hint of panic on their faces. Caroline was clutching the watermelon rose in her hand, as if it was her most precious possession. "Are you sure it's okay for them to stay here?" she asked.

"We might be heading into a storm," Billie whispered, turning back to Cara. "You better go back to the kitchen in case you have to pack up."

22

"Guys, you have one hour to clean and wrap up; we're closing early tonight."

Cara took the massive roll of cling film that Chef Claudio handed her, unsure of what to do with it. "I'm sorry, Chef. I don't understand. What's this for?"

"Did no one brief you on the procedures?" He shot her an annoyed look. "The storm. It's against safety policy to be in the kitchen during a storm, so we're all leaving early. Make sure nothing can fall off the shelves."

"Here, I'll help you." Ben came to the rescue. He took the roll from her and tied the plastic sheet to the rail above Cara's workstation. Then he started walking around it, making sure all utensils were covered, before securing it on the other side of the shelf. "Basically, we just wrap up the whole kitchen. Simple as that." He pointed at her set of drawers. "And don't forget those. We don't want to have knives all over the floor when we come in tomorrow morning."

"Will it be that bad?" Cara asked, giving her section one last clean before wrapping it up.

"Probably not, but we have to take precautions. Better to be safe than sorry." Ben started wrapping up his own station, fast and methodical. "You first storm, huh?"

Cara nodded. "Should I be worried?"

"Not unless you get seasick. In that case, you'll be in for a long night." Ben laughed. "Hey, don't be scared, it's a good thing. We get to leave at eight, and there will be a party downstairs. You'll join us, right?"

Cara looked around the kitchen and noticed the cheerful faces. "Yeah, sure. Sounds fun." She had noticed the wind had picked up already by the way the ship was tilting. A stool in the corner slid towards her, and she wrapped it tight against a pole before scanning the kitchen for any other loose objects. "What if the guests want to eat?"

She passed the cling film over to Ibrahim, who shot her an amused look. "They haven't told you anything, have they?"

Cara shook her head. "I guess not."

Ibrahim removed the microwave plug from the socket and wrapped it against the railing. "The guests will have a cold buffet in Brasserie Six. We can't have hot soup or curries flying around, burning people, so in case of a storm the staff of Brasserie Six are basically screwed. They'll be up all night plating salads and making sandwiches for the whole ship." The ship tilted again, and Cara almost lost her balance. "Come on," Ben said. "Time to leave before any accidents happen."

The party had already started in the communal staff area, where loud music was playing out of the speakers. The five people behind the bar were singing along as they pulled one pint after the other. It was the first time that

Cara was spending time with the kitchen staff outside of work, and it was nice to see them relax and drop the stern determination and the stressed looks that they usually carried during service hours. Everyone seemed to be in a good mood, praising the storm for their night off. Cara accepted a beer from Ben and toasted with the guys, finally feeling like she was one of them.

Arnie and the deck crew joined the fun too. He was soaked from the rain, but it didn't seem to bother him. "Deck is closed!" he roared like a lion. "Me and my crew need some shots, and we need them now!"

"Feels like a frat party," Cara said. She watched the deck crew as they downed shots in every colour on the spectrum.

Ben laughed. "You're right. Most of us are normal, hard-working people, but when a storm comes, we all turn into a bunch of students." He nodded towards the deck crew at the bar. "They're the party crowd, no doubt about that. And we..." He looked around their table. "We're the ones that never come out because we're always too busy. I mean, look at us, it's pathetic. Ibrahim is making a prep list for tomorrow, and Chef Claudio is on the phone placing orders."

A loud cheer came from across the room. Cara turned around and saw that the commotion was caused by the animation team that had just walked in. Their presence was clearly appreciated by the deck crew.

"And here come the mean girls," Ben chuckled. Several men whistled as Billie and her colleagues crossed the room.

Billie was wearing her sequined magician's assistant costume that left little to the imagination, and she seemed to be just fine with that. Her face lit up when she saw Cara. "Hey, I was hoping you'd be off too." She looked around the crowded room, searching for an empty chair. Then she sighed at the lack of one and sat down on Cara's lap. "This will do if you don't mind. My feet are killing me in these shoes." She kicked off her high heels and closed her eyes. "God, that feels good."

Cara laughed. "Be my guest." She was aware of the other chefs staring at them, and she felt a twinge of pride. It felt nice to have Billie close, so she wrapped an arm around her waist and handed Billie her glass. "Drink?"

"Thank you, darling." Billie took a sip of the beer and looked around the table. "What's up with you guys? You look like you've seen a ghost."

One of the sous-chefs chuckled. "We've just watched one of the hottest girls on this ship sit down on our female fruit carver's lap. It doesn't seem fair, somehow."

"Agreed," Ben said, handing them both a beer. "I take it you guys know each other?"

Cara and Billie both nodded. "We bunk together. Billie is the one who recommended me for this job." Cara smiled. "She also managed to get us a room for two, so I basically owe her my life."

"You guys are in a room for two?" Ben's eyes widened. "How on earth did you do that? I've been here for ten years and never managed to get into anything smaller than a four-bed."

Billie laughed. "I told them that I needed space for all my costumes, which is true. Plus, I manage a pretty big team, and the higher rank helps too." She put her arm around Cara's shoulders and squeezed her. "I couldn't have wished for a better roomie. I just don't get to see her enough, but guess what?" She shot Cara an excited grin.

"What?" Cara couldn't help but laugh at her enthusiasm.

"I've managed to get two days off. We're going to Cape Town!"

"Whaaat?!" Cara hugged her, unable to hide her happiness.

"I saw on your schedule that you were off when we dock in Cape Town," Billie continued, "so I swapped shifts."

Their eyes met, and Cara felt a tingle of excitement in her lower abdomen. *What's going on? Dan's your best friend, don't even think about it.* "That's great news, Billie. It will be so much more fun going with you." She tried to distract her mind from Billie's legs, but it was impossible. Billie looked great tonight, radiant even. It wasn't the costume, or the hair, or the make-up. Cara had seen that many times before. No, it was her attitude and the look on her face. It was mischievous and carefree. Cara felt herself blush and looked away, winking at her tablemates. At that moment their entire company, including the table and chairs, shifted, as the ship tilted to the left.

"Pick up your glasses," one of the bartenders shouted. There were screams and cheers, but no one sounded terrified. Cara held her breath as she took her glass and leaned to the right, waiting for the ship's body to steady itself again.

"Zero broken glasses!" The crowd cheered again at the bartender's announcement.

"Please tell me we're not going to die," Cara said, pleading.

Billie giggled, holding on to her as their chair moved back. "We won't, but we don't often get these big storms either. It's exciting, don't you think?"

Cara shot her a cynical look. "If you say so. I'm not sure how I feel about it yet."

Ibrahim stood up and finished his beer. "Enough of this," he said. "I'm going to take a sleeping pill and strap myself to the bed. Don't forget me if we start sinking." He walked off on unsteady legs, leaning in as the ship tilted again.

Cara looked at Ibrahim's empty chair next to her. Billie glanced at it too. "Do you want me to move?"

Cara shrugged and raised an eyebrow. "Whatever is comfortable for you, Billie-Boo," she said in Arnie's Australian accent.

They both laughed, and Billie shook her head. "In that case, I think I'll stay right here." She wiggled her bottom and moved further onto Cara's lap, leaning in close.

Cara's heart was beating fast in her throat. *Oh God, she's flirting with me. Was I flirting too?* She felt adrenaline run through her veins and wasn't sure whether she was excited or terrified, both from the storm and Billie's close presence. The room tilted again, and she quickly grabbed her glass from the table, steadying her feet on the floor to stop the chair from sliding.

"It's even worse upstairs," Billie said.

Cara laughed. "Worse than this?"

"Yeah. We're below sea level here, so we don't feel the full effect of the waves. Upstairs, you can see the sea splashing up against the windows and hear the wind blowing over the deck. Do you want to go upstairs and have a look? It's quite impressive."

Cara frowned. "I'm not sure I can take any more of this, but being reminded that we're under sea level during a storm isn't making me feel any better either, so I guess I'd be quite happy with some distraction." She looked down at her hand that was resting on Billie's bare thigh and removed it. "Do we need to get changed?"

Billie pointed at Cara's whites. "What are you wearing underneath that?" To Cara's surprise, she started unbuttoning it, revealing a white tank top. "Perfect, that will do."

Then she produced a cardigan and a pair of flip-flops from her bag and unpinned her hair. Cara watched her blonde locks fall over her shoulders and felt a sudden urge to run her hand through them. *Don't you dare. Stay away from her.* Before she had the chance to do anything stupid, Billie stood up and took her hand.

"Come on."

23

The upper decks were still full of people, but there was a strange atmosphere. It was quiet, as if everyone was holding their breath, waiting for the next wave to hit them. Crowds had gathered in front of the windows, filming and taking pictures. Cara watched water splash up against the side of the ship, causing it to shake. She shivered.

"I had no idea it was this bad." A large plant pot had fallen over, and a couple of staff members were sweeping up the mess while others were tying chairs and tables to poles in the middle of the room. "Should we help them?"

Billie shook her head. "No, we're not supposed to be here. Besides, we've been drinking, so we're not allowed to mingle with the guests." She led them up the flight of stairs towards the wellness floor and knocked on the door to the library.

Margret's cheerful face appeared. "Hi girls, come in. I was just about to close for the night. It's a bit too shaky for me up here."

"Thanks," Billie said. "Are you sure you don't mind?"

Margret laughed. "Of course not, dear. Just keep the door shut. Nobody comes here late at night, so you should be fine. There's still some tea left in the pot, and there's some Baileys behind the coffee machine. Make yourselves at home." Margret handed Billie the key. "Drop this in my post box tonight, will you? I'll pick it up tomorrow morning." She turned at the door. "Oh, and if anyone sees you when you come out, tell them I was seasick and that you were closing down for me, okay?"

Billie nodded. "Of course. Thank you, Margret." She closed the door behind her and turned to Cara. "Help me move that couch over to the window, will you?"

The ship tilted from left to right as they dragged the leather sofa away from the glass doors, but they managed to hold their balance. Cara sat down in front of the window and draped her chef's jacket back over her shoulders. When Billie switched off the music and dimmed the lights, she could see and hear the raging ocean, like an angry monster below them. She folded her legs underneath her and leaned back, in awe of the show that was playing out in front of her. The unease she had felt was gone, replaced by wonderment and a strange sense of calm. For a split second, the lightning struck, and the sky lit up, allowing them a view over the daunting horizon.

Billie rummaged behind the bar and came back with two takeaway cups. "Caramel tea with milk and a shot of Baileys. Sounds weird, but it's surprisingly good."

Cara inhaled the scent of the hot drink and closed her eyes before taking a sip. "It's good. Thank you."

"Margret's favourite drink," Billie explained. "Apparently it makes you sleep like a baby."

She leaned against Cara and draped a blanket over their legs. Cara held her breath when she felt Billie's body against her own. It felt different tonight. It wasn't like a hug or a friendly squeeze. The contact was intentional, and it terrified her.

"You don't mind, do you?"

Cara shook her head. "Of course I don't." Her hand was still on the back of the sofa, and she wasn't sure what to do with it. Finally, she exhaled and let it fall around Billie's neck. She watched the ocean and tried to relax.

"Thank you for bringing me here, Billie. It's beautiful."

Billie looked up at her and smiled. "You're welcome. You know, I wouldn't want to watch this with anyone else. I feel comfortable around you. We've been in that tiny cabin for weeks now, and I'm not even enjoying my precious time alone in there." She hesitated. "I like having you around."

Cara smiled. "Me too. I'm glad I came." She swallowed, carefully weighing her words. "Billie, I feel like I owe you the world. I don't know how I can ever repay you. I'm happier than I've been in years and it's all because of you and this job."

Billie laughed. "I didn't do anything. You're so talented, and you don't even know it." She paused. "You seem to have a real passion for food and cooking. Have you ever considered doing this for a living? I mean, permanently?"

Cara thought about that. She did love cooking, she always had. "I guess it's crossed my mind. But journalism is in my blood; it's what I was raised to do."

Billie looked up and frowned. "Explain. Are your parents journalists?"

Cara nodded. "My father is. He used to be a war correspondent, but he's currently working on a project involving missing people in Saudi Arabia. It's incredible he's still alive, after all the places he's been stationed. I don't see him very often, never have."

"Did you miss him as a child?" Billie's voice was soft as she looked up at Cara.

Cara lingered for a moment, captivated by Billie's eyes. They caused an internal explosion of butterflies, each time she looked into them. *She's so beautiful...*

"I didn't know any better," Cara said, her voice unsteady. "It was just the way things were. He used to come home four to five times a year but now that I'm older and my parents are divorced, I hardly see him anymore. He lives for his job." She sighed. "I always admired that about him. The dedication, the courage... I wanted to be just like him when I grew up. That's why I studied journalism."

"And now?" Billie asked.

"Now, I'm not so sure anymore. It's been hard to find good jobs in the field, and last year, I didn't work at all." Cara shrugged. "Maybe I'm just not good enough."

Billie took Cara's hand from her shoulder and pulled it down against her chest. "Or maybe you just don't love it as much as you hoped you would." She took a sip of her tea and put the cup on the floor. "And your mother? What about her?"

"My mother works at the British Embassy in Abu Dhabi. She moved there after she divorced my father."

"That's impressive," Billie said. "Are you close to her?"

Cara shifted on the couch, aware that they were now almost lying down together. She straightened her back, determined not to give in to her growing desire to pull Billie on top of her. "Not really. We speak on Skype now and then, and we text. I haven't seen her in a year, but I guess that's my fault. I've been ignoring her." Cara hesitated, unsure of how far she was prepared to open up. But she had already started talking, and it felt good to say things out loud. To say things the way they were. She trusted Billie. "I can't help but feel like a failure. My parents are both successful, and I'm generally unemployed. I guess I could have asked them to pay my rent or buy me a ticket so I could stay with either of them for a while. They could easily afford it, and I'm sure they'd be more than happy to help, but I didn't want them to know that I couldn't find a job, so I moved in with Dan."

Billie squeezed her hand at the sound of his name. "They don't know you're here, do they?"

Cara shook her head. "No, they don't. They think I still work for The Times. They were so proud when I got the job; I didn't have the heart to tell them about my redundancy." She took a long drink of her tea, savouring the effect of the alcohol, numbing her senses.

"So, what about your family? Tell me about them. I know you have a sister who's going to have a baby, but that's about it."

Billie chuckled. "Not as impressive as your family, I'm afraid. My parents are both teachers. My father is a maths teacher at the local college, and my mother teaches at a school for special needs children. I've got two sisters, one who's about to be a single mother and one who's married with children. And then, there's me. I have a teaching degree, as I've told you. But I've also studied finance on the side, so I'm a qualified accountant too, believe it or not."

Cara laughed. "You're not even joking, are you?"

"Nope." Billie cast her a flirty smile. "I look pretty hot with my glasses on."

Cara felt her cheeks blush. "I don't doubt that for a second. So why are you not crunching numbers or teaching?"

Billie chuckled. "Do you really have to ask? This, teaching or accountancy?" She rolled her eyes. "I don't know what I was thinking. Maybe I just wanted to follow in my parents' footsteps, like you. I planned on securing myself a safe, low-risk future with a steady income. It seemed like such a good idea at the time." She paused. "After I graduated, I saw a job advert for the animation team on this ship and applied. I figured a year out wouldn't do any harm to my career prospects, and I wanted to do something fun before I started working full-time. I was lucky to be petite and got scouted as a magician's assistant for my first season. It raised my profile and gave me a head start. Now, eight years later, I'm a team leader. I get to dance, entertain, scout talent, and I get to go to amazing places. I love it." She sighed. "I can't see myself doing anything else."

"What do you do the other half of the year?" Cara asked. "When you're not on the ship?"

Billie smiled, looking out over the ocean. "I complain about not being at sea and not seeing the people I love to work with. I go to the beach a lot, even when it's cold, and I do some entertainment work for hotel chains and charities, but it's not the same. I can't do another cruise either because the seasons overlap." She turned towards Cara and put an arm around her waist.

Cara shivered. The touch made the hairs on the back of her neck stand up. With the intimacy of their conversation and the way Billie was looking at her, it was hard to focus on what she was saying. Billie seemed to move closer with every sentence she spoke.

"The cruise company we work for is starting ten-month cruises next year, and I want to be a part of it."

Cara arched an eyebrow. "Are you telling me there are people in this world who go on holiday for ten months of the year?"

"Yeah, apparently there are. I've applied for Head of

Entertainment. It's a big responsibility, but I think I can do it."

Cara smiled, aware of Billie's lips, so close to hers now. "That sounds great. I'm sure you're going to be amazing," she said in a soft voice. Billie's eyes met hers again, and they lingered for a moment.

Cara put her cup down and reached out to touch her face. "I'm sorry. I..." She retracted her hand.

"It's okay." Billie kept her gaze fixed on her.

Cara could see by the longing in her eyes that they were both fighting the same battle, terrified to make a move, and terrified not to. *Don't do anything. This is wrong.* But Cara had already lost. She closed her eyes and felt Billie's breath on her face. Her chest was heaving, and her heart was pounding in her throat. She felt Billie move closer, until soft lips touched hers, ever so lightly.

"This is wrong. We shouldn't even be thinking about this," she mumbled against Billie's mouth. Her hands were balled into fists, her nails digging into her own skin.

"I know," Billie whispered. But she pressed harder and let her tongue slide over Cara's upper lip.

Cara gasped. Billie's teasing was too much for her feeble resolve, and she couldn't hold back any longer. She opened her mouth and turned, pulling Billie on top of her, claiming her with her tongue. It felt so right, so natural, that she was unable to think about what she was doing. They both moaned and sank deeper into the kiss, finally giving in to the longing that left them both defenceless. Cara laced her hands through Billie's hair and pulled her closer. She could feel the heat of Billie's thigh pressing against her centre and gasped at the sensation. *What the hell are you doing? Stop it. Now.*

Suddenly, they both pulled out of the kiss, startled, and

stared at each other for what felt like an eternity. Billie was the first to speak.

"I'm so sorry, Cara," she stammered. "This is all my fault. I shouldn't have kissed you. I just... I couldn't resist." Her eyes wandered down to Cara's lips. "Your mouth..." She sighed and moved off Cara, burying her face in her hands. "Oh God, I'm a bad person."

"You're not a bad person." Cara tried to steady her voice as she sat up too. Every part of her was trembling, and she watched her own shaking hand as she brought it to her lips. She closed her eyes. "I wanted it just as much as you did. We're both responsible." She hesitated. "We shouldn't have done it. But it happened. It must have been the alcohol."

"Yeah," Billie whispered. "The alcohol." She paused. "This is awkward. What do we do now?"

Cara stared into nowhere. She was still trying to grasp what had just happened. "I don't know, Billie. Let's go to bed and sleep it off. I don't think I'm capable of having a rational conversation right now. Is that okay?"

Billie nodded. "Yes, that's probably a good idea." She turned and looked over her shoulder. "Hey, did you see that?"

Cara turned too, narrowing her eyes as she stared into the dark behind them. She caught a glimpse of a shadow, disappearing into the corridor. "Was someone there? I think I saw someone too..." There was panic in Cara's voice now.

Billie shrugged and turned again to check the door. It was wide open. "I don't know; I'm pretty sure I closed the door. But then maybe I didn't. Or maybe we just imagined it." She sighed. "If there was someone, I guess we'll hear about it tomorrow. Nothing stays secret for very long around here." Billie got up from the couch. "It's all my fault. I should have thought about the consequences before I..."

"It's not your fault," Cara interrupted her. "Stop saying that. We both know that there's been this thing between us for a while now. I thought I was stronger but clearly, I underestimated the situation."

"Me too." Billie still looked flustered. "Let's get out of here. I don't think I'm in a state to talk now either."

24

"Don't you dare make me wear that, Billie. I can't wear green; it's not a good colour on me. Can't you tell it's going to clash with my delicate complexion?" Dorian held up the new green polo shirt Billie had handed him and shook his head in disgust. "How on earth am I going to find a rich boyfriend wearing this?"

"He's right," Josipa chipped in. "I feel like a toad. A big fat toad. It's not just the colour, it's unflattering." She stared at her reflection in the dressing room mirror, pulling the excess fabric back.

Billie sighed in frustration, refusing to take back the shirts. "Hey, don't shoot the messenger. It wasn't my idea. Head office decided that everyone working on the mini golf range should wear these from now on, and there's nothing I can do about that." She silently thanked her lucky stars that she wasn't the one doing the golf shifts. The shirts were hideous indeed. The colour reminded her of insects, and the Pelican crest embroidered on the left side of the chest was far too big compared to the sorry excuse for a collar that stuck up against Josipa's neck like it was trying to choke her.

Billie managed to suppress a laugh, not wanting to provoke her any further. There were four green buttons down the chest, and a red one at the bottom. Some graduate in the branding department who had attempted to be creative, Billie guessed.

"It's not that bad, guys." She tried to sound positive.

Josipa rolled her eyes. "Yeah, right. Can we at least do something about the fit? Take it to the tailor for some adjustments?"

Billie took a deep breath. "Okay, I suppose they're yours now, so do with them what you want." She had no energy left to argue with them. "Take them to the tailor. Tell him to put it on the animation budget. He can call me for authorization." She gave them both a warning look before she headed out the door. "But no funny business, okay? I don't want to see cropped T-shirts or extreme cleavages on either of you tomorrow." She almost crashed into Arnie as she headed outside.

"There you are," he said, smiling. "Gwen is waiting for you at the bar. She asked me to come and get you."

"I can't right now, Arnie." She looked up at the sky in despair, balling her hands into fists. Gwen was the last person she wanted to speak to. "I'm really busy, and I have to be at the managers' meeting in twenty minutes."

"That's alright." Gwen poked her head over Arnie's shoulder. "I only need five minutes. Can you spare five?"

Billie's eyes widened. "Oh, hi Gwen. I didn't see you there. How are you?"

"I'm good, just a bit bored," Gwen said, matter-of-factly. "And you? I see you survived the storm?" She hesitated. "I was looking for you last night. Thought you might have the evening off."

"Yeah, that was quite a storm, huh? I started to feel seasick, so I went to bed early," Billie lied.

Gwen nodded slowly, pursing her lips. "You poor thing. Well, you look like you're back to your old self today. Anyway, I was wondering if you'd like to have dinner with me tonight? My treat. I've reserved a table at La Mer." She giggled and batted her eyelashes. "Forgive me, but I checked your schedule with one of your colleagues, so I'd be sure you were off at eight."

"That's very kind of you, Gwen." Billie's mind was going full blast, trying to come up with an excuse. "Unfortunately, someone's called in sick, so I have to teach the yoga class tonight."

Gwen looked disappointed, but she collected herself. "No worries. I could always join the class? I could do with some exercise."

"Sounds good." Arnie put an arm around Gwen's shoulder and winked. "Maybe I'll come too. We could have dinner first and then go to yoga together?"

Gwen arched an eyebrow, ignoring his suggestion. There was an awkward silence, and Billie was desperate to get away from them.

"Okay, great," she stammered. "I'll see you both in class tonight, then." She gave Gwen and Arnie a cheerful wave and hurried to her meeting. *Damn it.* Now she would have to give the yoga instructor a night off and take over from her, resulting in a thirteen-hour shift if she counted the preparations for the class. This was not a good day.

Billie's phone vibrated in her pocket. She took it out but put it away as soon as she saw the message was from Dan. She didn't want to read it. She couldn't read it. Contrary to what she'd expected, Dan's affection for her seemed only to have grown since she'd left. At first, she liked that, and talking to him cheered her up. His sweet messages and funny voicemails had made her laugh. But now Cara was the only thing on her mind, and for the first time in her life, Billie had no idea how to deal with the situation.

25

"We need to talk." Cara leaned over the edge of her bed, looking down at Billie. "Billie?" She raised her voice. "Come on, I know you're not sleeping, you always snore when you do. You can't keep ignoring me forever."

Billie opened her eyes and sighed. "I know." She looked up at Cara and held her gaze. Cara tried to ignore the butterflies she felt, but that had proven close to impossible so far. "I should tell him, right?" Billie said. "That we kissed?"

"No." Cara waved her hand. "That's the thing. I don't think you should. It would break his heart if he knew I did that to him. I've known Dan since our first year of University, and I love him. He'll be devastated if he finds out." She sighed. "It feels like a betrayal. God, what am I saying? It is a betrayal. I've been a terrible friend, and I'm pretty sure he would never speak to me again if you told him. I can't lose him, Billie."

Billie stood up and leaned against the railing of Cara's bed. She was wearing Cara's Rolling Stones T-shirt and white briefs, low on her hips. Cara's gaze fleeted down to her exposed belly button and then back up to the messy blonde hair and her full, peach coloured lips.

"I'm sorry. I shouldn't have kissed you," Billie said, nervously shifting from one foot to another. "I put both you and myself in a difficult situation and that was never my intention. Last night..." She shook her head. "Everything was so perfect. You and me in that library with the storm roaring outside. I felt like I could talk to you. I felt safe with you, and I think you felt safe with me." She swallowed hard. "I tried to fight the attraction, but you looked at me in a way no one ever has before. That look of tenderness and desire in your eyes. I couldn't resist." She shivered at the memories of the previous night. "Or maybe I just imagined that. Anyway, I got carried away. It won't happen again, and if you don't want me to tell Dan, then our secret is safe with me."

Cara rolled onto her side, facing Billie. "Thank you. I really don't want him to find out. If we leave it at this, there's not much harm done, right?" She turned to Billie for consolation, although she knew deep down that what they had done was wrong, no matter how much she tried to rationalize it.

"Yeah," Billie said, not looking too sure of herself either. "I guess so."

Cara sighed in relief at their agreement. "For the record, Billie, you didn't imagine anything. I like you. And I mean, really like you. Sometimes, it's hard not to stare at you, because you're so beautiful and funny and charming." She put her hand on Billie's, resting on the railing. "It doesn't make it any easier, sharing a room with you. I mean, you get undressed in front of me, and flirt with me..." Cara paused, distracted by Billie's mouth. It was like a magnet, pulling her closer and closer, no matter how hard she fought. Billie's lips were parted as if she were holding her breath, and her eyes were darker than normal. It was clear that they were still very much on the same wavelength, and that the attraction between them would be a hard thing to ignore. *Not again. Don't do it.*

"Thank you for telling me," Billie whispered. "It's nice to know you feel the same way. And you're right. This..." She gestured to the room around them. "This doesn't make it any easier."

Cara removed her hand and turned her attention to the red night light on the ceiling. "What we need to do, Billie, is pretend it never happened and try to be friends. Can you do that?"

Billie nodded slowly. "I think I can do that. I'll try. Can you?"

Cara nodded too. "Yes. We have to." She pulled the cover over her shoulders and closed her eyes as Billie got back into bed. She missed her touch already.

"Cara?" Billie called from the bottom bunk.

"Yes?"

"Do I really snore?" Cara chuckled.

"You do. And it's cute. Goodnight, Billie."

26

Billie sneaked out of bed the next morning, determined to avoid Cara, who was still fast asleep. She tiptoed around the room and gathered her gym gear, before heading out to the deck. It was only six am but the sun was already poking its first light over the horizon, leaving a golden trail of ripples. Mornings were beautiful at sea, and the silence on the deck this time of day was a welcome break from the usually noisy poolside after breakfast.

She took a deep breath, looking up at the sky. The night had left the scent of rain in the air, but other than that, the ocean was still. She hadn't exercised by herself in a while. It was something she deemed unnecessary, with all the gym classes she taught weekly, but she needed to clear her head. To her relief, the track around the ship was deserted, so she tightened her laces and took off at a slow pace. As much as she tried to focus on her breathing, Billie couldn't seem to erase Cara from her thoughts. She ran faster and faster, attempting to exhaust herself, but it seemed impossible to erase their kiss from her mind. Each time her memory flashed back, a shiver shot down her spine, leaving her hungry and even more restless than before.

"Hey there, early bird." Billie winced at Arnie's voice behind her. *Not him. Why can't I just get a minute to myself?*

"What are you doing here?" she asked, sounding crankier than she intended.

"I come here every morning," he answered cheerfully. Billie accelerated, but Arnie caught up with her and grinned. "Someone got out on the wrong side of the bed. Still hung over from the storm party? I didn't see much of you yesterday either, the way you took off right after yoga."

"I'm fine." Billie panted. "Mind your own business, Arnie." There was no point trying to stay ahead of him; he was in much better shape than she was.

"I'm sorry, I can't do that." He was running next to her, trying to make eye contact. "You don't seem fine to me, and I want to help you."

"You can't help me." Billie rolled her eyes. "Look, I'm sorry to be so blunt, but I just don't want to talk right now, okay?" She realized she was out of breath, after only four laps of the deck.

"Did you have a fight with your roomie?" Billie shot him a furious look, but Arnie still didn't get the message. "Because she seems like a decent person to me, and I'm sure she'll be chill if you apologize for whatever you did."

"Stop it, Arnie. Just stop, please." Billie came to a halt at the back end of the ship. She sat down panting, resting her head on her crossed arms. To her annoyance, Arnie stopped too and sat down next to her. He placed a hand on her back. "Listen," Billie said, "I know you want to help, but this is not the right time. If you could just…"

"I know what's bothering you, Billie-Boo," he interrupted her. "It's Cara, right? You two have this thing going on. There's no shame in that."

"Great," Billie whispered. "That's just great." She finally met Arnie's gaze. "How did you know? Was that you, sneaking around the library last night?"

Arnie shrugged. "I wasn't anywhere near the library. Why would I go there? I haven't read a book since college." He grinned. "Call it intuition. It was just a guess. But you just admitted it."

"And I suppose your so-called intuition made sure the whole ship knows about Cara and me too?"

Arnie shook his head. "No. I didn't discuss it with anyone."

Billie shot him an angry look. "Yeah, right. Just like you didn't tell Gwen about me and that chick from the casino a couple of years ago."

Arnie seemed taken aback by that. He held up both hands in defence. "Hey, I didn't know that was a secret. It's not like every man and his dog on this ship doesn't know about it already. Gwen asked me if I thought you were into women. I told her I didn't know but that you had a fling with a woman once, so it wasn't out of the question. How is that so terrible?" He sighed. "I'm sorry. I didn't realize it would get you in trouble."

Billie shook her head. "Never mind. It's okay. And just so we're clear, there's nothing going on between Cara and me, okay? We were drunk and we kissed. That's all."

"Sure," Arnie said, picking on a torn fingernail. "Whatever you say, nothing's going on. But even if the two of you were a couple, I want you to know that it wouldn't bother me if you were a lezzer." Billie rolled her eyes at that, but the oblivious Arnie continued. "I'm a pretty liberal guy, you know, and you need to do what feels right for you." He pressed a hand against his heart. "In here, Billie."

Billie didn't know whether to laugh or cry. Their conversation was getting too ridiculous for words, but Arnie was trying his best to be a good friend, and it was kind of endearing. "Thanks, Arnie. As I already told you, there is nothing between Cara and me, but it's great to know that I have your permission to sleep with women and that you will still respect me if I turn out to be a lesbian." Her tone was sarcastic, but Arnie seemed perfectly satisfied with her reply.

He stood up and held out a hand. "I won't mention it again. Race you to the finish line?"

Billie let him help her up and nodded, grateful he had finally dropped the subject.

27

"You, with the dark hair, in the back." Cara looked up from the pineapple she was carving, shivering at the sound of Chef Claudio's raised voice. He nodded when she met his stern gaze. "Yeah, you. Get your skinny ass over here."

She put her knife down and walked over to his meeting table, straightening her jacket and tucking stray strands of hair back into her cap. Her legs were shaking, and her heart was pounding. *What have I done?* Chef Claudio looked angry. Not that that was anything unusual, but the fact that he had singled her out was worrying.

"Yes, Chef?" She took a deep breath, trying to calm her nerves.

"Cara, right?"

Cara nodded. "Yes, Chef. Is something wrong?"

He frowned and gestured to Ben's empty workstation. "Ben broke his leg. The idiot fell down the stairs after one too many drinks last night. We'll be sending him back when we get to the next port, and I need you to take over his section tonight. How far are you with the fruit carving?"

Cara let out a sigh of relief. "I'm about an hour away from finishing, Chef."

Chef Claudio looked at his watch. "An hour is too much. You'll have twenty minutes after you've finished prepping the starters. I'll get someone to walk you through the menu and show you how things are done."

"No need," Cara interrupted him. "I know the menu. I used to help Ben after finishing the centrepieces."

Chef Claudio cocked his head, and the frown between his eyebrows reappeared. "Are you saying the lazy bastard couldn't manage on his own? You know how to make the starters? All of them?"

Cara nodded. "Ben was fine working by himself, Chef. I just wanted to learn so I offered to help him. I've made most of the dishes more than once."

"Very well." Chef Claudio sniffed. "Back to work then." He gestured for her to leave. "And don't fuck it up," she heard him yell after her as she walked back to her section.

Cara smiled. She felt sorry for Ben, but at the same time she couldn't wait to get her hands on the starters. It meant she'd have to work a double shift, but it felt like a blessing today. Finally, she had the chance to show them what she could do. She started gathering her ingredients, working off the prep list that was hanging down from the top shelf. After making a schedule, she started chopping, frying and boiling with the focus of a heart surgeon. Her hands were shaking as she carefully put all the ingredients together, ensuring nothing went to waste.

Two hours later, Chef Claudio was back. He barged into the kitchen with the notepad that seemed to be permanently attached to his left hand. "Plate your dishes, everyone. You have thirty minutes. I want to see and taste perfection, and nothing but perfection."

Cara nudged the chef next to her, a middle-aged Vietnamese man who went by the name of Kim. "I didn't know he was going to taste today. Did you?"

Kim shook his head. "He does this sometimes. Wants to keep us on our toes, I guess. Or maybe he's testing you." Kim started whipping up a hollandaise sauce as if his life depended on it.

Cara went to work with her soups, salads, tuna carpaccio and deep-fried Camembert. She was slightly behind and wasn't looking forward to the tasting. Despite her excitement at the opportunity she'd been given, and her eagerness to prove her worth to Chef Claudio, she couldn't help being distracted by mental images of Billie, which kept popping up in her head, making her heart race.

They hadn't exchanged more than the necessary words lately, and that had been hard. Billie had already been asleep when Cara came back to their room the past couple of nights, or maybe she'd just been pretending to sleep. The mornings had been quiet too, and the usually chatty Billie had gone out on the deck with her coffee. It bothered Cara, the way their relationship had changed after their kiss, although they both knew that keeping a distance was the right thing to do. Avoidance was better than temptation, in their case. The issue between her and Billie made things tricky, especially on a day like this. She had already managed to burn her hand, and her plating didn't look exactly the way she wanted. Unfortunately, there was no room for mistakes in Chef Claudio's kitchen, and Cara was dreading she might fall victim to one of his vicious verbal attacks. She dressed her salad leaves, topped them with pickled beetroot and the mackerel pâté she had prepared earlier. She carefully poured the watercress soup and the minestrone into bowls and drizzled the garnish on top. Then she marinated her Camembert and deep fried it, before placing it on a bed of rocket and tomato chutney. The carpaccio was the hardest. The slices were so thin that Cara had to use food wrap to transfer them onto the plates, trying to arrange them in a perfect circle, with no more than half an inch of overlap. She barely managed to put the herbs and dressing on top before Chef Claudio shouted:

"Step back from your stations!" His voice was loud and confident as he walked up to them with the force of an army commander, a stark contrast to his skinny frame and his almost skull-like face.

He started at the front with the desserts. "Nadine, your ice-cream is far too sweet. Did you follow the recipe?"

Nadine nodded.

"Nonsense." He took another bite. "If you had followed the recipe, your ice-cream would be tangy, not syrupy like this crap." He gestured towards the box of ice-cream. "Throw that away and start over. Use the blast chiller, and you should be ready in time for service." Cara watched Nadine's shoulders drop. She looked like she'd lost the will to live, but she didn't protest. Nobody ever did.

Danny was next in line, with a variety of fish dishes. "Nice flavour, Danny. Keep up the good work." A ratty grin spread across the Chef's face, which was an unusual occurrence.

Danny beamed with pride. "Thank you, Chef."

Chef Claudio skimmed over the next dishes without many comments. The relief on the faces of the chefs who passed would have been comical to Cara, if it hadn't been for the fact that she was up next. She looked up at Chef Claudio as he cracked the cheese that oozed out of its nut crust, and she felt a sudden need to make excuses for her sloppy plating.

"I'm sorry, Chef. It's been a bit hectic today. I'm not sure if I..."

"Don't defend the food, Cara," he interrupted her. "Let it speak for itself. It is what it is." He took a bite from each dish in front of him, inspecting the food for missing ingredients or flaws. Then he shook his head. "Just a bit more colour on the Camembert. Other than that, it's spot-on. Well done."

Cara let out a sigh of relief. "Thank you. I mean, thank you, Chef." Her eyes lit up when she saw him smiling before he walked off. *I'm getting good at this! I can cook!* And although the smile was just a small gesture, to Cara, it meant the world. It was exactly what she needed to boost her confidence in the kitchen. She couldn't wait to tell Billie.

28

After her shift, Cara headed for the night shop to buy a newspaper. Finally, she would have two full days off. She couldn't remember the last time she'd had the time to read a full newspaper front to back over many, many coffees. She slowed down as she passed the theatre. A wave of applause told her Mr. Lombardi's show was still on. Cara was drawn to the doors as soon as she heard him call Billie's name. She pushed open one of them and peeked through the gap. There was Billie on stage, in her red sequined dress. She was standing centre stage, next to Mr. Lombardi. The spotlight was on her, as she smiled at the audience. She looked radiant, Cara thought, the way she stood there with confidence, striking flirty poses as she handed Mr. Lombardi a red scarf.

Cara opened the door further and scanned the rows of chairs for an empty seat at the back before slipping into the theatre. She knew it was against staff policy, but she was unable to resist the temptation of watching Billie on stage. Mr. Lombardi tied a scarf around Billie's ponytail. She jumped up, acted surprised and put her hands in front of her mouth when a white dove came flying out of her hair. Cara laughed at her startled expression when another dove appeared. Billie was good, and she knew how to get the audience going. Her movements were elegant, as she stepped into a wooden box, kicking her legs up in the air before Mr. Lombardi closed the lid. She shot the audience a terrified look when he started sawing the box in half. There were gasps from every corner of the theatre. Billie's head was still sticking out. She was perfectly still, and her eyes were closed now. Although Billie had mentioned it was a boring old trick that practically every magician used, it seemed to work, and applause broke out when Mr. Lombardi separated the two halves and spun them around. Then he put them back together and covered them with a red velvet throw. When he removed it, Billie was gone from the box.

Cara looked around the theatre along with everyone else in the audience, trying to figure out where she'd gone, until the spotlight moved over the stage towards the curtains behind Mr. Lombardi. The curtains opened, and there was Billie. She spread out her arms and smiled, greeting the audience.

Cara sighed as she watched, feeling her heart swell with emotion at the mere sight of her. *She's amazing.* Billie looked beautiful. She bowed for the applause and gestured towards Mr. Lombardi, thanking him for his performance.

"Look at those legs," the man next to Cara said to his friend. "I wonder what's underneath that little dress."

Cara turned to him, and an overwhelming sense of protectiveness took over when he whistled. She nudged him. "Hey, watch your mouth, primate."

He turned to her and laughed, along with his friend. They were both in their late forties and looked like they were having a night out without their wives. The smell of beer was oozing out of his pores. "And you are?"

Cara cocked her head, studying his frumpy comb-over. "It doesn't matter who I am, just have a little respect, okay?"

The man chuckled, clearly uncomfortable with Cara, who refused to break her warning stare. He stood up and nodded towards the exit. "Come on, Tiger. Let's go and get a drink before the little lady here gets all upset."

Cara wanted to pull him back by his hair and punch him, but remembered that she wasn't supposed to be there in the first place. She tried to compose herself, as she watched her hands shaking with rage and sat back, wondering what the hell had come over her.

29

Billie walked into the dressing room to find Cara sitting in her chair. Her heart skipped a beat, and she suddenly felt self-conscious in her presence. Cara was still in her chef's whites, the jacket open and the sleeves rolled up, exposing the rose tattoos on her right arm. Underneath, she was wearing her usual white vest top. A red bandana was wrapped around her head and tied at the front, holding back her fringe. Although it was almost midnight, she looked like she was full of energy. Her eyes were sparkling with excitement, and she smiled broadly when Billie greeted her.

"Cara, what a nice surprise. I didn't expect to see you here."

"Hey, Billie. I sneaked into the theatre and managed to catch the last part of the show. You were so great up there."

Billie rolled her eyes and laughed. "Thank you. But I didn't do very much, apart from striking stupid poses and pretending to be scared."

"Well, I didn't think it was stupid. You were so charismatic and so..." She shook her head. "I'm sorry. I didn't even ask you if I could come in. Do you want me to leave?" She stood up to give Billie her chair back.

"No, of course not. Sit back down. I need to get changed anyway; the laundry lady is finally picking up this monstrosity of a garment to be dry-cleaned." She looked down at the sequined red dress she'd been wearing for five shows now. Broken sequins were poking into her skin, and she couldn't wait to get out of it. She hesitated when she took hold of the hem to pull it over her head. "Do you mind?"

Cara frowned in confusion, then the penny dropped. "Oh of course, sorry." She giggled nervously as she swivelled the chair around, so she had her back to Billie. It didn't help much, as she could still see Billie in the mirror that was right in front of her now. Billie laughed as Cara closed her eyes, covering her face with her hands. It wasn't anything she hadn't seen before, but things were different now. And if they were going to keep their distance, they would have to stop seeing each other half naked.

"I'm glad you're here," Billie said, as she struggled with the heavy red dress. "I've missed talking to you." She hesitated. "And I feel like we've been avoiding each other. Well I have, to be honest with you. I'm just not sure how to deal with this." She slipped the dress over the hanger and zipped up the bag around it before stepping into her own jersey dress. "You can turn around now."

Cara laughed. "That's better. It looked painful, the way you were squeezed into that red tube." Then her face turned serious. "I've missed you too." She sighed. "I had a wonderful day in the kitchen, and I really wanted to tell you about it." She held up a takeaway box. "I made you a seared tuna sesame salad in case you were hungry. There's extra wasabi in there, just the way you like it."

Billie smiled as she took the box. "Oh Cara, you're the best. Let's go outside, I want to hear all about your day."

T he night was chilly on the Atlantic, but comfortable enough to sit on the deck. They went for their usual spot on one of the front benches with the best view over the ocean. After Billie had eaten her salad, she snuggled against Cara, who put an arm around her shoulder. Cara's heart started beating faster as soon as Billie's face touched her chest.

"So much for distance, huh?" Cara remarked. But she couldn't stop her hand from reaching out and stroking Billie's hair.

Billie shook her head and inhaled deep against the fabric of Cara's vest top underneath her open jacket. "Just five minutes, please. You smell so good."

"I smell of food," Cara said, laughing. "And smoke, and probably sweat too. Can't imagine that being very enticing."

Billie ignored her and pulled Cara's arm further down over her shoulders. She held it there and looked up. "So, tell me. What happened tonight?"

Cara chuckled. Feeling Billie close to her had made her forget the whole reason she wanted to speak to her in the first place. "Chef Claudio told me I'll be replacing Ben on the starters. Ben got drunk last night and broke his leg, so he's going home."

"Oh no. Poor Ben." Billie winced. "So you took over from him?"

Cara smiled, thinking of the rare compliment she had been given. "Yes. It was the most stressful shift so far, but it went really well. Chef Claudio did a tasting, and he liked my food. It was the best feeling ever. I'm not just a fruit carver now, Billie. I'm a chef de partie, and tonight, I was pretty good at my job." She laughed. "It was eye-opening. I loved every second of it, and I think I know what I want to do with my life now. Long-term, I mean. I want to get really good at cooking and make it my career."

"That's great." Billie looked up at her. "I'm so happy you've found something you're passionate about. And I'm so proud of you." She met Cara's smile with a cheeky grin. "Does that mean you might come back with me next season?"

Cara shrugged. "Maybe. Depends..."

"Depends on what?"

"I don't know, Billie. It's hard to be around you. I'm hoping that these feelings I have will go away and that everything will be easier then. But even if they do, I'll have to make my own choices, not follow you around. We're not a couple."

"You're right," Billie whispered. "Forget what I said, I don't know what I was thinking."

"Billie..." Cara swallowed hard. "I'm sorry. That sounded harsh, and I didn't mean to hurt you. But you know what I mean, right?"

Billie looked up at the sky. Thousands of stars were glistening in the darkness. "I know. It's just that I'm going to miss you when we get back home. I'm going to miss seeing you every night, and talking to you whenever I want."

"Yeah." Cara sighed. "Same here." There was a brief silence. "How was your day?" she asked, changing the subject. "Did anything exciting happen? Any gossip?"

Billie shrugged. "Not much. We had a full house at the show tonight, so that was nice. And I received the new shirts from head office a couple of days ago. They look awful, and my team won't stop giving me grief about it. You know how vain young girls can be, right? And that includes Dorian."

Cara laughed. "That bad?"

Billie nodded, the corners of her mouth pulling up into a tiny smile. "Let's just say I'm happy I won't have to wear them." The wind picked up, causing Billie to shiver.

"Are you cold?" Cara rubbed her arm. "Do you want to go back inside?"

"No." Billie shook her head. "I'm fine. Could we just stay here for a little longer?"

"Of course." Cara kissed the top of Billie's head, inhaling the scent of her shampoo. "We can stay as long as you want."

30

"How's the sexy chef doing?"

"Dan... good to hear your voice." Cara's heart sank at his cheerful tone. She checked to see if the bathroom door was closed. Billie was in there, getting ready for the night's performance. She sneaked into the hallway.

"How are you, Cara?" Dan laughed. "Why are you whispering? Are you working?"

"No, just trying not to wake anyone up," Cara lied. "Some people are taking a nap after their shift, and these walls are like cardboard." She sat down on the stained carpet at the end of the corridor and leaned against the emergency exit door, waiting for Dan's face to appear on her screen. His hair was wet, and water was still dripping down his face as if he hadn't bothered to dry himself off after his shower.

"All righty then." Dan lowered his voice too. "Just wanted to check up on you. I saw there had been a storm along your route, and I wanted to know if you were safe."

"Eh yeah..." Cara stammered. "It was pretty wild, but we got through it. Apparently, it was one of the worst ones they've had in years. It was okay though. They gave us a night off, so we had a staff party."

"Sounds good." Dan chuckled. "Have you and Billie been partying a lot then? You do look tired, if you don't mind me saying."

Cara smiled and swallowed hard. "Not really," she lied again. "In fact, we hardly ever see each other. I work late; she works funny shifts... you know how it goes."

"Okay. Well, Billie told me you guys were going to Cape Town together."

"Oh yes, I was going to tell you that. How could I forget!" Cara shouted with way too much enthusiasm. Damn it. She was such a bad liar. "I'm really looking forward to it." She managed to produce a chuckle. "We'll send you a postcard and some fridge magnets. I know how much you love them."

Dan laughed. "And Billie? How is she?"

"She's fine," Cara answered immediately. "Why do you ask? You speak to her, don't you?" Again, that stupid, defensive tone. Why did she do that? She balled her free hand into a fist and bit her knuckle.

"I don't know." Dan sighed. "She sounded different when I last spoke to her, that's all. Just made me wonder if she's okay." There was a pause. "She hasn't met anyone, has she? Because if she has, you need to tell me. I'm not going to waste my time on her if she's messing around with someone else. You would tell me, wouldn't you?"

"No, of course she hasn't." Cara shook her head. "And if she had, I'd tell you straight away. You know I'll always be on your side, Dan. No matter what happens."

"I'm not worried," Dan said defensively. "I just want to know the score, that's all. I mean, I've been behaving myself, but it's getting harder and harder when she's not around."

He groaned. "Oh God, I sound like a total loser now, don't I? I've always said I'll never be one of those..."

"You're not a loser," Cara interrupted him. "You're a good person. You're decent. And that's why I love you."

Dan smiled at her from behind the kitchen table. "I love you too, Cara." He turned the camera. "I'm cleaning. Can you believe that?"

Cara laughed. "What happened to you, Dan? First Billie and now you're cleaning? Hey, wait. Is that an apron?"

Dan grinned and directed the camera towards the strawberry printed apron over his bare chest. "It sure is. I'm holding open house and interviews next week. Just a temporary tenant," he quickly added. "I'm putting your room up for rent for four months. The microbrewery thing didn't work out." He laughed. "Turns out it's hard work, making beer."

Cara smiled. "So, you're trying to lure people into paying for that shithole now."

Dan nodded. "Yup. And you have no idea how filthy this place is. I never noticed it before, but now I see dust and grease everywhere. I've had three showers already today." He turned towards the wall. "Hey, look at this. I found some paintings at the flea market. Thought they might spruce up the décor."

Cara regarded the paintings with an amused look. Three heavy wooden frames with carved flowers held paintings of horses, running on a beach. "Nice Dan. Interesting choice." She laughed. "And the frames... I hope you didn't pay much for them."

Dan laughed too. "Well, that's not all. You see, there was this house clearance, and the deceased was clearly a big fan of horses, so I decided to go all the way and coordinate the accessories." He winked. "Get it?"

"Show me," Cara said, ready to face the damage. "Just get it over with." She had almost forgotten how much Dan made her laugh.

Dan pointed the camera at a life-size pony sculpture in the hallway. It was showing its teeth, smiling into the lens. More horse paintings were leaning against it, and several porcelain horse figures were displayed on the floor.

"Still need to find a home for these bad boys," Dan said. "I was thinking maybe the living room."

"The living room sounds like an excellent choice. And don't forget to save some of that crap for my room. I can't wait to see the result of your styling attempts when I get back." She looked at her watch. Billie would be leaving their cabin soon.

"I have to go, Dan. I need to get dressed for work. Can I call you back later?"

Dan blew her a kiss. "No need. I just wanted to see you, that's all." He paused. "I miss you, Cara. I miss you both. Say hi to Billie for me, will you?"

Cara nodded. "I will. Speak soon."

31

"Do you know where we're going, or do you want me to turn on my satnav?" Cara asked, waving her phone around.

The Duncan Dock in Cape Town was a lively place. Taxis and shuttles were picking up and dropping off, large cruise ships and vessels were departing and arriving, and tour guides were leading their charges to their excursion buses. She looked out over the city that spread between Table Mountain and the sea, and felt a rush of excitement at the idea of two full days in a new place. There wasn't much exploring left to do on the ship. By now, she knew it inside out and was dying for a change of scenery.

"Nope. I've been here a couple of times. I think I still remember," Billie said, leading the way. "Let's walk to the V&A Waterfront and have a coffee first; we can take a bus from there." The sun hit them as they moved out of the shade of the cruise terminal.

"It's so much warmer here than on the ship. I'm glad I only brought a small backpack." Cara took off her cardigan and tied it around her waist.

"Wait till you start climbing." Billie laughed. "Table Mountain is no joke. People tend to underestimate how hard the climb is because it's a tourist attraction, but I've got a feeling we'll be sleeping like babies tonight."

They walked along the waterfront, passing a mixture of colonial and industrial buildings, until they reached a narrow footbridge, leading to the marina. The waterfront was crowded with locals eating their breakfast on the benches along the water, tourists browsing through the souvenir shops and the galleries, and yachts docking at the bay. Most restaurants and cafes were situated along the water, with generous outside space and big white parasols sheltering the tables from the bright sun. They found a free table at a brunch restaurant and took a seat in the shade, facing the harbour.

"I feel like I'm on holiday," Cara giggled. "It's sunny, there's a promenade, and I've got both feet on steady ground." She ordered an iced coffee and leaned back in her chair.

"I'll have a cappuccino please," Billie said to the waiter, before turning back to Cara. "Me too. I've been looking forward to this. Two full days off, what a treat. I suppose we could sleep on the boat tonight, but it wouldn't be the same, right?"

Cara shook her head. "No, let's stay here and enjoy the city for as long as we can. I'm sure we'll find somewhere cheap and cheerful later." She smiled. "It's nice to spend some time together, isn't it?"

"Yeah." Billie sighed. "It's nice to be with you. Just the two of us." She gave Cara a playful wink. "And I promise you I'll behave if you do the same."

Cara laughed. "I can't promise you anything if you're planning on wearing that today." She pointed at Billie's short, figure-hugging jersey dress.

"What's wrong with it?" Billie stood up and wiggled her hips. "This is perfectly fine climbing attire. I took freedom of movement into great consideration when I put my outfit together this morning."

"Nothing's wrong with it. It's just very short, that's all. That dress could be distracting in a life or death situation. And since we're climbing..."

"You'll just have to walk up front then," Billie interrupted her playfully. "And with that, I'm handing the role of navigator over to you."

There was a long queue at the cable car station. Cara noticed a sign that said: 'Waiting time from here 1 hour.' She laughed. "Serves them right for taking the easy way."

Billie looked up at the majestic Table Mountain that towered above them and frowned. "Or maybe they're just smart."

Cara gave her a nudge. "You're not backing out now. It was your idea to hike all the way up there."

Billie shot her a cynical look. "Yeah right. No way am I backing out. Let's talk in an hour, if you haven't fallen too far behind, that is." She checked her backpack. "I've got water, do you?" Cara nodded. "Great. Stay there; I'm going to get us a picnic."

Billie ran over to a passing food truck, waving at the driver to stop. A couple of minutes later, she came back with two large takeaway boxes. "You're going to love this," she said with a grin. She stashed the boxes in her backpack and adjusted her shoulder straps. "Are you ready for a hike?"

Cara lowered the visor on her cap as they walked up the narrow, cobblestone path. After a little while, the path turned into wonky stairs made of large rocks, which led them up the hill to the bottom of the mountain. It was green and untouched for as far as she could see. Billie's bare legs offered an attractive addition to the already beautiful view, and Cara tried to walk behind her as much as she could.

She was well aware that she wasn't exactly practicing what she preached, as she had been pushing Billie to keep a distance, telling her over and over that she wanted to be loyal to Dan, yet here she was again, staring up at Billie's behind. Her reason was telling her one thing, but her whole body and being were screaming another. Was she fooling herself, thinking she could maintain control over her actions? Cara's resolve was slowly crumbling in the face of the magnetic effect that Billie seemed to have on her. She was also aware that she had the option of moving out of the room, removing herself from all temptation. But she didn't want to make that choice, because Billie was like a drug, and she needed her.

"Cara, are you coming?" Billie's voice calling her name startled Cara, and she ran up the steps to catch up with her.

They climbed up through a steep ravine, with rocks that reached high on either side, and stopped in the shade to catch their breath.

"I'm not used to exercising anymore," Cara said, bending down. She rested her elbows on her knees.

Billie nodded, leaning against the mountain wall as she took a sip from her water bottle. "Same here. I thought I'd be in good shape with all the classes I teach, but it's much harder than I thought it would be." She laughed. "We're over halfway. Do you want to take a break?"

Cara nodded, still out of breath. They sat down on a flat

surface, looking out over the coastline, the city centre, and the southern suburbs. Cara leaned back on her elbows, giving her lower back a rest.

"It's beautiful here, and we're not even at the top." There was no one around, apart from two other hikers, and after they had passed, it was silent. Cara shielded her eyes from the sun when she saw something moving close by. "Hey, what's that?" A pair of tiny eyes were staring at her from underneath a rock. The rabbit-sized creature was furry and brown, and its nose came sticking out as if it was trying to figure out if they had food on them.

Billie's eyes widened in excitement. "It's a dassie! Oh, look how cute he is." She bent forward to take a peek underneath the rock. "Come here, sweetie." The dassie came out of its hiding place, carefully approaching them. He looked like a giant guinea pig, with small ears and funny feet. "They're descended from African elephants, believe it or not," Billie whispered, slowly reaching out her hand. "They're very common around here." She pointed at his feet. "They've got hoof-like nails on the tips of their toes, see?"

Cara kept quiet as the dassie approached them, curiously sniffing Billie's hand. It looked nothing like an elephant, not even a tiny one, but Cara took her word for it. When his curiosity was satisfied, he looked up at Cara, and then eyed up the bag in her lap.

"He's adorable," Cara said, sticking out her hand too. "Are you hungry, little fella?"

"We're not supposed to feed them," Billie said. "But I suppose a banana wouldn't hurt?" While Billie rummaged through her bag the dassie sat down, staring up at them. His little hands eagerly reached out for the banana, and he snatched it away, retreating to his cave. "You're welcome," Billie laughed.

She turned to Cara. "And you? Are you hungry too?" She handed Cara one of the takeaway boxes.

Cara smiled when she opened it. It smelled delicious, and the food was still warm. "Wow, what is this?"

"I have no idea," Billie laughed. "The sign said lamb and pondweed stew, whatever that may be." She took a bite and closed her eyes. "But it sure tastes good."

After a final steep climb, Cara let herself fall onto the paved surface of one of the highest points of Table Mountain. Billie dropped down next to her, equally exhausted. It was full of people, taking pictures in front of the panoramic view.

"We did it, Cara. All the way to the top." She placed a hand on Cara's in between them and looked up at the sky. A cloud drifted over them, and it was so close that she could almost touch it. Billie pointed down at the spider's web of cobbled paths they had climbed. "Look how far we've come."

Cara leaned forward then hastily moved back from the edge. "Shit, this is high."

They could see the Pelican amongst other cruise ships, waiting for their return in the harbour. Smaller ships were coming in and out of the V&A berths, one of them heading for an island in the distance.

"That's Robben Island," Billie said. "The famous island that held South Africa's political prisoners, including Nelson Mandela." Then she pointed to the north of the city, where the only piece of flat land was situated. "And if I'm not mistaken, those are the Cape Flats, the apartheid's dumping grounds. It was a desolate piece of land, where all the non-whites were moved during the apartheid. There were no facilities, and it was dry and sandy, making agriculture hard. It's still a very poor and dangerous area, full of gangs and with high crime rates."

"I've read about it," Cara said. "It's hard to believe that the apartheid only ended in the nineties, right?"

"Yeah." Billie nodded. "It's unfortunate, but Cape Town is still quite segregated. Do you see that patch, halfway up that hill over there?" Cara nodded. "That's the Malay Quarter, home of the Indian and Malaysian community. And at the bottom of Table Mountain is the rich area, as you can tell by the villas with large gardens and pools. That's predominantly white." Billie pointed at a road next to it. "On the other side of that road are the poor black townships. Life is still rough in most of those areas, although some of them are slowly transforming into artistic neighbourhoods, with galleries and small businesses."

A cloud was moving in, and patches of low hanging mist cascaded over the edge of the cliff, like a waterfall in slow motion. Cara ran her hand through its cool dampness. It was breathtaking. They could see the other mountain ranges, partially covered in clouds. She leaned into Billie and rested her cheek on her shoulder. A sense of calm overcame her. She felt exhausted, but the accomplishment of the hike, and Billie's closeness, made up for it tenfold.

"Hey, Billie?"

"What?" Billie smiled.

"Can we please take the cable car down? I think I'm just about done walking for today."

"So, you're admitting defeat?" Billie said in a teasing tone.

"Come on." Cara nudged her. "Don't tell me you're up for walking down, because I know your legs hurt just as much as mine. You just don't want to admit it."

"I'll admit defeat if you walk down by yourself."

Cara shook her head. "But I'd rather you come with me."

Billie laughed. "I don't want to walk down either." She winked. "And I certainly don't want to spend two hours away from you."

"Can you handle a casual stroll, or are you too tired?" Billie asked when they got out of the cable car.

Cara nodded. "I sure can. I think I've got my energy back now. Where do you suggest we go?"

"Bo-Kaap. It's the Malay quarter I just pointed out. I've never been there before, but I've heard it's a nice neighbourhood. We'll have to get a cab, though." She held up her hand to hail a taxi.

Cara and Billie looked around in amazement when they entered the vibrant Bo-Kaap with its cobbled streets and colourful homes. The township was built on the slopes of a hill, above the city centre, and the views were breathtaking. Above them was Table Mountain, and below the city and the harbour.

To her surprise, Cara spotted a mosque. "It almost feels like a different country."

"You're right." Billie took a picture of a charming row of townhouses, built on a slope against the mountain wall. "During the apartheid, the Bo-Kaap quarter was declared a Muslims only area," she explained. "It's now also known as the Malay Quarter, the oldest residential area in Cape Town."

"Everything is so well taken care of," Cara said, as they started walking down the hill. The houses were painted in bright pink, green, yellow, red, turquoise and purple, and stood out against the clear blue sky. Their balconies and verandas were painted in contrasting colours and decorated with plants and flowers, hanging over the balustrades. There weren't many cars, but there was an abundance of scooters, also brightly coloured. They passed spice shops, small family run restaurants, and a rehearsal studio, where an afro-jazz band was playing with the windows and doors wide open. Billie clapped her hands to the rhythm and shook her shoulders, bumping her hips against Cara's every four beats.

Cara laughed. "You're never going to get me to dance, no matter what you do, so spare yourself the effort." She let her gaze wander over Billie's body and winked. "Although you do look delightful, shaking your booty like that."

Billie shot her a flirty smile. "Oh yeah? Are you sure you don't want to dance with me?"

Cara shook her head and rolled her eyes in amusement. "Positive." She pointed up to the roof terrace of a red building. People were hanging over the balustrade with beers in their hands, moving to the rhythm of the music. "But I'll have a drink while I watch you dance."

They sat down at a table by the edge of the terrace, with a wide view over the neighbourhood. The bar felt both traditional and eclectic, carefully curated with creative flair. A large, low hanging straw parasol above their table provided shade and a feeling of intimacy. Empty fruit tins functioned as plant pots on the tables and drinks were served out of jam jars. Yellow painted car tyres had been transformed into seats for the lower tables, each with a straw backrest. The clientele consisted mostly of young locals, cheering for the DJ, who had just put on a popular tune.

Cara leaned back in her chair and ordered two beers for

them. "It's weird to be away from the ship, isn't it? It felt funny to walk on steady ground for the first hour, as if I'd suddenly sobered up after weeks of intoxication."

"Me too." Billie took their drinks from the waiter. She took a sip and closed her eyes. "Oh God, that's so nice." She put her glass down and leaned over the table. "Don't get me wrong, I love my job, but sometimes I just need to get away."

"I'm surprised your girlfriend Gwen didn't come along," Cara said, trying to keep a straight face.

Billie shot her a warning look. "Don't call her that, please. I'm traumatized by her advances enough as it is. She asked me to move in with her, did I tell you that?"

Cara burst into laughter. "No, she didn't."

Billie nodded. "Yep, she did. But I kindly declined." She shrugged. "Anyway, Gwen packed her bags and left for the airport this morning. I guess she finally got bored. She's catching a flight to Sydney instead."

"Thank God for that." Cara held up her glass. "Cheers, Billie. I didn't mean to come across as jealous." She grinned. "But maybe I was."

Billie kicked her under the table. "Maybe?"

"Okay." Cara laughed. "I was jealous. But it's not like it would have made any difference." She sighed and leaned forward too, allowing her eyes to wander over Billie's face and neck. "I've been staring at your neck for most of the day, trying to imagine what it tastes like." She watched Billie shiver as goosebumps appeared on her arms. "But I'll behave."

"And I'm not going to put my mouth on your lips either, as much as I'm dying to," Billie whispered. She shot Cara a mischievous glance. "But we can still talk about it, right? No harm in a little bit of sexy-talk?"

Cara laughed and covered her eyes with her hands. "I

can't believe you just said that. I don't think sexy-talk, as you call it, is something friends do amongst each other, nor is it a good idea for two people who are trying to maintain boundaries."

"Fine," Billie said. "But you started this by admitting you were lusting after my soft and delicious neck. So, you better keep your end of the bargain too. And speaking of bargains..." She picked up the check that the waiter had left on their table and waved it in front of Cara. "The drinks here are dirt cheap. I think we should have a night out together."

Cara laughed. "That sounds good. I'm done walking for the day." She looked down at her bare feet that were resting on her shoes under the table. "And I haven't had a fun night out in a very, very long time."

The crowd started clapping when a lady in traditional African attire came up to the roof. She waved and smiled at familiar faces and yelled something in Afrikaans before lighting up the grill next to the DJ.

"We're in luck today," Billie said. "They're doing a traditional barbeque. Gathering from the reaction of the locals, we might be in for a real treat."

Cara gestured to the waiter for another round. The sun had started to set and the light cast a warm glow over the rooftops of Bo-Kaap. The streets were quiet now, but on the roof, the evening had only just started. The DJ switched to dance music, and salads, bread, dips and something that resembled porridge, called 'pap,' were brought out and displayed on a long table next to the grill, alongside paper plates and plastic cutlery.

"Hey there." Billie and Cara both looked up in surprise at the woman in a denim skirt and a white T-shirt who was trying to get their attention. Her long dreads were pulled back into a ponytail, and she had a piercing in her cheek. "My name is Ayanda." She hesitated and gestured to her friends. "We were just curious about the two of you as we've never seen you here. Are you tourists?"

Cara grimaced. "We are. I'm so sorry, is this a private party? We didn't realize..."

"No, not at all," Ayanda interrupted her. "But we rarely get non-residents here. It's always the same crowd on a Friday night, so it's refreshing to see some new faces. Would you like to join us?"

"Sure," Billie and Cara said in unison. Then they looked at each other and laughed.

"I'm Cara. Nice to meet you," Cara said, still chuckling.

Billie waved. "And I'm Billie." She glanced over at the bar. "You go ahead, Cara. I'll get a bottle. We don't want to arrive at a party empty-handed, do we?"

Ayanda's friends reshuffled their seats to make space for Cara and Billie. They all cleared the table, bought tickets for the barbeque and helped themselves to delicious salads and meats from the grill. They were mainly local artists like Ayanda herself, selling paintings and pottery in galleries at the markets.

"So, you both work on a cruise ship? Wow, that must be fun, traveling the world while you work." Ayanda seemed fascinated with Cara and Billie's lifestyle, and Cara suddenly realized how lucky she was. Ever since she'd stepped onto the Pelican, she'd been either working or obsessing over Billie, and she hadn't given her new life much thought.

"Yeah, it's fun," she said. "It's my first season. Billie got me the job, she's been doing it for years."

"And is this your first time in Cape Town?" one of the guys asked.

Cara nodded. "It is for me." That answer brought cheering from the group.

"You're in luck," he said. You've found the best people and the best place to hang out on your first visit." He winked. "And we're going to show you a good time."

32

"Oh God, I don't feel too well." Billie tried unsuccessfully to walk towards the guesthouse in a straight line. "You need to do the talking, Cara. I'm not sure I can speak anymore."

"Don't worry," Cara said, holding Billie up with one arm. "Do you still have your bag and your passport?"

"Yeah. I think it's hanging over my shoulder." She looked to the side, then slipped the rucksack off her arm, almost losing her balance in the process. Cara managed to catch her before she landed on the front steps. "Oops." Billie laughed. "I'm glad I've got my prince charming with me." She batted her eyelashes, laughing at her tipsy state.

Cara didn't feel too stable herself, but at least she could walk and talk. She had also managed to book them a room online, nearby the rooftop bar, where they'd been dancing all night long.

It was a quaint little place, painted in pastel blue. The window frames were white, matching the rocking chairs on the porch next to the front door. The lady of the house looked sleepy when she opened the door to let them in. Her

LISE GOLD

hair was tied in a net, and she wore a blue velvet robe and big fluffy pink slippers.

"You English girls sure know how to party," she said with a friendly smile. "My name is Blossom. It's a pleasure to meet you." Blossom continued talking as she hobbled towards her reception desk. "I usually don't let people in this late, but I always make an exception for women on their own. You never know what can happen to tourists stumbling around at this hour, looking for a place to sleep. I hope you took a taxi?"

Cara nodded. "We did. And thank you for accepting the reservation. We appreciate it." She looked at Billie, who was now sleeping standing up, resting her head on her shoulder. "Does she need to sign anywhere?"

"No, dear. Just your signature will be enough." Blossom put on her reading glasses and glanced over her clipboard. "I'm afraid I've only got a double bed, I figured you wouldn't be too fussed this time at night." She handed Cara the key and led them upstairs. "Don't let her throw up on the bed if she gets sick. I'm too old to clean it up. There's a bucket in the bathroom. Put it next to the bed and keep an eye on her, okay? Breakfast is between nine and eleven. I can bring it to your room if you want?"

"That would be great." Cara gave Blossom a grateful smile while she dragged Billie into the room. "Come on, Billie. Just a couple more steps, let's get you into bed."

Cara wondered how a person so small could feel so heavy. She lowered Billie onto the bed, then grabbed her by the ankles and moved her onto the left side, next to the bathroom. She found the bucket, placed it next to the bed, and put a glass of water on the nightstand. It was warm in the room, so she switched on the ventilator and opened the doors to the balcony. She closed her eyes at the slight breeze. Only an hour ago, she'd felt pretty intoxicated herself, but Billie's helplessness had sobered her up the moment she realized she'd have to take care of her.

"Cara, is that you?" Billie mumbled.

Cara smiled and walked over to her. "Yeah, it's me. Can I get you some water?"

Billie regarded her through one eye. "No, I feel sick. Help me take my clothes off, please. It's too warm in here. I don't think I can sit up without throwing up all over the bed."

Cara felt her heart rate accelerate. She hesitated as she looked down at Billie. Her blonde hair was tossed over the pillow; her head turned to the side. Even drunk, she was the most stunning creature she'd ever seen.

"I'm not sure that's a good idea," she heard herself say.

"Come on, Cara. Help me. I'm boiling."

Cara sighed as she lifted the hem of Billie's dress, revealing her tanned thighs. She felt a stir of excitement deep down in her belly and cursed herself for even looking at them. *Think of something else. Anything.*

"Lift your arms, Billie." Billie obeyed. She lifted up her arms, then let them fall over her head. Cara struggled with the dress but managed to get it off. She tried to ignore the cream-colored bra and panties with lace edging and pulled the bedsheet from underneath Billie, covering her half-naked body.

Billie turned on her side and kicked off the sheets. "Come here, Cara." She patted the other side of the bed, closing her eyes. "I want to hold you."

Cara glanced around the room, looking for a suitable surface to sleep on, but there was nothing except for a vintage dressing table and a chair, matching the blue and white ditsy pattern in the curtains. The floor didn't look comfortable either, with its rough, wooden floorboards. "I'll be right there," she whispered, stroking Billie's hair. "Just go to sleep."

She walked out onto the balcony, gasping for air. Just the thought of getting in the bed next to Billie had heightened her senses to the point where she couldn't think straight anymore. She was angry with herself for feeling the way she did. Her feelings for Billie were supposed to die a slow death, not grow to uncontrollable proportions.

Leaning over the balcony railing, she looked out over the backyard. It was dark, but she could make out the silhouettes of trees around a gazebo, and something that looked like a vegetable patch. Apart from the crickets in the garden, it was quiet. Cara smiled at the monotone sound of Billie's deep and steady breathing, indicating she was sleeping now, and she let out a sigh of relief. Cara had done everything in her power to resist temptation, but Billie's drunken flirting hadn't made it easy. She scrolled through her missed calls and messages on her phone. Her stomach turned when she saw a message from Dan.

Hey Cara! How's my sailor doing? Miss you both. My new tenant hasn't even moved in yet, and she's already cleaned the kitchen! But don't worry, I'm not replacing you, even though she's perfect. I told her she had to be out by the time you're back. Dan. X

Cara sat down on one of the cast iron chairs on the balcony and rubbed her temples. Every moment she spent with Billie felt like a betrayal, even though they had technically managed to keep their distance. If only things were different. If only Billie and Dan had never met... Cara shook her head. Then she wouldn't be here now, on a balcony in Cape Town. She wouldn't have discovered her passion for cooking, and she wouldn't have known Billie. And that would have been worse because frankly, knowing Billie was one of the best things that had ever happened to her.

The breeze picked up, and raindrops started to fall, cooling her skin. Thoughts came and went, although none of them bore solutions to Cara's internal dilemma. She longed for Billie. She longed for her kiss, her touch, and her closeness. But they could never be more than friends. Cara knew she would have to choose between Dan and Billie. And in that case, Dan would always come first. It was the only way.

33

---

here am I? Billie blinked against the sunlight that was streaming in through the balcony doors. It took her a while to remember, dozing in and out of a light sleep. Although she was more than comfortable, it felt different from other mornings. Her arm was draped over something next to her, and she was pretty sure it wasn't a pillow. She lifted her head but let it drop again when what felt like a lightning bolt shot through it.

Slowly, flashes of their night on the rooftop came back to her. She still had no idea how they had gotten here, but the room looked nice and the bed linen smelt fresh. She assessed the situation, digging through her hazy memory. Drinks, music, barbeque, then more drinks. And lots of dancing.

She opened her eyes and saw that she was spooning Cara. Her leg was squeezed in between Cara's thighs, and her face was buried in freshly washed dark hair. It felt so good. A light breeze told her she was in her underwear. Cara was dressed in a white T-shirt and jersey shorts. Billie guessed that unlike her, she'd freshened up before going to bed. Cara was still fast asleep, and Billie couldn't decide whether to have a shower or stay there just a little bit longer, enjoying Cara's warm body against hers. She noticed Cara was lying at the very edge of the bed and grimaced at her neediness. Perhaps this spooning thing was what she'd been trying to avoid? *Shit. I hope I didn't make a fool of myself.* Billie untangled herself from Cara and sat up in bed. Next to her on the nightstand was a glass of water and two painkillers. She smiled at the sweet gesture, then swallowed them both before heading into the bathroom.

"Good Morning," Cara said, looking over her shoulder. She was sitting in the sun on the balcony, her bare legs resting on the balustrade. "How are you feeling?"

Billie felt a tingle of excitement when she met her broad smile. Cara looked hot as hell in her white T-shirt and shades. The red and black tattoos on her right arm matched the red flowers in the pots, next to the breakfast table. It would have made a beautiful picture, she thought. She tied her white robe and joined Cara outside.

"Much better after those painkillers. Thank you." She chuckled. "I'm sorry if I harassed you last night."

"Not at all," Cara said, handing her a glass of orange juice. "You were fast asleep within two minutes." She failed to mention waking up to find Billie holding her. She'd pretended to be asleep to make it last just a little bit longer. "Here, help yourself to coffee and breakfast. Blossom brought it up five minutes ago. The croissants are still warm."

"Who's Blossom?" Billie narrowed her eyes in confusion, then shook her head. "You know what? Never mind. It smells delicious, and I'm dying for a coffee." She put her legs up too while pouring herself a coffee and looked out over the back garden. "Good find, Cara. It's so pretty here. Kind of idyllic, with all the fruit trees and the little stream running through the back there. How did you find it?"

Cara shrugged. "Just lucky. We're in a residential neighbourhood, not far from where we were last night."

Billie smiled and met Cara's gaze. "It was a fun night, wasn't it? Thank you for taking care of me." She glanced at the lush surroundings. "In a really, really great way."

Cara winked over the rim of her coffee cup. "It was a pleasure. Hey, your phone has been ringing all morning. I think you should check your messages; it might be important."

Billie winced as she looked over at her bag in the far corner of the room. It looked impossibly far away from the comfortable position she was in now, and quite frankly, she was dreading to look. She vaguely remembered her phone ringing throughout the night, and that was rarely good news.

Finally, Cara stood up to get Billie's bag and handed her the phone from the front pocket. "Here. Just get it over with."

"Thanks." Billie's worried face lit up as she scrolled through her messages. "I'm an auntie!" she exclaimed. "Helen's had a little girl. She's five weeks early, but she's fine. They both are." She smiled at Cara. "Her name is Daisy. Pretty name, don't you think?"

"It is." Cara felt happy just watching Billie's delighted smile. "Do you have a picture?"

"Just loading now," Billie said. She stood up and sat down on Cara's lap with an arm around her neck and her phone in front of them. She pressed her cheek against Cara's as she looked at the pictures that popped up one by one. "She's beautiful," Billie said in a whisper. "I've never seen anything so tiny."

Cara smiled and placed a soft kiss on her cheek. "She's perfect. Congratulations, Auntie. I'm glad everything is okay."

"Me too." Billie rang her sister and waited for her to pick up.

She clearly had no intention of moving off Cara's lap, but Cara didn't mind. It was a beautiful morning, with blue skies and sunshine, and the fact that Billie wanted to share her big moment with her made it even more perfect.

"Billie?" Helen's voice sounded sleepy, but she was smiling from the hospital bed.

"I'm sorry, Helen. You were sleeping. I can call you back..."

"Don't you dare," Helen interrupted her. She sat up in bed and waved into the camera. "Who's your friend attached to your cheek?"

"Oh yes. Of course. This is Cara," Billie said, laughing. "We're in a hotel in Cape Town."

Cara waved back at her. "Congratulations, Helen. Billie's told me a lot about you."

Helen waved back. "Hey there. Likewise. I'm glad you're taking care of her." She got up from the bed and walked over to the cot next to it. The baby was wrapped up tight in a blanket. A tube was coming out of her nose, and she had numerous wires attached to her arms and wrists. "Meet Daisy." Helen smiled as she stroked Daisy's cheek. "Don't worry. I know she looks fragile, but the doctors have assured me she's as healthy as a five-week premature baby can be. They're keeping her here for a week, and if everything is fine, and she's growing, I can take her home with me after that."

Billie stared at the little girl with tears in her eyes. "I'm so sorry I can't be there for you, Helen. Will you please update me every day? And how are you? You must be exhausted..."

Helen shrugged. "I'm okay. Tired, yes. But I'm glad she's here. They're taking excellent care of her. And mum's going to be staying with me for the first two weeks when Daisy comes home. The birth was quick. She couldn't wait to get out, apparently. The nurses told me it was one of the easiest births they had ever seen, but I'm not sure I agree with that."

Billie smiled. "I can't believe she came out of you." She leaned in closer to Cara, as if she needed the contact.

Daisy started crying, and a nurse walked over, disconnecting the tube from her nose. Helen shot them both an apologetic look. "I have to go now. We're going to try and get her to breastfeed. She's been refusing until now, so I'm going to lie back down. Love you, Billie. Take care."

Billie waved. "Love you, Helen." She blew her sister a kiss before hanging up. Then she put her phone back on the table and hugged Cara, burying her face in her neck. Cara tightened her grip and held her until Billie finally let go and looked at her. "I'm so glad you were here to meet Helen and Daisy," she said, getting up.

"I feel honoured. Your sister seems nice." She reluctantly let go of Billie. "Hey, are you up for some sightseeing today, or do you need a rest?"

Billie shook her head. "No, I'd love to do something. I suddenly feel full of energy. What did you have in mind?"

_____

34

Simon's Town was only a short train ride from Cape Town, and within two hours, Billie found herself following Cara through the white dunes of Foxy Beach. The dense vegetation that grew higher towards the shore provided shade in the morning sun, and they walked in a comfortable silence, admiring the spectacular coastline. The three-mile walk was nothing compared to their hike up Table Mountain the previous day, and Billie felt energetic, despite her slight hangover.

"I can't believe I haven't been here before. It's beautiful."

"It is." Cara stopped and looked out over the ocean. The sea was calm today. "Foxy Beach is a quiet beach. Apparently, most people go to the more touristy Boulders Beach because there's a penguin colony there." She grinned. "But Ayanda assured me there would be penguins here too, so fingers crossed."

Billie reached out for her hand as they strolled further down the path towards the beach. Cara hesitated but gave up when Billie took a tight hold. She shot her a goofy grin. Holding someone's hand wasn't a crime, was it? It felt right, especially with how much she was missing their closeness from that morning.

"You look cute today," she said, without thinking.

Billie chuckled and looked down at her denim shorts and creased white top. "Thank you." She winked. "Thought I'd get my legs out for you again."

Cara laughed. "I appreciate it." She paused, listening to the noise that seemed to come from behind the dune in front of them. It sounded like a slaughterhouse. "Do you hear that? Unless someone is being murdered over there, I'm pretty sure that's what penguins sound like. Come on; I think we're close."

They made their way over the hill, which led them towards a footbridge with benches facing the beach. They stalled at the sight of a group of penguins. They looked like they were gossiping, the way they were standing there with their heads close together, and their wings flapping up and down.

Billie held her hands in front of her mouth. "This is incredible," she whispered. "Look at them. They're so cute. And so funny." The penguins looked up for a moment, but soon lost interest, and continued whatever it was they were doing. "Let's try to get closer."

They slowly walked towards the end of the bridge and sat down on a bench. The penguins turned to them once again, but they didn't seem frightened. Instead, they stared at them curiously. Billie waved as if she'd just spotted an old friend, and one of the penguins nodded back at her, making both her and Cara laugh. The water along the beach was shallow, with big rocks, breaking up the waves. On top of them, more penguins were resting or sleeping in the sun. Soon, another group came bouncing out of the water, one by one. They stopped for a moment and looked up at Cara and Billie, then joined the others in their conversation.

"Do you miss your family?" Cara asked.

"Not usually." Billie shrugged. "But on days like these, sure, I miss them. I wish I could be there for my sister right now and hold my niece, but that's the sacrifice that comes with the job, right?" She leaned back on her elbows and lifted her head towards the sun. "On the upside," she continued, "I do have a lot of free time when I'm home, so I make up for it then. Sometimes it's even too much, especially when I stay with my parents." She turned to Cara. "I've been thinking of buying an apartment, so I have my own personal space in between jobs."

"You have? I'm impressed." Cara took a sip from her water bottle, then handed it to Billie.

"I've been saving up. I don't spend much when I'm at sea, and when I live with my parents I don't pay rent, so I think this might be the year that I'm finally going to do it."

"Smart move," Cara said. "In London?"

Billie sighed. "No, that would be out of my price range. Maybe just outside, near the airport. I could rent it out to airport staff when I'm not there." She cocked her head. "Are you moving back in with Dan?"

Cara shrugged. "That's the plan. I might look for a job in a restaurant when I'm back. Maybe expand my knowledge, learn about Asian cuisine, or Middle Eastern."

"So, you have a plan now?" Billie grinned. "You've certainly got your shit together for someone who had no idea what they wanted only three months ago."

Cara laughed. "Thanks to you, Billie. I don't know how I can thank you for what you've done for me." She paused. "I think you might be the best thing that's ever happened to me." Their eyes locked and she could see Billie was touched by her confession. A soft smile spread across Cara's face. "I'm sorry, I'm not usually this dramatic. I…"

"No," Billie interrupted her. "Don't apologize. I feel the same."

"But I didn't do anything."

"It doesn't matter. It's how I feel." Billie placed her hand on Cara's and squeezed it. "You're important to me, and I want you to be in my life."

Cara closed her eyes and sighed. "Billie, I can't see you when I'm back living with Dan." She moved her hand away and immediately regretted it. "It will be awkward."

"I'm breaking up with Dan," Billie protested. "I just haven't found the right moment yet. Besides, it's not like we're doing anything wrong. It was one kiss. Just once."

Cara turned towards Billie, facing her. She stared into the blue depths that made her go weak and defenceless, time and time again. "But it doesn't feel that way, does it?"

Billie shook her head, meeting her gaze. "No, it doesn't."

35

"You look like you could do with some fresh air," Billie laughed when Cara came stumbling into their room, drenched in sweat.

Cara held up a hand. "Can't speak. Need a shower first." She took off her whites and stepped straight into the shower.

Billie listened to the water running and heard Cara sigh in relief. The door was open, and she had to restrain herself from peaking around the corner. Billie loved watching her. She watched Cara in the kitchen, whenever she had the chance. She always acted like she was on top of everything, even though she was still on the verge of panic most of the time. She also watched Cara getting undressed at the end of the night, talking to her before she fell into a deep coma from complete exhaustion. And although she knew it was creepy, she even loved watching Cara sleep. Whenever she got up at night to use the bathroom, she would steal a glance at her naked thighs that peeked out from beneath the sheets. That was possibly the highlight of her day.

"That was the best shower I've ever had." Cara stepped

out of the bathroom a little later with a towel wrapped around her, her hair still dripping wet. She looked down at Billie. "Were you serious about the fresh air? Because I could definitely do with some of that right now."

Billie jumped off her bed and put on a pair of shorts. "Sure. Usual spot?"

The wind was chilly, and Billie shivered when they crossed the deck towards the benches at the front of the ship.

"Do you want my jacket?" Cara rubbed Billie's bare arms. "You look cold. Here, take it."

Billie shook her head but gave in when Cara insisted. "Thank you. You're such a... gentleman?" They both laughed as they sat down, looking out over the restless ocean. The sky was filled with dark, low hanging clouds.

"So, this is the Indian Ocean," Cara said. "Never thought I'd be drifting in the middle of it."

Billie pulled the jacket over her shoulders, covering her arms. "I thought the Indian Ocean was supposed to be the warmest of all. It's still beautiful, though. I never get tired of the view and the sound of the waves, even when the weather is bad." She sighed. "Does it ever bother you, not seeing land?"

"At first, I thought I might panic," Cara said. She hesitated, then leaned back, pulling Billie towards her on the bench. "But now I like it. Where we go is something I can't control, and I've surrendered to it now. It's almost comforting, in a way." She paused. "And I love sitting here with you after work. It feels like coming home. Like I'm exactly where I'm supposed to be."

Billie looked up at her from the crook of her arm and

opened her mouth to speak. When nothing came out, she looked down at her hands, blushing. Cara cursed herself for being so honest yet again. But it felt right, and she knew Billie felt the same. They had sat here so many nights, so many hours. Sometimes talking and eating, sometimes in silence. They were comfortable with each other, and the only thing that stood in their way was the tension of that ever-present pull between them, which could break everything in a heartbeat.

"I was on mains today," Cara said, breaking the silence.

"Really? That's fantastic." Billie sounded genuinely happy for her. "How come?"

"Eduardo came in drunk. Everyone could tell, he smelled like a brewery." Cara chuckled. "Chef Claudio only realized he was intoxicated because he couldn't stop grinning, and that's unusual because Eduardo never smiles."

"Well too bad for him but good for you. I assume it was hard, from the state you were in when you came back tonight?"

Cara nodded. "It was. And even though it was only a one-night thing, I did it, and it went well. Sure, I made some mistakes but nothing major." She paused. "I don't think I've ever felt so happy in a job before."

Billie snuggled deeper into the crook of her arm and Cara could feel herself starting to relax. "I'm glad. And you know what that means, right?"

Cara shook her head. "What does it mean?"

"It means you're a part of the crew now. You can come back next season and pick your station."

"Do you think so?"

"Yeah. If they can count on you and you do your job well, the Pelican will take you back. It's just how it works." She put a hand on Cara's knee. "Listen, I know what you said about making your own choices and that we're not in a relationship. And I get that. But there's no point denying yourself something you enjoy either. You happen to love your job, so why not think about coming back? It's not like we have to share a room. You could always move in with those filthy boys from the pool deck."

Cara laughed. "Yes, I suppose you're right. Although I think I'll pass on sharing a room with Arnie and his friends."

Billie rolled her eyes. "I've been there. And believe me, it's not great." She shifted in her seat. "Sorry, do you mind if I lie down for a bit? My back is killing me after all the dance classes today. I stood in for three people who were sick after that stupid staff party." She sighed. "I bet Eduardo was with my girls. I had to give them an official warning, and I always hate doing that. Makes me feel like the bad cop." She turned and stretched out on the bench, resting her head in Cara's lap.

Cara's hands gravitated towards Billie's hair and she laced her fingers through it. "Maybe you're right," she said. "For the first time in my life, I can see where I'm going, and you have no idea how good that feels."

It was a strange thought, knowing she could have a future at sea. Cara hadn't considered the idea before, but now that she was sitting on the top deck of a ship, crossing the ocean with Billie's head in her lap, it didn't seem so crazy.

36

"Hey, wake up." Cara touched Billie's face, careful not to scare her. "We're in Vietnam, and we only have ten hours. Get up!"

"Fuck." Billie sat up in bed and looked around the room with one eye open. "I'm sure I set my alarm clock. Are we there already?"

The loud beep of the ship told them that they were, just before the cruise director's high-pitched voice penetrated their ears. "Ladies and gentlemen, welcome to..."

"Oh God, please make him stop! How do other people bear that voice?" Billie pulled the pillow over her head, trying to block out the noise. "I'm so tired."

"I know you're tired," Cara said in a pleading tone. "But if you sleep through this, we're both going to miss out on Vietnam." She raised her voice when Billie didn't reply. "Come on. We've missed the last two ports already, and I haven't left the ship in weeks. I feel like I'm about to go crazy." She sighed. "I could go on my own, but it's not going to be half as fun, and you're going to regret it. Please, you promised me we'd have breakfast there."

Billie opened both eyes this time, trying to adjust to the bright light in the cabin. "Okay, just give me a minute. I'm awake, I think." She yawned and put on her sweetest smile. "Will you start the shower for me, please? I'll be up in two minutes."

"So, where are we going?" Billie asked an hour later. They were disembarking the ship alongside thousands of tourists. The port of Ho Chi Minh City was chaotic, compared to Cape Town, and the noise was almost too much to bear in the early morning.

Cara laughed. "I have no idea, never been here. But it's an amazing city for food, so the main question is, are you hungry?"

"I would love some breakfast." Billie glanced around the industrial port. "I'm too tired to think. How do we get around here?"

Cara pointed at the motorbike taxis, waiting in line at the taxi stand.

"Are you sure this is safe?" Billie asked, watching the motorbikes drive off with two or three people on the back.

"I don't know. But it seems like the fastest way to get to the Binh Tay Market, so let's not waste any time. I'm sure we'll be fine."

Billie got in the middle, and Cara got on the back, barely keeping her balance as the driver sped up, cutting off other motorbikes, cars, and even trucks. Billie screamed while Cara held on tight to Billie's waist. She steadied herself from the back with her other hand, worried she'd fly off if the driver came to an abrupt halt.

"This is the scariest thing I've ever done!" There was a hint of panic in Billie's voice.

"Just hold on to him, I've got you from the back," Cara said, trying to keep calm. She didn't want Billie to know she was terrified herself when her knee almost scraped the ground as they took a sharp bend.

"Where is Binh Tay Market?" Billie shouted. "Is it far?"

"I don't know!" Cara shouted back. "I don't know anything. I just read about this market where we can get great food, and that's where I asked him to take us."

They both burst into hysterical laughter, holding on for dear life. There were motorbikes and cars everywhere, so close that they bumped into them on several occasions. The traffic was chaotic, and as confident as their driver seemed; they were both holding their breath. Finally, they arrived at the market. The driver laughed at their shocked faces when they stepped down onto the pavement, grateful to still be alive.

"Where are you going?" he asked.

"What do you mean?" Cara frowned. "We're going here."

He laughed. "But what do you want? Do you want shopping or food?"

"Food!" Cara and Billie both shouted in unison.

The driver seemed amused at their eagerness to get something to eat and got back on his bike. "This market is very big. Let me drive you to the food."

Billie looked hesitant. "I'm not sure my heart can take it, Cara," she whispered.

Cara giggled. "We're already here, so we might as well get back on, it will be two minutes, tops. And look at this place." She gestured to the thousands of stalls. "It's a labyrinth, and the website is right, the food court is in the centre." With very little enthusiasm, Billie got back on the motorbike.

"I'll drive slowly," their driver promised, before speeding

off again. He cut off pedestrians and drove through stalls, catching Cara's foot in a bag of merchandise more than once.

When he stopped again, they found themselves in the biggest food court they'd ever seen. The set-up at most stalls was basic, with only two gas fires for the chefs to cook on, if they were lucky. There were meat and fish stalls, soup restaurants and dessert places, each with their own signature dish and considerable queues in front of them. It was noisy and crowded with locals doing their daily shopping. Children of the stall holders were running around, playing or helping out.

Billie dragged Cara over to a stall that served pink crepes with sticky coconut rice. "That's what I want," she said matter-of-factly, securing her place in line. "It smells so good; I can almost taste it."

A little later, they were sitting on the edge of a fountain, each with a crepe and an iced coffee. Billie was attacking hers with a big smile on her face. "I think I'm starting to wake up," she mumbled.

"You mean you hadn't woken up after that bike ride?" Cara laughed. "Because your eyes were like saucers when we got here, you looked like an owl on acid."

Billie rolled her eyes. "Okay, I might have been terrified, but it was worth it. This is so good." She closed her eyes, savouring every bite. "So, what's next, considering you're being such a great guide today?"

"Let's see..." Cara said, scrolling through her phone. "I think we should go to a floating market. Cai Be is the closest one to where we are now. With the heavy traffic, it's probably best if we take another motorbike taxi to save time, but it's up to you. If you're too scared, we can..."

"I'm not scared," Billie interrupted her. She shot Cara a

cheeky grin, unwilling to give in to the provocation. "That guy was driving like a lunatic. They can't all be driving like that, surely?"

Cara arched a brow and stood up. "You're right, they can't. Let's see if we can find someone to take us."

C ara couldn't stop laughing at the bewildered look on Billie's face when they finally got off the back of the motorbike in Cai Be. She was bending over as if she was feeling sick, steadying herself on her knees. "Well that answers that question. They do all drive like madmen." She looked at Cara, wide eyed. "Is this what an adrenaline rush feels like? When you think you're going to die but then you don't?"

Cara tried to keep a straight face, but she couldn't deny that the thought of dying had crossed her mind too. She was still shaking from the car they'd almost hit, only a couple of minutes ago. Their driver hadn't seemed rattled, though. He had laughed it off as par for the course. "Come here," she said, holding out her arms for Billie. Billie stood up and sank into the embrace, resting her head on Cara's shoulder. Cara shivered when she felt warm breath on her neck. She tried to block her mind from Billie's breasts pressed against hers, and focused on her surroundings.

The countryside was a stark contrast to the busy city. It was green and lush, with fruit farms and rice paddies stretched out over the fertile land. Farmers were unloading their produce at the docks, re-stocking their boats for the market.

"I'm sorry. I didn't realize it was a two-hour drive." Cara stretched her legs, tired from sitting in the same position on the back of the motorbike. "Maybe we should take a bus back. But now that we're here, let's go and see the Mekong Delta, shall we?"

She paid the driver and tipped him generously for the long ride. He smiled and pointed at his motorbike. "Thank you. Wait here?"

Cara and Billie both shook their heads frantically. "No thank you," they said in unison, and Billie held up a hand. "We're sorry, we didn't mean it like that. But we don't know how long we're going to be, so it's probably best if we go our separate ways now. Have a safe trip back."

He didn't seem to understand much of what she said, but he smiled and drove towards his next victims, a couple who were waiting along the roadside, waving at him.

"Okay," Cara said after he had disappeared. "You sit here and relax; I'll get us a boat. Would you like some water?"

"Don't be so cute, Cara. You know I can't handle it when you're being all sweet and worried about me."

Cara laughed. "What do you mean? I'm trying to be a good tour guide here."

Billie sat down and opened her handbag, producing a bottle of water. "I'm good, darling. But a boat would be great, my legs still feel like jelly after that near-death experience. I don't think I can walk yet."

"You need a boat?" An old lady jumped in between them. "I have. Cheap!" she shouted, waving her skinny arms around. It was clear that she had no intention of leaving them alone until they gave in.

Cara nodded. "Okay, thank you," she said, still too flustered to argue. She looked around. Cai Be was a sweet little town by one of the Mekong River distributaries. Most of the homes built on land had their own fruit and vegetable gardens, or large paddy fields. The majority of the homes however, were built on stilts in the water, connected by a network of bridges, leading to shops, restaurants, manufacturers and even a school. The bicycle seemed to be the transportation of choice on the narrow roads alongside small side canals, and life here was lived at a much slower pace.

Cara turned back to the old woman. "Where do we go?"

"Follow me," their toothless guide commanded, leading them towards her boat. "Sampan," she said, pointing at a long wooden boat with a small shelter at the back.

"Is that what it's called?" Cara asked. "And what's your name?"

The old lady grinned, exposing her gums. "Me, Bian."

"Nice to meet you, Bian," Cara said, struggling to get into the boat. "I'm Cara, and my friend here is Billie. We would like to see the floating market and the delta. Can you show us around?"

Bian nodded and pointed at the only intact bench in the back. When they were both seated, Bian lifted her paddle and pushed the boat away from the dock with surprising force for an old lady.

"How old do you think she is?" Billie asked. "I'm not sure I'm comfortable with this."

"I don't know. Too old to be doing this, for sure. I feel sorry for her." Cara waved at the old woman, trying to get her attention. "Would you like me to do that?" she asked. Bian looked at her blankly. "Me, handle the boat," Cara continued, making rowing gestures with her arms.

"You want to?" Bian pointed at her and laughed.

Cara nodded. "Yes, please. I would love to. You sit down and relax." She stood up and patted the seat next to Billie.

Bian continued to laugh as she handed the paddle to Cara and swapped places. "You crazy," she said, watching Cara struggle at first.

It didn't take long for her to get the hang of it though, and soon enough, they were off, with Cara sweating in the burning heat of the sun. She lowered the visor on her cap in an attempt to shade her face. Bian and Billie watched her in amusement from the comfort of the shelter.

"Let me know when you want me to take over," Billie shouted.

Bian leaned back and grinned. "Me, princess," she said, before breaking out in laughter again.

As they followed the river, it became busier with identical boats and more tourists. The locals laughed at Cara, who was desperately trying to avoid the other sampans. They seemed entertained by Bian too, who continuously shouted at them, making a point of being on the bench. When they got to the market, Bian took over.

"Okay," she shouted when they almost crashed into a lady selling pineapples. "You sit, me expert." She maneuvered them through the crowd with little effort, waving at people she knew. Farmers were selling flowers, fruit, fish, and meat from rafts and flatboats, while local women were preparing meals on cookers in the open air. Although it was a wholesale market, there were plenty of boats selling souvenirs, and Billie bought an ankle chain for herself, and a handmade leather rattle for little Daisy. Cara thought about getting something for Dan, but she didn't want to mention his name. It was the one subject they were trying to avoid, and so she shook her head at a young man selling outrageous lighters that Dan would have loved.

"Are you seriously buying a diary?" she asked in amusement when Billie started negotiating with one of the traders.

"Quiet Cara, you're throwing me off my game. I'm trying to get a good deal here." After a long and passionate haggle, Billie handed her a leather notebook with a hand-carved wooden pen. "It's for you," she said. "To write your recipes in."

Cara smiled, touched by the sweet gesture. "You didn't have to do that."

"No, I want to. You're doing so great in the kitchen; it would be a shame if you forgot the things you've learned. Besides, I want you to have something to remember me by. Something that you'll use." She paused and bit her lip. "I hope we'll still see each other when we get back home, but I know it's not going to be the same, so I don't want you to forget..."

Cara hugged her, interrupting her sentence. "Thanks, Billie. That means a lot to me." She studied the brown leather book with rough paper. "It's beautiful. I promise I'll use it." She let her gaze wander over the market.

"Hey, I want to get you something too." Billie was about to protest, but Cara stopped her from speaking. "I don't want you to forget about me either, so please let me." She asked Bian to stop by a boat that sold ceramic coffee mugs and bought the biggest and most beautiful mug they had. It was teal with orange at the top, randomly dripping down the sides. "Now you'll think of me every morning when you wake up."

Billie took the mug from her and carefully placed it in her bag. "Thank you, Cara." She lowered her head, avoiding Cara's gaze. "I was probably going to anyway."

Bian nodded in approval. "More shopping? Or hungry?" She asked, pushing the boat away from the stall.

"Yes, we are hungry," Billie answered with a smile. "Do you know where we can get food?"

Bian nodded. "We go to my friend. She make food."

They floated along the river, away from the noise, and were entering a more rural area now, with farms and lush strips of forest along the bank. Bian steered them towards a fruit orchard where she tied her boat to a tree and jumped out with the ease of a young ballerina.

Billie and Cara barely made it onto land, with Cara sliding into the water with one foot. "I've got you," Billie said, pulling her up.

"Thanks." Cara gladly used her near fall as an excuse to hold on to Billie a little longer, and they walked into the tangerine orchard, hand in hand. The garden was small and intimate, with only a handful of tables underneath the trees. Apart from a young family, Cara and Billie were the only guests. Bian led them to a table under a gazebo, where a jug of ice water was awaiting them.

"Are you not eating with us?" Cara asked, pulling a chair out for Bian.

Bian shook her head as she rooted through her bag, producing a set of false teeth. "I eat inside with my friend," she mumbled, popping the teeth into her mouth.

Bian's welcoming friend was about the same age as her, with long grey hair and a network of deep crow's feet around her eyes. She still seemed to have her own teeth though, and graced them with a broad smile, after greeting Bian.

"We have set menu every day. Traditional Vietnamese food. Okay?"

"That sounds great," Cara said, accepting the glass of tangerine juice that one of the younger staff members handed her. "You have a beautiful place here."

"Thank you," the lady said, beaming with pride. "Please relax. My staff will bring food."

Billie smiled at her before she turned back to Cara. "How lucky are we to end up here, right?"

Cara's eyes widened. "Lucky? I'm the tour guide, remember? I brought us here!"

Billie laughed. "All right. I have to admit; your guiding skills are exceptional." She met Cara's gaze and let her eyes linger. "That was sweet of you, what you did for Bian." She hesitated. "I couldn't stop looking at your arms when you were steering the boat. I wanted to touch them so badly, I nearly passed out."

Cara grinned. "Yeah?"

"Yeah," Billie whispered.

Cara stared at her in silence. Billie didn't shy away and didn't seem to regret what she'd said. She just sat there with her tousled hair and bright blue eyes, her white linen shirt hanging off one shoulder. She looked like she had just had sex. Or was about to, Cara thought. *I can't do this. I can't do this to Dan.*

Their waitress approached them, and they broke eye contact. Cara, who was still flustered by their flirtation, turned her attention towards the plate in front of them. She studied the translucent spring rolls, packed with greens and shrimp, accompanied by a dark peanut sauce. She was grateful for the distraction. Both the excitement and the guilt she felt had removed all sense of hunger, but she took a spring roll and dipped it in the sauce anyway.

"These are so good," Billie said, swallowing her first bite. There was a silence, and Billie hesitated before she spoke. "Cara, can I ask you something?"

"Sure." Cara cocked her head curiously. "Ask away."

"Do you miss your ex-girlfriend? I mean, would you take her back if she told you she'd made the biggest mistake of her life? If she told you she wanted to start over?"

Cara frowned. "Why do you ask?"

"Well..." Billie shrugged. "You never talk about her. You

haven't even mentioned her name once. All you told me was that she broke up with you after two years. That's quite a long time to be with someone. I guess I'm just wondering..."

"If I cheated on her?" Cara finished her sentence. "No, I didn't. She left me because I was a miserable person to be with. I don't blame her for it anymore. In fact, thinking back, I wouldn't have wanted to be around me either." She laughed.

"I find that hard to imagine," Billie said. There was a pause again. "So, would you?"

"Would I what?" Cara grinned, amused by Billie's sudden cautiousness. If she was going to be nosy, she'd have to spell the question out, too.

"Would you take her back?"

Cara shook her head. "Millie." She was surprised at how easy it was to say the name out loud. She felt so detached from that time in her life now that it was hard to imagine it had happened at all. "That's her name. And no, we would never get back together."

"Why not?"

Cara shot Billie a curious look. "Why do you want to know about my ex-girlfriend all of a sudden?"

"I'm not sure," Billie said. "I guess I've been wondering why someone would not want to be with you. I just find it hard to imagine." She lowered her head, breaking eye contact. "You're an amazing person. She must be crazy."

Cara blushed at the comment, and she could feel her heartbeat pumping in the vein at the side of her neck. "Thanks, Billie," she stammered. "That's the sweetest thing anyone's ever said to me." She transferred some clams on to her plate and speared a chopstick through a piece of bitter melon. "I'm sure Millie moved on the moment she left me. She moved in with a friend I'd never heard of. That says enough, doesn't it?" Cara didn't wait for an answer. "And as far as I'm concerned, we weren't right for each other in the first place. There was never that spark, you know?"

Billie nodded. "I know." Her eyes met Cara's again. "That spark that makes you feel crazy alive. When it's almost impossible to resist the other person." She held her gaze, and Cara felt Billie's bare foot on her chair, between her legs. She gasped at the contact.

Billie smiled at her reaction. "When a simple touch can send a jolt of electricity throughout your whole body, leaving you aching for more." She closed her eyes when Cara took her foot in her hands, gently massaging it. "I know what that feels like," Billie whispered.

She looked aroused, and Cara watched her bite her lip when she leaned forward and moved a hand up Billie's leg, caressing the soft skin of her inner thigh. She could feel her trembling. Cara was breathing fast when she finally leaned back and let go of Billie's leg that was still resting between hers. How had this happened? How had they gone from a conversation about exes, to openly flirting?

"Everything okay?" Their waitress asked.

Cara picked up her chopsticks and put the piece of bitter melon in her mouth. "It's great. Thank you," she mumbled through the mouthful. When the girl was out of sight, she turned back to Billie. "Why is it that, no matter how hard I try, I can't seem to stop wanting you?"

Billie took in a quick breath and smiled. "Because you have a thing for 'illies'." She laughed.

Cara swallowed a clam and frowned. "What does that mean?"

Billie shrugged. "Millie, Billie...what's next? Willie?"

Cara giggled and shook her head. "No, it's not the same. Nothing compares to you."

They sat there without breaking eye contact until the waiter came over with braised pork knuckles, a bowl of chili noodles and a Vietnamese salad.

"Dan-Dan," Billie said, pointing at the noodles.

"Great," Cara mumbled. "Dan-Dan." She took a bite and had to admit that the dish was delicious, despite its name that had ripped them right out of their steamy flirtation.

37

"Are you okay?" Margret glanced at Billie from behind the coffee maker. "You've been sitting there all by yourself for three hours, staring out of the window, and there's not even land in sight. Surely you could think of better things to do with your free afternoon? Billie?"

Billie woke up from her daydream when Margret raised her voice. "I'm fine, Margret. Thank you for asking. Just taking some time for myself, that's all."

Margret didn't seem convinced. "How's that boyfriend of yours doing? Is he still calling you?"

"Yes. Dan still calls me." Billie sighed. "But I wish he wouldn't." She turned to Margret, who was cleaning the bar like it was an elite racehorse. Long strokes of polish, only in one direction. "Something happened. I was in the wrong, but it doesn't feel wrong." She paused. "I want to end it with him, but every time I speak to him, he sounds so happy to hear my voice. It's killing me. He's a great guy, and I don't want to hurt him."

Margret continued her cleaning regime without looking up, the way she had for most of her life. The library was quiet, but that was nothing new. People preferred to read on their digital devices nowadays, while lounging on the deck with a cocktail.

"What was this big thing that happened?" she asked, still concentrating on her task. "Does it have something to do with a certain roommate, by any chance?"

Billie shifted on the sofa. "How did you know? I mean, how..."

Margret laughed. "It's rather obvious, darling." She smiled, finally looking up. "The way you two act around each other, looking for any excuse to make physical contact. You seem at your happiest whenever Cara's around, and you never spend your late nights reading in here anymore. Do you think I'm daft? I might be old, but I know that women can love other women. My older sister Beth lived with a lady, you know." She grinned. "Not so much of a lady perhaps, but a woman nevertheless."

"Really?" Billie turned to Margret and tucked her feet underneath her on the couch.

Margret nodded. "Her name was Sarah. Nice gal. My sister met her on a seniors' holiday in Spain. Before that, Beth had never introduced me to anyone special in her life, but after she came back from Spain, she was a different person." Margret smiled at the memory. "She said: 'Margret, I have to tell you something. I've met the love of my life, and we're moving in together. She's a woman, and I don't care if you think it's unnatural, life's too short to be alone when you've found that special someone.'"

Billie tilted her head and rested her cheek on the sofa's back. "That's sweet. So, you didn't know your sister was gay?"

Margret shook her head. "I had no idea. It was her best-kept secret for fifty-odd years of her life. Later, she told me she had been too scared to tell people when she was younger. Life was different back then, you know. People weren't as open-minded as they are nowadays. But when she got older, she stopped caring about what other people thought of her, and I admire her for that. Anyway, I told her I was happy for her and I meant it. I've never seen her glowing the way she did when she was with Sarah. If you ask me, it was the best thing that ever happened to her."

"What happened to Sarah?" Billie asked. "You said *was*, as if she's not in the picture anymore."

Margret put down her cloth and walked around the bar. She took a seat next to Billie by the window. "Sarah died of cancer a year after they signed their civil partnership. They only had five years together. My sister hasn't been the same since. She's picked up her life again and moved on, but her spark is gone. When I'm on my break, we spend our time in her summer cottage by the coast in Cornwall, looking out over the sea. She bought the cottage with Sarah. They loved walking on the beach together." Margret shrugged. "Now she'll have to make do with me. I think of my late husband, and Beth's thoughts are always with Sarah. It's our way of paying respect to them, I suppose." She swallowed hard. "But I'm glad we've both had the privilege to love and be loved. There's no greater thing to hope for, Billie."

Billie put a hand on Margret's. "Thanks, Margret. I'll remember that." She paused. "Your husband... you never told me you were married."

"You never asked."

Billie shot her an apologetic look. "I know. I'm sorry. I guess I've never been able to picture you having a life outside this ship."

Margret smiled. "It's fine. And I suppose you're right. This is the only life I know. I started working on cruise ships when I was nineteen. Not the Pelican, of course. The ship was called Star of the South." She sighed. "Those were my best years. I was young and pretty and eager to go wherever adventure would take me. I met my husband there, Charles. He was a mechanic, and a pretty good one too. We got married at sea, worked on the same ships, and spent our lives quite happily in those stuffy cabins. We didn't need much, just each other. Then, Charles died of a heart attack on the Atlantic Ocean in the early nineties." Margret looked down at her hands, resting in her lap. "I feel close to him when I'm at sea. I belong here."

Billie nodded slowly. "I'm so sorry about your husband, Margret."

"It's okay, sweetie." Margret mustered a brave face. "He's been gone for a long time now, and I'm fine."

"I think I belong here too," Billie said, surprised by her sudden openness. "I wasn't ready to admit it, at first. I just took it one year at a time, trying to fool my family into thinking that every time could be my last, I guess. That I might settle down after that." She took a deep breath. "But this year, I've finally admitted to myself that this is what I want to do for the rest of my life. I love it, and that's enough for me. Life is simple here. It is what it is, and there is nothing to worry about apart from doing my job and making sure I get the occasional day off to see something of the world." She paused. "I was lost before I first came here. I didn't know what I wanted to do with my life. All I knew was that it wasn't teaching, and it certainly wasn't accountancy. I think Cara was in the same place, that's why I got her a job here. I think I recognized myself in her." She hesitated. "Well that, and the fact that Dan wouldn't stop bugging me about it. Dan's her best friend, you see."

"Right. So that's where things get complicated." Margret nodded.

"Yeah." Billie shrugged. "I'd only met her a couple of times before we came on board, and I swear, I never saw this coming. If I had, I wouldn't have offered to share my room with her."

"And Cara?" Margret asked. "Is she happy here?"

Billie smiled. "Yeah. I think so. She seems very happy. Cara's changed. Or maybe she's just back to her old self now. She's funny and confident, and she's got this air about her that's... I don't know... Charming? Magnetic? Delightful?"

"You most certainly have a crush on her," Margret laughed, lightening the mood.

Billie grinned. "Okay, maybe I do." It was the first time she had said it out loud. "But Dan is her best friend, and that makes her a no-go."

"Sounds to me like you went there already." Margret lowered her glasses with an amused look. "And that puts the two of you in a sticky situation now, doesn't it?" She didn't wait for an answer. "Don't worry so much, Billie. You young-sters worry way too much for your own good. If this really is love, it's not a big deal in the grand scheme of a lifetime. Sure, Dan's feelings will get hurt. And it's going to be nasty. Cara might lose his friendship, but then maybe she won't. Eventually, Dan will find someone who can make him happy too, and you'll all look back on this in twenty years' time and agree that you've done the right thing."

Billie sighed. "That sounds so easy, Margret."

Margret stood up and squeezed Billie's shoulder. "When you get to my age, you're able to see the bigger picture in life. One of the few perks of growing older." She reached over the bar and came back with a large cup of coffee with something strong in it. "Here, drink this. It will help you relax."

"Thanks." Billie took a sip and winced. "You mean it's going to knock me out?" They both laughed.

"I think I might have one myself," Margret giggled as she made herself a drink in a takeaway cup. "It's almost time to close down anyway."

Billie raised her cup. "Thank you, Margret. For being here." She looked up into Margret's kind eyes. "It's really nice to have you around."

Margret smiled and raised her cup too. "Likewise, kiddo."

38

"We're over half way now," Billie said, pointing at the interactive map by the information desk. "The ship will be making a turn tomorrow, docking at Manilla, Sydney and then..." She spread her fingers, zooming in on a tiny island in the Indian Ocean. "Mauritius."

Cara bent forward, studying the map. "That's a long way till our next break."

Billie shrugged. "Every single one of my team members has begged me for days off in Sydney. I could hardly plan myself in. But the upside is, the ship will be nice and quiet. Most of our guests take four days in Sydney, so I'll be working part-time then."

"Great." Cara smiled. As long as she was with Billie, she didn't really care where she went. Even getting out of bed in the mornings was something to look forward to, knowing they would drink coffee together while sharing a newspaper. "In that case, will you go and see a movie with me next weekend? It's not a date," she hastily added. "I just haven't done anything like that in a long time."

Billie laughed. "Me neither. I would love to." She

lowered her voice and hooked her arm into Cara's as they walked back towards the elevator. "Will you take me to dinner before our non-date?"

"Maybe." Cara shook her head, the colour going to her cheeks. "Or maybe not. Dinner is very date-ish."

"Oh, come on, Cara. We can go to the buffet. That's not exactly romantic, is it?"

"I suppose so." Cara tried to force the goofy look off her face. She was very aware of herself, like always when Billie was near. "Buffet and an action movie, then?" She laughed and looked to Billie for confirmation.

"Sounds like my kind of night out." Billie shot her a flirty smile as they stepped into the elevator. "I'm in. Pick me up at seven," she joked as they went down.

Cara leaned back against the wall and looked into Billie's blue eyes. Billie was facing her from the other side of the elevator, giving her that look that was impossible to resist. Despite the silence that followed, they both held their gaze. The tension was electrifying, and Cara's heart was beating so fast, she was terrified Billie could hear it.

"Are you okay, Cara?" Billie teased without breaking eye contact. "You look a bit red in the cheeks."

"No, just warm in here, that's all." Cara shook her head but couldn't suppress a grin as she looked down at her feet. She sighed in relief when the doors opened, and a cleaner stepped in, dragging her laundry cart in between them.

39

"Thanks for your help guys, I'm off tonight so I'll see you all tomorrow." Billie put her clipboard in her bag and changed from her shorts and polo shirt into a white summer dress. She checked her hair in the mirror and put on some lip gloss before closing the staffroom door behind her.

"Hey there."

"Oh, hi." Billie was caught off guard by Cara sitting on one of the sun beds. She was wearing jeans and a tight T-shirt, showing off her athletic body. Her dark bob and fringe had been straightened, and the black eyeliner made her eyes stand out. She looked stunning, and for once, Billie was lost for words.

"Surprised to see me?" Cara asked. "I said I'd pick you up at seven, didn't I?"

Billie took a deep breath and collected herself. "Yes, of course. And you're on time."

Cara grinned. "Yes, I am." She stood up and looked Billie up and down. "You look nice, Billie."

"Thanks. You look nice too," Billie stammered. "Really

nice." Why was she acting like an insecure teenager? She always had the upper hand. Always. Except for today, apparently.

"Shall we go and get some food, or would you like to hang around the staffroom for a bit longer?" Cara asked with an amused smirk.

Billie laughed and shook her head as she hooked her arm into Cara's. "No, let's go. I don't know what's wrong with me today. The sun must have fried my brain."

Claudio's was quiet, and that was a rare occurrence, even when at port. "I'm not going to pull the chair out for you," Cara said, sitting down at the table. "Because we're not on a date."

Billie laughed. "I didn't expect you to. But you could order us some wine, though? That wouldn't be date-ish, would it?" She handed Cara the wine list. "I know next to nothing about wine, other than that I like most of them, so take your pick."

"Sure." Cara tried to look like she knew what she was doing. She studied the wine list and pointed out the Chablis to the waiter. It was the only wine she was remotely familiar with, apart from the cheap red wine she used to get from the night shop in London.

"Hey, you work in the kitchen, am I right?" their waiter said after taking the drinks order. He studied Cara's hair while adjusting his comb-over. "You clean up well. I didn't recognize you without your bandana and your whites."

Cara laughed. "I'm not sure how to take that but thanks anyway."

He smiled and gestured towards the kitchen door. "Shall I tell your colleagues that you're here?"

"No, please don't." Cara waved a hand. "I think I can handle a day without them. I was just curious what it was like on the other side of the pass, that's all. And I have to say, it's quite nice." She smiled up at him.

"I'm glad you like it. We do try." He poured them a glass of water and lit the candle on the table. "So, is there a special occasion for tonight, ladies?" He looked from Cara to Billie and back. "I could bring some more candles over, since it's quiet." He bent down in between them and lowered his voice. "We also have the lovers' cocktail on offer this week." Cara and Billie stared back at him in amusement.

"Well..." Cara looked at his nametag. "Frank. I have the evening off, so I would say that's pretty special, yes."

"Me too," Billie chipped in. "But if you're asking if we're on a date... no we're not." She giggled. "This is very much a non-date."

"Right," Frank said. He got up again. "I apologize, I didn't mean to pry." His cheeks were rosy as he took a step back. "I'll have someone bring the wine over for you. Enjoy your dinner."

"He's annoying," Billie said after he had left. "But he is right. You do clean up nice. I mean, not that you don't look nice normally. But I can see that you've gone through a bit more trouble today. Did you do that for me?" Her tone was teasing.

Cara leaned in closer. "What about that dress you're wearing? Did you do that for me? Because I know you weren't wearing it this morning, so you must have put it in your bag before you left."

Billie smiled. "Come on, Cara. Don't answer a question with a question. It's not fair. But yes, if you must know, I put on a dress for you." She stood up and walked towards the buffet. Cara felt her insides flutter at the sight of Billie's legs in her short, white dress. *Behave, Cara.*

"Did you check if there's a good movie on later?" Billie

asked when they were back at the table with plates full of grilled artichokes, crab cakes and a bowl of lemon mayonnaise. She poured them both a glass of wine from the cooler next to her. Although their conversation was back to normal, the tension was still lingering between them.

"I did." Cara grimaced. "The Bodyguard is the only movie on tonight, I'm afraid. They've got some kind of back-to-the-nineties week on at the cinema."

Billie, who was just about to help herself to the food, dropped her fork back on her plate and laughed. "You're joking, right?"

Cara shook her head and laughed too. "No, I'm not, so if you still want to go, that's our only option."

Billie sat back in her chair, weighing her options. "No, I want to go. You promised me a movie so that's what we'll do. Besides, I've never seen it before." She went back to concentrating on the food, amusement written all over her face. "Mmm, this is good," she mumbled, after taking a bite of the crab cake. "Not bad for buffet food."

"You're right," Cara said, dipping an artichoke in the mayonnaise. "It is good. I made this yesterday. Five litres, it took me two hours."

Billie's eyes widened. "Really? That's amazing. You're a mayo genius, did you know that?"

Cara beamed with pride at Billie's compliment. She looked over to the buffet to check if there was anything else on it that she might have made, but her sight was hindered by two men in chef's whites who were looking their way. Cara buried her face in her hands. "Oh God. Please tell me that's not Eduardo and that creepy little kitchen porter."

"Your colleagues?" Billie turned and waved at them.

"What are you doing?" Cara whispered. "I was trying to ignore them."

"Why?" Billie nodded towards them. "Look, they're waving back. I'm sure they're just being friendly."

"They're never just friendly." Cara put on a polite smile and waved too, hoping that would make them go away. "And they never leave the kitchen, especially Eduardo, he doesn't like people." She sighed. "That waiter must have told them we're here, and now they're going to think we're on a date."

Billie chuckled. "So what? Let them. I don't mind."

"You don't?"

"No." Billie scooped another crab cake onto her plate. "Who cares what they think?" She put her hand on top of Cara's, resting on the table. "I'm sure they'd be super jealous of me if they thought I was dating you." She wiggled her eyebrows. "And I think that's kind of cool."

Cara relaxed back into her seat, but kept her hand on the table. Billie was stroking her wrist, giving her goose-bumps. "I think it's more likely to be the other way around, Billie. You should hear the things they say about you in the kitchen." They both laughed.

"Well in that case," Billie said, "they can be jealous of both of us." She stood up and put a hand on Cara's shoulder. "I want to try the sushi now. Want me to get you anything?"

L ater that night, they were sitting in the back row of the cinema. Billie was crunching away with a supersize box of caramel popcorn on her lap. There were only about ten other people there, most of them seated at the front. Billie put her legs up on the back of the empty seat in front of her and slumped in her chair.

"I don't think I've ever been on a cinema date before," she said, leaning into Cara.

Cara smiled in amusement, sipping her coke. "It's not a date, Billie."

She contradicted herself by putting an arm around Billie's shoulders, allowing Billie to rest her head on her chest. It was nothing new. They had sat like this many times before, outside on the deck, but somehow it felt different tonight. Cara's hand searched for a lock of Billie's hair, and she twirled it around her finger, causing Billie to shiver. When the lights went out, and the curtains opened, Cara put her feet up too and pulled Billie in closer. She was warm and soft, and her hair smelt of peaches. Each time Cara got a waft of the scent, it stirred something inside of her. *God, she smells good.* She let her gaze wander over Billie's legs. Her thighs were highlighted by flashes from the screen. They were smooth and toned. *Look at the screen. Don't go too far.* The movie had started now, but she could barely concentrate with Billie sitting next to her.

"Popcorn?" Billie whispered, looking up at her. She held one up in front of Cara's mouth. Cara parted her lips and let Billie feed her. Her hand lingered there, touching Cara's lips lightly.

Cara held her breath at the craving that suddenly seemed to overtake her entire body. When Billie retracted her hand, Cara caught her wrist in a reflex, and put it back against her mouth. She closed her eyes as she folded her lips over the tip of Billie's index finger. Billie moaned and threw her head back against Cara's arm. The overwhelming reaction to the simple touch surprised them both. Cara was unable to hold back, as she sucked Billie's finger deeper into her mouth. Billie gasped, flexing her hips in her seat. It caused the hem of her dress to hike up, revealing more of her thighs. As if she had no control over it, Cara's hand let go of Billie's wrist, and made its way down to her knee, moving upwards as she stroked her, squeezing the inside of Billie's thigh. Billie offered her other fingers, gasping each time Cara took one into her mouth. There was a vague sense of a soundtrack playing in the background, but other than that, they were unaware of their surroundings. Cara felt Billie's muscles tense as she moved her hand between her legs, barely touching the lace of her panties.

They jumped up when the security guard's flashlight shone on them from the end of their row of chairs. Billie took her feet off the seat and sat straight up in a split second, pulling down the hem of her dress. Cara held up her hands, as if he was going to shoot her. She couldn't see his face in the dark, and that made it hard to assess the situation.

"Everything okay back there, ladies?" he shouted. The other people in the cinema turned at the sound of his voice.

"We're good," Billie said in a high-pitched voice. "Thanks for asking."

He nodded. "No shoes on the chairs." He moved the flashlight towards Cara's feet. "That means you too."

Cara almost fell off her chair when she threw her legs up in the air, removing them as quickly as she could. "Sorry," she said, trying to look as regretful as she could.

He nodded. "No worries. Just keep them down." With that, he had turned off the flashlight and walked back to the door.

Cara sunk deep into her chair and tried to concentrate on the dialogue, wondering if things could possibly get anymore awkward than they were. *Oh God. Control yourself, you idiot.* Billie looked flustered too. She was staring at the screen, pretending to watch the movie. There an obvious silence amongst the noise, and for the duration of the movie, they were both waiting for the other to speak.

When the end credits started rolling, Cara couldn't take it anymore.

"Billie," she whispered. "Are you okay?"

Billie turned; her face still flushed. "Yeah," she said, keeping her voice down. "I think I got a bit carried away just then."

Cara was relieved to see her face breaking into an amused smile. "I think I did too." She laughed. "Turns out this was a date after all."

40

It had been another hectic day, and after fourteen long hours, Billie finally sat down on the couch in the staffroom.

"This is crazy," she said, putting her feet up on the footstool. "People can be so demanding without distraction." They had been at sea for five days now, working non-stop and she was looking forward to having some time off. It was dark, and the last guests had finally left the pool deck. "Just one more day."

"Tell me about it." Josipa slouched down next to her. She held a plant mister in front of her face and exhaled as she sprayed the cool mist against her face.

"Hey, give me that." Billie took it and sprayed her own face. "That feels so good. Where did you get that thing?"

"The gardener," Josipa said. "I mean the plant lady." She frowned. "What do you call someone who deals with plants? I can't think, I'm too tired." She took the mister back and sprayed into her top.

Billie shrugged. "No idea, but it's the best thing I've felt all day."

Her phone beeped, and she picked it up from the table without thinking. She flinched when she saw it was a message from Dan. *Miss you.* That was all it said, except for a heart emoji at the end. It had been a while since Dan had sent her a message. Maybe he was busy. Or maybe he had sensed that she wasn't so keen anymore.

"Your boyfriend?" Josipa asked, looking at the phone in Billie's hands.

Billie sighed. "Yeah." She wanted to stand up to avoid a conversation on the subject, but she was too exhausted.

"And?" Josipa's attention suddenly spiked. "Can I see a picture? I didn't know you were seeing someone."

"I don't have a picture," Billie lied.

"But surely he must be on social media?" Josipa had no intention of giving up. She took her phone out of her pocket and typed in her pin code. "What's his name?"

Billie couldn't take it anymore. "I'm going to break up with him," she said. "I've been meaning to for the past week, but I keep on putting it off." She felt sick at the thought of making the call.

"Right." Josipa seemed to process that information. "Is it the distance?" She hesitated. "Or did you meet someone else?"

Billie rubbed her eyes. They were sore from looking into the sun all day. "I have met someone else," she heard herself say. *Why am I telling her this?* "Not that it matters. It's not going to work out."

Josipa opened her mouth to say something but decided against it. Instead, she walked over to the storage room and found a bottle of whiskey in one of the old fancy dress boxes. "Arnie's secret stash," she said, holding up the bottle. "Want one?"

Billie nodded. She watched Josipa pour them both a

glass of the lukewarm liquid, accepted it, and knocked it back in one go. Then she held her glass out again for a refill. "I'll buy him a new bottle tomorrow," she said.

"Are you in love?" Josipa asked.

Billie nodded slowly. "Yes."

41

"I'm so glad we were able to catch the last hour of sun," Cara said as she strolled next to Billie at a slow pace. The sand was warm, and now and then they moved closer to the ocean to cool their feet. Billie had her flip-flops in one hand and a towel in the other. The idyllic beachfront along a row of independent hotels consisted of nothing but white sand and palm trees, thick grass and tropical plants. Apart from the music playing in the beach bars, it was quiet along the coast. Even the sea was calm, as if the island had decided to take a break. The famous clear water that drew tourists to the beaches of Mauritius was turquoise in the shallows, and a deep shade of jade further out. A handful of fishing boats were making their way back to the wooden pier, where hotel staff were waiting with cooler bags to pick up the catch of the day.

"I never thought I'd be in Mauritius." Cara's eyes sparkled as she looked around. "It's a whole new level of perfect here." A shoal of iridescent fish moved through the water in natural, fluid motions. Crabs that were flushed ashore were trying to get back to the sea, struggling against the tide.

"You're right. It's more than perfect." Billie sighed. "I could get used to this." She turned to Cara. "I've barely seen you in the past week. Not since our non-date." She shot Cara an amused glance and they both laughed. "With all the double shifts I've been working, I pass out as soon as I hit the bed. We've lost four team members already due to illness and injury, and our newbie got off in Sydney because she was homesick."

Cara shrugged. "It hasn't been much better in the kitchen. It's like people feel the need to eat everything in sight after they've been off the ship for a few days. Just because it's free. And we still haven't found a replacement for Ben." She smiled. "But hey, who cares. We're here now."

Billie inhaled and closed her eyes. "Do you smell that? It smells awesome."

Cara stuck her nose up in the air and got a waft of garlic, coriander and curry leaves. Drawn towards the aroma of fresh seafood, they followed a sign that said Kiosk Magique. The food shack was situated underneath a thick roof of trees, providing shade for the picnic tables around it. Crates and barrels, painted in green and yellow, functioned as seats, and there was a small bottle of vanilla rum on each table. It was filled with people, both locals and tourists.

"English?" A waiter approached them and pointed at a free table in the grass.

"Yes, thank you." Cara smiled at him and took a seat opposite Billie, examining the rum. "Want some?"

Billie laughed. "Hell yeah. When in Mauritius..." She held out two glasses for Cara, who poured them both a generous amount, and scrambled for the ice cubes in the bucket next to them. A little later they were feasting on king prawns, dorado and a variety of curry dishes.

"I need to know how to make this," Cara said, pointing at the fish curry. "It's so good; I'm surprised it's even legal." She scooped some more onto her plate, while Billie refilled their glasses.

"And I need to buy some of this rum. It's going straight to my head, but I don't care. It's delicious. Anyway, we don't have to be back at work until eleven tomorrow morning, so the night is young." Billie raised her glass and took a sip. "Oh Cara, I wish we could stay here tonight. Wouldn't that be nice? Waking up to this?" She gestured to the beach and the food with a beaming smile.

The sky was bright blue, running into a gradient of orange and then a bright red, just above the horizon. It was darkening by the minute, and the soft light of dusk left a glow on Billie's face, making her look even more radiant than before. Cara couldn't stop looking at her. It was almost magical, the way the low sun skimmed her blonde hair. She felt a flutter in her stomach when Billie stared back at her, just a little bit too long.

"Why not," Cara suddenly heard herself say. "We could ask around, see if any of those chalets are available?" She gestured to the wooden cabins with straw roofs that were scattered along the beach. "We just need to find a driver to take us back tomorrow morning. Apart from that, nothing is stopping us, right?"

"You need a cabin?" A big, bald man at the table next to them yelled in a heavy French accent. He had obviously been listening to their conversation. "I know the owner, Dinesh. I'll get you ladies a chalet. It's cheap during the week, and I'm sure Dinesh will be happy to drive you back to where you need to be tomorrow morning. Just tell him you need to leave an hour earlier, and you'll be fine. He's not so good with timekeeping." He laughed, pointing at his watch.

"Wow, thank you!" Billie cast him her most generous smile and wiggled on her seat in excitement. "That sounds like a perfect plan."

The beach was almost deserted by the time Cara and Billie had finished their food and secured a chalet. The few people left were packing their bags and shaking out their towels, zombified after a long day in the sun. Cara spread a blanket out over the sand, then sat down and let her gaze wander over Billie, who looked dangerously sexy in her white summer dress. The bottle of rum was still in her hand, but she had stopped drinking from it. She had a natural dark tan, and all the sun exposure had highlighted her blonde hair, making her blue eyes stand out and impossible to ignore.

Cara tried not to stare and patted the space next to her. "Come on. Sit down. You're not scared of me, are you?"

Billie laughed and shook her head. "By now, I'm not sure of anything anymore." She sat down next to Cara. "All I know is that it scares me how good you look tonight."

Cara's legs and arms were toned from working in the kitchen, and her black hair was tangled in a messy beach look. Cara blushed at the compliment. "I was just thinking the same thing." She turned to face Billie and pulled her legs up, resting her chin on her knees. Her expression turned serious. "It feels like we're doing something wrong, just by admitting that."

Billie cocked her head and cast her a sad smile. "I don't know. Maybe." She sighed, playing with the hem of her dress. "I spoke to Dan last week. I broke up with him."

Cara's eyes widened. "I had no idea. You didn't tell me..."

Billie shrugged. "I didn't want to bring up the subject. It feels awkward every time we talk about him."

"Oh God, you didn't mention me, did you?"

Billie shook her head. "No, I didn't, but I did tell him that I'd met someone and that it would be best if we stopped calling each other. And by that, I meant him calling me because that's how it's been lately."

"Why didn't you tell me? Was he okay? What did he say?" Cara's stomach dropped at the thought of Dan being turned down by the only woman who had ever managed to keep his interest for more than a week.

Billie shrugged. "Would it have made a difference if I'd told you?" She didn't wait for a reply. "He seemed fine. Or as fine as one can be in that situation. He said that he was disappointed, but that he understood." She paused. "I'm pretty sure he wasn't angry. I think I would have heard it in his voice."

"That easy, huh?" Cara frowned in suspicion, but the spark of hope she felt was so much stronger than her doubt. She wanted nothing more than to believe that Dan was okay. "And you're sure he wasn't just saying that?"

"I don't know." Billie rested her head on Cara's shoulder and looked out over the ocean. "I don't think I know him well enough to gauge how he's feeling. But he was calm and even funny, just before we hung up. All I know is that I should have told him weeks ago. I was putting it off, and that was wrong."

Cara closed her eyes and shivered at the feeling of Billie's hair, tickling her cheek. "So where does that leave us?" The words were out before she'd had time to think them through.

Billie smiled and lifted her head to meet Cara's eyes. "It leaves us wherever you want us to be." She paused. "But I thought you didn't want anything to happen between us, regardless of Dan and me."

Cara nodded, lowering her voice. "Yeah. I know I said that." There was silence between them, as they listened to the sound of the gentle waves and the cacophony of birdsong, saying goodbye to another day. The last sliver of light disappeared behind the horizon, isolating them from the view of the last people left on the beach. She held her breath, terrified to break the spell of that moment in which everything seemed to be perfect. She looked down at Billie's mouth and then back up into the depths of the blue eyes that drew her closer and closer until she felt the softness of Billie's lips on hers. A warm glow spread through her body, leaving her helpless and craving more.

Billie's voice was hoarse with longing. "I want you," she whispered. "I need to feel you, Cara. Everywhere. I need you to kiss me, and I need your hands on me, and I need them now."

Cara couldn't move. For a moment, she felt paralyzed, staring at the beautiful face of the woman she had been longing to touch for so long. She put her hand behind Billie's neck, pulled her in closer, and parted her lips to claim her mouth. To take whatever she'd been dreaming about since their first kiss. Butterflies started flapping around in her stomach and went straight to her head, leaving her dizzy and unable to think. She felt Billie's tongue, dancing around hers, as their kiss deepened. Billie moaned, sinking her hands into Cara's hair. Cara slipped her hand under Billie's dress and ran it over her leg and her bottom, while lowering her onto the towel with her other hand. Billie's skin was firm and smooth and warm. She felt the curves of her hips as Billie pulled her on top and wrapped a leg around her thigh.

"Take me," she mumbled. "Please."

Cara pulled back before she lost herself. She opened her eyes to meet Billie's aroused expression. "I think we should move inside," she said, out of breath. She scanned the beach. It was dark now, and she could barely make out a silhouette of someone coming their way.

Billie nodded, struggling to speak. Her hair was messy, and her dress was hanging off one shoulder. Cara took her hand and led them to the cabin, where she lit the candles next to the double bed. It was clean and simple, with white bedsheets and a mosquito net draped across it. Billie lifted the net and threw herself onto the bed, waiting for Cara to follow. "I need you," she said, her eyes begging.

Cara took Billie's face in her hands and kissed her gently. "Let me take off your dress," she whispered against her mouth.

Billie lifted her shaking arms, allowing Cara to pull the dress over her head, revealing her yellow bikini and tanned skin. Cara gasped as she traced a finger down from Billie's collarbone to the top of her bikini. Billie drew a quick breath and shivered when the finger skimmed underneath the edge. Cara moved her hands around Billie's back and untied the strings, undoing her bikini top. Then she pulled it off, finally allowing herself to look.

"You're so beautiful," she whispered. Billie's breasts were full and firm, with small, hard nipples. She traced her sides, encouraged by Billie's ragged breathing. Cara let her gaze travel over her nearly-naked body and felt a desperate need to take her. She ripped off her own T-shirt and bikini top before lowering herself on top of Billie.

They both closed their eyes, savouring the first moment of the warm contact. Billie pulled Cara's face towards her, opening her mouth to meet Cara's lips and tongue in a passionate kiss that drew the breath from them both. Cara moved her hand over Billie's breast and kissed her neck. First softly, then harder, gently biting the warm skin that smelled of lavender soap and sea breeze. Billie buckled underneath her and lifted her hips when Cara's hand moved down in between them, sliding over her stomach. She stopped when she reached the edge of the bikini bottom and lifted her head to look down at Billie.

Billie nodded. "Please, Cara. I need you to touch me."

Cara untied the strings and moved her hand down underneath the fabric, caressing the soft curls between Billie's thighs. She gasped at the wetness against her fingers when Billie opened her legs. She took a nipple into her mouth and bit it softly while she moved her fingers through the slick folds, causing Billie to cry out. Billie's reaction to her touch was pure and raw. Her nails dug into Cara's skin when she pulled her up to kiss her hard and deep while grinding her hips up against Cara's thigh. Cara bit Billie's bottom lip as she entered her with two fingers. She was wet and warm and so ready.

"Oh God!" Billie broke the kiss and threw her head back when Cara pushed deeper before pulling back, arching her fingers inside of her. She could feel Billie's body trembling at her touch, and so she moved inside her again, penetrating her in slow and deep motions until she found a steady rhythm between their bodies. Billie moved with her like they were one, holding on to Cara's back. Cara watched her eyelids flutter as she bit her lip.

"Is that good?" she mumbled against Billie's mouth.

Billie nodded. "Hmm... So good."

She threw her head back again, and Cara knew she was close. She moved her thumb over Billie's centre and kissed her while she held Billie's hand on the pillow above her head. Cara couldn't remember a time she'd felt closer to someone than she did now, and she opened her eyes and lifted her head to watch Billie tremble underneath her before she tightened around Cara's fingers, holding her breath. Cara held on to Billie while she rode out the last waves of her orgasm, buckling in her arms. She was perfect. Blonde locks were stuck to her neck and her forehead, damp and glistening with grains of sand.

Tiny drops of sweat trickled down Billie's face, as she stared up at Cara with a look of surprise and relief on her face. "Wow...okay..." she let out a deep sigh. "That was incredible." Her hand reached out to touch Cara's face. "You're incredible."

Cara laughed. "It's not me. I think it's a thing called chemistry. Maybe you've heard about it?"

Billie giggled. "Chemistry?" She pushed Cara off her and turned them over, straddling her. "You mean that thing that makes me want to eat you alive?"

Billie bent down and kissed the soft skin under Cara's ear, trailing her tongue down to her nipple. Cara moaned in pleasure when Billie's hot breath blew over her breasts. She moved slow and seductive, careful not to miss a single inch of her body. Cara felt Billie's feminine curves under her fingertips, as she followed her spine down to her bottom. She held it with both hands and drew Billie closer towards her. Billie turned Cara's face to the side and kissed her neck, and her ear. Her mouth lingered there. "I want to make you feel good too," she whispered. "But I don't know what I'm doing so you need to tell me what you like."

Cara moaned when Billie lowered herself on top of her. "No need, Billie. You're doing great." She was still trying to grasp the fact that this was Billie, in bed with her. Billie, whom she'd been longing for and dying to touch. Cara watched Billie kiss around her bellybutton, and trace her hips down towards her thighs, stroking the inside of her legs from her knees upwards, until Cara couldn't take it anymore. "Touch me. Please."

Billie smiled as she traced the edge of Cara's briefs with her fingertips, before pulling them off. Without hesitation, she lowered herself between Cara's legs and spread them apart. She closed her eyes and let her tongue run over the full length of Cara's centre, before looking up at her and repeating the movement, with more pressure this time. Cara gasped when Billie's tongue circled her clit. She lifted her hips from the mattress and threw herself back in the pillows. Billie was moaning between her legs, as she slowly brought Cara towards a climax.

Cara took Billie's face in her hands and pulled her up towards her own. "Wait. I want to kiss you when I..." Billie kissed her hard, interrupting her sentence. She lowered a hand in between them and entered Cara with one finger, then another one before pushing into her with her full weight. "Oh God!"

"When you what?" Billie looked down at her with a look of dark desire, as she pressed a teasing hand down on Cara's clit.

Cara claimed her mouth again before she wrapped her legs around Billie, pulling her into a tight embrace. The internal explosions grew stronger until her vision went blank. She held her breath. "Stay there. Don't let go," Cara said as her body shook.

Their bodies were damp and tired when they both sighed in relief. She looked up at Billie, who was hovering above her, looking pretty pleased with herself. "You don't seem to have a problem with inexperience," Cara said in a teasing tone.

Billie laughed. "Maybe you're just easy to please."

42

Cara woke up in the middle of the night. She reached out for Billie, but she wasn't there. She sat up and blinked a couple of times, letting her eyes adjust to the dark before scanning the room. *What's happened? Did she change her mind? Did I scare her?* She felt panic spreading across her chest. She couldn't lose Billie. Not now. She put on her briefs and T-shirt and opened the door. The wind ran through her hair, cooling her neck from the heat of the cabin.

To her relief, she saw Billie on the beach. She was sitting in the sand, facing the ocean, her legs stretched out in front of her. Cara sighed and held on to her stomach, which seemed to do a little dance each time she saw her. She approached Billie, careful not to scare her.

"This feels like a dream, doesn't it?" Billie looked up at Cara and gestured to the spot next to her. She pulled her bare legs up under her chin and wrapped her arms around them. Cara sat down next to her. It was dark, but not dark enough to miss how beautiful Billie looked, sitting there at the edge of the ocean, the water washing over her feet.

"Only if you don't mind. Are you okay?"

Billie nodded. "Don't worry. I'm more than okay. I couldn't sleep so I came out here." She smiled. "It's lovely, don't you think?"

"It is." Cara stretched her legs out in front of her and leaned back on her elbows. "And so quiet."

"It's weird," Billie said in a soft voice. "We spend most of our time out on the ocean, but we rarely get to feel it on our skin. I wish we could stay here a little while longer."

Cara nodded. "We could always come back. Just you and me."

"What do you mean?" Billie whispered. "Last week, you told me we could never be a thing, and now you're saying this. Don't mess with me, Cara. I don't need any promises, but I do need to know where I stand. What are we?"

Cara kissed her softly on the cheek. She could feel Billie's long eyelashes fluttering against her skin. "You're right. I shouldn't have said that." There was a pause. "I don't know what we are," she answered honestly. "I'm not ready to choose between you and my best friend. But I do know that I've never been happier than I am now."

Cara shook her head. "Oh God, Billie. You have no idea how crazy I am about you." She moved to sit behind Billie, enveloping her with her legs. She folded her arms around Billie's waist and kissed her neck down to her shoulders. "It's hard to even look your way without throwing myself on top of you, now that I know how good that feels."

Billie giggled, relaxing into Cara's grip. "Please do, I have no problem with that." She hesitated, turning her head. "Last night was amazing, Cara. It's still amazing. And a little bit overwhelming. To me, anyway. You know, I've been intrigued by you ever since we first kissed." She shook her head. "No, wait. It was before that."

Cara cocked her head and smiled. "Really?"

Billie nodded. "Yeah." She blushed. "I tried to ignore it, but it was impossible. The way you look when you come in at night, with your hair all messy and the sleeves of your whites rolled up, showing those tattoos. You look so cool and capable. You do this thing where you take off your jacket in one movement, leaving you in one of those white vest tops you always wear underneath. It's like a free strip-tease." Billie grinned. "And then you lie down on the bed, collecting yourself before you have a shower. It's my favourite moment of the day."

Cara smiled sheepishly. "I had no idea." She chuckled. "I think my favourite moments are when you get back from one of your stage nights, in that sequined dress with feathers on your head. You look stunning and sexy. But then you strip yourself off all the bling and accessories and make-up, and you're so breathtakingly beautiful, just the way you are. Your hair and your skin, your eyes and that gorgeous body, only covered in lingerie. I look at you when you get undressed, whenever I get the chance."

"I know," Billie arched a teasing eyebrow. "I love the way you look at me; it's such a turn-on."

"You've noticed that?"

"It's hard not to," Billie said with a grin. "One time you pretended to read with the newspaper upside down."

Cara laughed. "I had no idea you knew." She buried her head in Billie's neck. "Oh God, I feel like a pervert now."

"Don't." Billie lifted Cara's chin, forcing her to look into her eyes. "No one's ever looked at me the way you do. You make me feel wanted and sexy and alive. That's how I feel right now. I feel like I can handle anything."

"Me too," Cara admitted. "I know it's wrong, but I need you. It's like you're feeding me with your presence, and I'm always hungry when you're not around. And now, time seems so precious all of a sudden." She shook her head. "This hasn't gone according to plan, has it?"

"It certainly wasn't my plan," Billie said. "I liked you when we had dinner together that night at Dan's house, but other than that, I honestly couldn't care less about you. I only offered to help you out with a job because Dan had had been bugging me about it."

Cara's eyes widened. "I can't believe it. How cheeky! He never told me that. I thought it was a spontaneous thing."

Billie laughed. "No, it wasn't. But I wanted to help you. I really did. I was happy you turned out to be such a good fruit carver. It made it a lot easier to fit you in somewhere." She sighed. "Dan was worried about you. He talked about you a lot, said you hadn't been yourself in a long time."

"I know." Cara covered Billie's hand with her own. "I wasn't myself. And I know Dan just wanted to help me. He texted me to say that he couldn't wait to have me back as his miserable roommate." She laughed. "You know, Dan is the closest thing I've ever had to real family. My parents were never around, and I moved from boarding school to boarding school, depending on where my father worked. They might as well have left me in one place, I hardly saw them anyway. But when I went to University and met Dan, I knew I had finally found someone I could rely on to stick around. We did everything together. When he switched to Fine Arts, we still saw each other twice a week, catching up in the pub. He wasn't the kind of guy to have a lot of male friends, and my company was safe because we would never end up in bed together. I guess you could say the same for me." She sighed. "Being with you feels so good, Billie. But it's not fair to Dan."

Billie snuggled closer against Cara. "I know. But we're

here now, and we've already gone too far. I don't regret anything. Do you?"

Cara shook her head. "No, I don't."

"Good." Billie let out a sigh of relief. "Ignoring each other isn't going to change anything. We'd be denying ourselves so much." Her gaze gravitated towards Cara's mouth. "Here's my proposal. Why don't we just enjoy our time together? We only have five weeks left, and I would love to spend every free minute with you. After that, we'll go our separate ways and pretend nothing ever happened, even if it's the hardest thing we'll ever have to do." She traced Cara's cheeks down to her mouth and let her thumb rest on her bottom lip. "I'd rather have you for a little while than not have you at all." Cara took Billie's hand and kissed the finger on her mouth.

"Okay," she said in a whisper. "I think I can agree to that."

43

"Good morning, gorgeous." Billie opened her eyes to find Cara standing over her, holding two coffees. "I managed to get these at a hotel down the beach." She kissed Billie's forehead before crawling back into bed. "You looked so peaceful sleeping. I didn't want to wake you."

Billie blinked against the sunlight that was now streaming in through the window and smiled. "Good morning to you too." She wrapped an arm around Cara's waist and yawned. "Thank you for the coffee. What time is it?"

"Nine. Almost time to go. But we've still got twenty minutes." Cara took off her T-shirt and snuggled up against Billie, who let out a deep sigh.

"Shit. I should have set my alarm. It's such a waste of time to sleep when I'm here with you." She pulled Cara closer. "Mmm... You feel so good." She smiled when their eyes met. "I feel so happy, Cara. Last night was amazing, wasn't it?"

Cara felt her insides flutter as the flashbacks of the previous night set off in her head like fireworks. They had made love over and over again until they were exhausted and fell into a deep sleep, entangled in each other's arms. And Billie was still here, naked in bed with her. She moved a hand up from Billie's thigh towards her breast.

"It was."

Billie shivered at the touch. "You don't regret it, do you?"

"No." Cara shook her head and smiled. "I still don't. Do you?"

"Not for a second." Billie traced the inside of Cara's thigh, making her tremble with anticipation. She rolled on top and pressed her thigh between Cara's legs. Cara gasped and closed her eyes, opening up to Billie.

"I didn't know it was possible..." Billie whispered in her ear, "to crave someone this much." She gently bit down on Cara's earlobe.

Cara shivered and turned her head sideways to give Billie access to her neck. The instant arousal she felt at the touch of her tongue left her raging with desire. She stroked Billie's back down to her bottom and lowered her hand between her legs. Billie moaned. Her expression went from seductive to downright dark in a matter of seconds.

Billie stared at Cara in surprise, breathing fast. "Oh, God. Please do that again."

Cara smiled, cupping Billie's centre from behind. She extended a finger towards her clit and circled it slowly. Billie let herself fall back down. She arched her back, burying her face in Cara's neck. Cara felt the wetness between Billie's legs, and it almost sent her over the edge. There was something about Billie that made her lose all control. All she could think about was pleasing her in ways she had never even dreamed about.

"Yes. Like that. Don't stop," Billie begged.

They were interrupted by a knock on the door. "Ladies,

it's Dinesh here. Are you ready for me to take you to the harbour?"

Cara and Billie looked up, flustered, and tried not to laugh. "I thought he was supposed to be late," Cara said, keeping her voice down.

Billie shrugged, easing herself away from Cara. "Hey Dinesh, we're coming, just give us a few minutes!"

44

Billie let go of Cara's hand when they approached the Pelican. "Sorry. Most of our guests know me, and not everyone is as open-minded as they like to think they are." Hundreds of tourists were waiting with their passports in hand, ready to board.

"Of course." Cara searched for her staff pass in her bag and joined Billie in the queue. They couldn't resist leaning into each other, shoulder to shoulder, the backs of their hands lightly touching as they waited.

"I'm happy Arnie's not here." Billie giggled. "He'd be on to us straight away. I can't seem to stop smiling." She tried to relax her mouth, but it bounced straight back into a broad grin.

Cara laughed. "Same here," she said.

"Oh look, it's the fruit carver!" Cara looked up to find the lady who had complimented her display, waving at her. Then her gaze turned to Billie with the enthusiasm of a ten-year-old. "And the line-dancing lady!"

Cara and Billie smiled and greeted them.

"Hi, Caroline." Cara was surprised she remembered her

name. She turned to Caroline's husband. "I'm sorry – I've forgotten your name."

"Edward," he said.

"That's right. Caroline and Edward. Did you have a good time in Mauritius? You've caught the sun, I see?" Cara gestured to Caroline's forehead. Her face and neck were red, but her forehead and nose had taken on a darker shade, bordering on purple. It looked painful.

Caroline beamed, rubbing her sore nose. "Oh yes! It was marvellous. Wasn't it, Edward? We went on a bus tour yesterday, and visited the most beautiful beach we've ever seen." She rolled her eyes in delight. "We decided to spend the night in a hotel there. It's been the trip of a lifetime so far. All the staff has been so kind and welcoming. I wish it could last forever." Caroline took a step closer and whispered. "But Edward is a little bit homesick, the poor sod. He misses his Monday night darts club and his local."

Billie tried to steer the topic away from Caroline's husband, who didn't seem too pleased with the turn the conversation was taking. "That's all right. We all miss home now and then. So, what's the occasion for the cruise? Just a well-deserved holiday?"

Caroline shook her head. "Oh no dear, we could never afford a holiday like this. Our son gave it to us as a present for our fortieth anniversary." She took her husband's hand and smiled at him lovingly. "It's the day after tomorrow."

"Wow, forty years!" Cara gasped. "That's quite something! And how nice of your son. You must have raised him well."

Edward nodded, delighted with the compliment. "He's a good lad. Started his own building company when he was twenty, and he's never shied away from a hard day's work since. He's done well for himself, hasn't he, Caroline?"

Caroline grinned from ear to ear. "Oh yes. We've been ever so blessed with our Toby. I would happily introduce him to either of you nice young ladies, but I'm afraid he's getting married next year, so he's off the market."

Cara chuckled. "I guess that's our loss, but good for him. And are you two lovebirds doing anything to celebrate your anniversary?" Cara asked, looking from Caroline to Edward and back.

They both laughed. "Not really," Caroline said. "Waking up on the Pelican every day is grand enough as it is. We'll be going to our usual buffet restaurant, and having a quiet night on our balcony. That's just how we like it." She articulated the word 'balcony,' making sure everyone around them knew they had a balcony suite.

"Well that sounds nice," Billie said, rubbing Caroline's shoulder. "You two have a lovely day tomorrow."

"Thank you, dear. You're so kind." The queue was moving quicker than usual, and Caroline was rummaging through her bag, searching for their passports. "And you girls? What have you been up to? Chasing the local boys? They're quite handsome here, aren't they?" She giggled.

"No, nothing like that," Cara laughed. "We've just been relaxing and enjoying a day off."

"Oh well, you both deserve a break. I suppose there are plenty of handsome boys on the ship anyway." She frowned and closed one eye as if going through the list of potential matches in her mind.

"Come on Caroline; you're holding up the queue. Where are the passports?" Edward was getting impatient, gesturing towards the customs officer who was waiting for them to go through.

"I've got them, Edward, calm down." She turned around one more time. "It was lovely to see you girls. I hope to speak to you again before we're back in Southampton."

Cara nudged Billie after saying goodbye. "You're so good with people."

"Me? I can't believe you remembered her name."

Cara smiled. "They're sweet. We should do something special for them."

"I know what you mean." Billie waved back at a group of people who had been trying to catch her attention. "But we're not supposed to. Ninety percent of our guests are here for a special reason, so if we started doing that we'd have our hands full, running around with roses and sparklers every night. If we do something for them and others see it, they'll all want special treatment, and we don't have enough staff or the means to do that."

Cara nodded. "Okay. I get that. But what if no one sees it?"

Billie shrugged. "Then it would be okay, I suppose." She sighed. A couple of her team members were waiting for her by the entrance. Josipa was wearing her green monstrosity of a shirt, and she didn't look happy.

Cara squeezed Billie's hand by means of goodbye. "Duty calls, I see. Good luck."

45

———

"Hey there, chef." Billie was leaning against the doorpost at the kitchen entrance.

Cara's face broke into a huge smile when she saw her. "Hey there, dancer. Are you waiting for me?"

Billie winked. She was still wearing her sportswear from the last class of the day. The grey leggings, matching crop top and the black cardigan, tied around her hips, looked dangerously good on her.

"You bet I am." Billie straightened herself and took a step closer. "I'm free for the rest of the night. What about you? Any plans?" Her mischievous grin left no question as to what she was hinting at. She lowered her voice. "I thought maybe you and I could have a shower together? I think we both need one."

Cara blushed and turned to find Ibrahim staring at them with interest. She rolled her eyes. "Haven't you got things to do, Ibrahim? Like cleaning up your station, maybe?" Cara pointed at the saucepans in front of him. "You could take those to the kitchen porter to start with," she suggested.

Ibrahim shook his head as if waking up from a

daydream. "Yeah. Sure. Want me to take yours as well?" He shot them both one last look before turning back to the mess.

Cara looked Billie up and down. She'd been thinking about her the whole day, fantasizing about what she'd do to her in the blissful privacy of their cabin, and she knew Billie had done the same. "Hold that thought," Cara said to Billie, still feeling flushed by her proposition. "I need five minutes; I'm almost done."

She had a funny feeling everyone was looking at them now, even though they couldn't hear what they were saying over the noise of the extractor fans and the industrial dish-washers. But that wasn't the end of the world. Cara felt a funny sense of pride. Billie was one of the most beautiful and charismatic women on the ship, and she would be spending the night with her.

Billie looked over her shoulder and winked before she walked off. "Great. I'll see you in five."

The bathroom door was open when Cara got back to their cabin. Not that that was anything unusual. Billie often left the door open while she had a shower. But Cara had always retreated to her bed, pretending to read. She had always tried to ignore her thoughts of Billie, naked under the running water. Tonight, everything was different. The open door was an invitation, and Cara undressed as fast as she could, trembling with anticipation.

"There you are." Billie looked up as she ran both hands through her shampooed hair. She was stunning, and the water trickling over her face and her body only enhanced her natural beauty.

"Here I am," Cara said in a soft voice.

She walked over to Billie and hesitated for a moment, before kissing her. Billie closed her eyes and moaned softly, grinding her body against Cara's. Cara let out a deep sigh, as she lowered her hands towards Billie's bottom. She couldn't remember ever being so turned on by anyone. It was almost too much, and she had to force herself to go slow when she felt Billie's tongue caressing hers.

"Don't hold back," Billie whispered. "I want you just as much as you want me. Just take me, please." Her pupils had expanded, and her eyes were dark as she looked into Cara's, begging for release.

Cara bit her lip and nodded slowly. Then she turned Billie around and pushed her against the shower wall. She stood behind her, her mouth against Billie's ear. "Are you sure?"

Billie nodded. "Yes. I'm sure."

Cara ran her tongue over Billie's neck and traced her breasts with one hand, while she ran her other hand over Billie's stomach, down to the hairline between her thighs. She felt Billie's legs give way underneath her when she entered her with two fingers. Billie moaned and pushed her bottom into Cara's centre, her hips moving seductively.

"Yes, Cara. Fuck me."

Cara put a hand in front of Billie's mouth when she pulled back and pushed inside her again. "Our neighbours are going to hear us," she whispered.

"I don't care." Billie threw her head back against Cara's shoulder. Her entire body was moving, as Cara brought her other hand down, pushing down on her clit.

"Oh God, yes!" Billie's cry was even louder this time, and Cara closed her eyes, biting down on her shoulder.

She felt the tension build up in her lower abdomen, when Billie pushed back hard against her centre, arching her back. Billie started breathing faster and shaking before she let her head fall back again and gasped in delight. Her body stiffened as she contracted around Cara's fingers. Cara held her tight under the hot shower, stroking her until the last waves of her orgasm had subsided and Billie was limp in her arms. She was still trembling, barely able to stand, when she turned around to face Cara.

"That was amazing." Billie sighed as she traced Cara's jawline and kissed her. "But now it's your turn." She pinned Cara against the wall and faced her.

Cara gasped when Billie bent down and licked her way towards her stomach. Her hands were still above her head, her nails scraping over Cara's breasts. Cara's chest was heaving. She felt dizzy and held her breath when Billie's mouth moved between her legs, touching her lightly with the tip of her tongue. Her legs went limp. They felt like jelly, and she grabbed the shower head to steady herself when Billie entered her with her tongue, grasping her bottom with both hands.

"Is that good?" Billie whispered, looking up at her.

Cara nodded, unable to speak. She opened her mouth to scream when Billie entered her again, then remembered the neighbours and bit her lip as Billie moved two fingers inside her while tickling her clit with her tongue. Her head banged back against the wall. "Yes. Right there."

Billie looked up at her. "Here?" She ran her tongue over Cara's centre again and sucked hard when Cara moaned louder.

Cara closed her eyes when she thought her body was going to melt. She was shaking, surprised at her own reaction. Billie stood up and kissed her as she cupped her centre and pushed inside, penetrating her in slow motions. Cara was still holding on to the shower head when she felt deep contractions building up to an explosion, so overwhelming that she lost her bearings for a moment.

When she opened her eyes again, she met Billie's beautiful smile under the streaming water. She was too flustered to speak, so smiled and embraced the silence. Cara sighed and buried her face in Billie's neck, while Billie held her tight with both arms. Billie felt natural against her skin, as if she had always been there.

46

Cara yawned when she entered the kitchen. Seven in the morning was way too early for her. She usually didn't wake up before nine, and she certainly never got up without having a coffee first. She took a sip from the steaming hot latte in her takeaway cup before heading into the pantry, searching for ingredients. It was strange, being in the kitchen all alone. The usual noise was absent, and so was the steam and the overwhelming smell of garlic and grilled food. She wasn't even sure if it was against the rules, but who could fault her for trying to please guests?

Cara was tired, and her mood had been unpredictable since they'd got back from Mauritius. When she looked at Billie, everything fell into place, and she was calm and happy. As soon as Billie left the room, her guilt played up, and she felt the heavy knot in her stomach tighten. Cara shook it off. Time to focus. She picked up a box from the floor in the corner and filled it with eggs, parsley, salmon and avocado. Then she went to work.

A little later, she knocked on the door of suite number 234. Caroline's sunburnt face appeared in the door. "Oh, good heavens! Look, Edward, it's the chef!" She opened the door wider and looked down at the covered serving tray in Cara's hands.

"Congratulations," Cara said, smiling. "I thought I'd bring you a little something for breakfast, to celebrate your anniversary."

Caroline opened the door, and for a moment, Cara thought she was going to cry. "You didn't need to do that," she shrieked. Her eyes were tearing up as she moved away from the door, letting Cara into the room. "Well isn't this a nice surprise. How lovely of you."

Edward stood up, putting away his newspaper and coffee cup. "It certainly is. Good morning, young lady."

"I'm sorry to barge in like this," Cara said. "Where would you like me to put it down?"

Caroline opened the balcony doors and cleared the table so that Cara could put down their breakfast. "Here we go. Smoked salmon, poached eggs, avocado and fresh fruit."

Cara lifted the cloche. She had arranged the smoked salmon in the shape of roses on the plates, and had poached the eggs in heart-shaped Eddingtons. The avocado was mashed and spread over two grilled crumpets, still steaming hot. The fruit bowl resembled a bouquet of flowers, cut from a variety of fruits.

Cara winked. "And a small bottle of bubbly." She handed Caroline a miniature sized Champagne bottle and two glasses from a plastic bag, dangling on her wrist. "Enjoy your breakfast. I hope you like smoked salmon?"

To Cara's surprise, Caroline flew around her neck, almost choking her in the embrace. "It's beautiful! This is so romantic." She took a step back releasing Cara from her fleshy arms. "You're too kind, my dear. How can we possibly thank you?"

She shot her husband a warning look. "Don't you dare touch that before I've taken a picture, Edward."

Edward laughed. "I wouldn't dare." He turned to Cara. "Thank you, Cara. It's lovely. You've really made our day."

"No need to thank me," Cara giggled. She looked at her watch. "I'd better get back to work now. Enjoy your anniversary."

"What are you grinning about?" Kenneth, one of the sous-chefs, studied Cara's face when she got back to the kitchen. The morning shift had started, and she was just in time for the briefing. Chef Claudio was already at the pass, rummaging through his paperwork.

"Nothing. Just a nice start to the day, that's all."

Ibrahim followed them to the back of the group of kitchen staff, who had gathered around Chef Claudio. "She got laid, that's what happened," he whispered. "It was Billie, that hot blonde chick from the animation team."

One of the commis chefs and two kitchen porters turned around and looked from Ibrahim to Cara and back. Chef Claudio looked up from his clipboard wide-eyed and opened his mouth as if to say something, then lowered his head again, shaking it in disbelief.

Cara shot Ibrahim a fierce look, elbowing him in the ribs. "Shut up and mind your own business. Privacy, remember?" She tried to scowl at him, but it was hard to get rid of the stupid grin that had been plastered on her face since she got up. She felt exhausted from making love to Billie all night, then getting up at the crack of dawn to make breakfast for Caroline and Edward. But nothing could ruin her day, and clearly, nothing could ruin her mood either. She shivered when she thought of Billie in the shower.

"Cara, are you okay with that?" Cara straightened up at the sound of Chef Claudio calling her name.

"I'm sorry, Chef. I didn't hear you."

Chef Claudio shot her an annoyed look. "Is there something wrong with your ears, Cara? Or is your mind elsewhere?" He looked over the rim of his reading glasses, seemingly amused. "I asked if you could take over prep from Achmed today. He's not feeling well. You'll have to work through lunch. Is that a problem?"

Cara shook her head. "No Chef. That's not a problem."

She ignored the grinning faces of her co-workers. By now, everyone seemed to know about her and Billie. *Damn you, Ibrahim.*

47

"Come on, ladies. You can do better than that. Lift those arms. Higher, higher." Billie watched fifteen women struggle to keep their arms above water as they were hopping from one leg to another. "We're almost done. Now give it everything you've got for the last three minutes."

The relief on the faces in front of her was comical, and most of them seemed to gain a new lease of life just by knowing the end was near. Patty and Sonya, the line-dancing enthusiasts, were at the front as usual, flaunting their matching pink bathing suits. They were both wearing their shades, and couldn't have looked more misplaced in an aqua aerobics class if they tried. Billie loved having them in her classes. They were full of energy, and always got other people to join in with their extreme enthusiasm for just about anything. It was only two in the afternoon, and although they were still fairly sober, Patty and Sonya looked like they were about to pass out, along with the other thirteen ladies in the group. Billie decided it was time to wrap it up before someone had a heart attack. They weren't the youngest bunch, after all.

"Ten, nine, eight..." she counted backwards, and although they still had seven seconds to go, the majority of her group lowered their arms and sank into the water, skipping the final moves. "Seven, two, one!" She clapped, and they all clapped along with her. "Well done, everybody. You should be proud of yourselves. That was a hard one today."

Billie took a deep breath and dipped her head into the water. She was exhausted herself, and hadn't realized the routine was probably a step too far for her intermediates. Then again, she hadn't exactly been clear-headed lately. She had spent the week in a blissful haze, daydreaming at work, knowing she would see Cara in the evening. It was the most wonderful feeling, knowing Cara wanted her too, and that she would have all night with her. Every night.

"Are you trying to kill them?" Billie turned to find Cara standing at the edge of the pool. Her oversized denim shirt was tied loosely at the waist. Underneath it, she was wearing a pair of black sports shorts and a black bikini top. Cara's lean frame and relatively pale colour stood out in the crowd of well-fed sunburnt tourists. She had straightened her hair that Billie had cut the previous night, and looked incredibly sexy, the way she carried herself with confidence and a hint of boyish mischief.

Billie moved closer to the edge when Cara bent down to face her. "Are you trying to kill me?"

Cara laughed. "I'd rather not. Then I wouldn't be able to watch you in your Baywatch suit, being all sexy in the pool." She leaned in closer and lowered her voice. "I could look at you all day."

Billie tried to suppress a grin and looked around the pool to make sure no one had seen her. "Not here, Cara. Everyone will be able to tell, the way you keep forcing this stupid smile on my face." She shielded her eyes from the sun with her hand. "How's your day off?"

Cara shrugged and sat down, lowering her feet into the water. "It's nice. Not nearly as nice as it would've been if you were off too, but I'm coping. I'm reading, actually." She held up a paper file. "My dad sent me his pre-work on a project he's working on in Saudi Arabia. Missing person cases, I told you about it. It's interesting. He's just signed a contract with a big publisher to research the case and write a book about it."

"Oh wow. So, he's writing a book now? That's cool." Billie pulled herself up and sat down next to Cara.

"Yeah, it is. He seemed excited about the initial research, so I thought I'd have a read-through." Cara blushed when Billie smiled at her. It was their first time by the pool together, and she was pretty sure the deck staff were keeping a close eye on them, including Arnie, who was shamelessly staring their way.

Billie spotted him too, but she ignored him and turned her focus back to Cara. "That sounds interesting. Can I read it sometime? Or you could tell me all about it tonight when I finish?"

"Sure. I'll tell you about it tonight." Tonight. That word was like music to Cara's ears. Tonight was all she'd been able to think about all day, every day.

Billie narrowed her eyes and looked at her with a teasing smile. "Are you blushing, Cara?" She didn't wait for an answer. "Oh my God. You're blushing. Do I make you blush?"

Cara laughed. "Yeah, you do. All the time." She nodded in Arnie's direction. "I feel like everyone knows about us. Did you tell anyone?"

Billie shrugged and shifted her eyes. "I might have told

Arnie." She held her hands up in defence. "He dragged it out of me, I swear. And I can't lie to him, can I? He's my friend. But I didn't tell anyone else, I swear."

Cara smiled and gave Arnie, who was still focused on them, the finger. "It's okay. The whole kitchen knows too. I guess the word spreads fast." She shook her head. "But there's a silver lining to it. You see, I'm their hero now. They all look up to me because I'm sleeping with the hottest girl on the ship, and you know what that means in a testosterone filled kitchen... I'm the boss." They both laughed.

"I've got to do my afternoon briefing now," Billie said. "Are you staying?"

Cara nodded towards the deckchairs. "I'm not supposed to be here, but I've been told a couple of hours won't get me into trouble."

48

"Hey, it's Dan." Dan's voice sounded far away, and even with the volume turned up, she had to focus hard to hear him.

Cara winced at the sound of his voice and cursed herself for picking up. "Dan! How are you? I don't know why the connection is so bad today. Maybe it's best if I call you back later?"

"Yeah well, don't worry, it won't be a long conversation." His voice was flat, with an edge to it.

"Is everything okay?" Cara asked. A funny feeling built up in her stomach, and for a moment, she thought she might be sick.

Dan sighed. "No, everything is not okay," he said. "I know what you've been up to. It seems like you're having a blast over there, wherever you are."

Cara stiffened. "It's going well," she stuttered. "My job is great, I'm getting better at it. And I've moved from fruit carving to starters." She paused. "You sound angry..."

"I'm glad to hear my best friend is doing well," Dan interrupted her. "But I already knew that. You see, I had an interesting message from a girl named Gwen yesterday. Claims she's the Captain's daughter."

Cara let out a deep sigh and sat down on Billie's bed. Her head dropped into the palm of her hand. "I know who she is, Dan. What did she..."

"Right." Dan sounded even angrier now. "Of course, you know who she is, and she knows who you are. She sent me a picture. You and Billie were both in it, and in a rather compromising position, if I may add."

Cara winced. *Seriously? That woman took pictures?* "Please, Dan. Let me explain..."

"You were kissing her, Cara. How do you explain that? You were kissing my ex-girlfriend and not only that, you were kissing her while we were still together." He raised his voice. "And even if we'd broken up before you two left, that's not something you do to a friend, is it?"

Cara clenched the phone in her hand. The anger in Dan's voice cut through her like a knife. "I'm so sorry, Dan. I didn't plan this. We never meant for this to happen."

"She was on top of you, on a couch in a library." Dan paused. "She was on top of you, and you were kissing her." His voice broke. "Are you the one she left me for?" Cara was silent. "You of all people. She was the first woman who actually meant something to me. Did you know that?"

The sound of his pain brought tears to Cara's eyes. "I didn't know, Dan. I didn't. Something grew between us, and I had no idea you were so serious about her. Or maybe I didn't want to know. Either way, it doesn't make it right." Cara's shoulders were shaking now, as she cried silently. It made it hard to speak. "I've been a terrible friend. The worst. And I understand if you..."

There was a click and then silence. Cara tried to call him again, but the call went straight to voicemail. Panic hit her when she realized Dan was done speaking to her, perhaps even for good. *I've lost him. Oh God, I've lost him.* The knot in her stomach made her feel sick, and she turned to her side on the bed and curled up, determined to fall asleep and never wake up again.

49

——————

"Hey, Dad." Cara leaned back in her chair at the call centre. She'd found a quiet corner. It was strange to hear her father's voice after such a long time. They'd sent the occasional email or text back and forth, but Cara hadn't spoken to him since she'd boarded the Pelican.

"Cara, sweetie. How are you? I've tried to call you a couple of times, but all I got back were passive aggressive texts. Are you alright?"

"Yes, I'm okay.... I think." She paused. "Not really."

"Baby girl, tell me. You're not ill, are you?" Her father sounded concerned now.

"No, I just messed up. I'd rather not talk about it."

There was an awkward silence. Cara's father had never been much of a talker, at least not with her. "I emailed Dan last week," he finally said. "I thought he might know why you'd been so quiet. He told me you're at sea. What the hell are you doing on a cruise ship?"

"I'm working." Cara sighed. "It's a long story. I'm a chef, Dad. I love it, and I'm getting pretty good now. I was made redundant in the restructure at the paper, and I didn't want to tell you and mum before I'd found another job." She paused. "I wasn't getting anywhere, so when this opportunity presented itself, I was happy to have something to focus on."

Cara tried not to cry, but it was all too much. Her voice broke when she continued. "I finally thought I'd found a place where I belonged, and then I messed it all up like I've been messing everything up the past couple of years." She searched for a tissue in her bag and blew her nose. "I had to move in with Dan because I couldn't afford the rent anymore. He's been so kind to me but I betrayed him. I don't think he wants to speak to me ever again. I slept with his girlfriend, and now he hates me, which I totally deserve. I'll be finishing here next month, and I can't go back there."

"Oh Cara, please don't cry. We all make mistakes; God only knows I have. But the best thing to do is to learn from them and move on. Make new friends, new memories. Life's too short to dwell on your mistakes." He paused. "Maybe you just need a new challenge, and I might have something for you. You see, I tried to call you with a job offer, but I couldn't get hold of you. It's about project Riyadh. Did you read the work I sent you?"

"Yes." Cara sniffed. "Looks like you've made a good start."

"Well," her father continued, "I'll need a research assistant."

Cara's attention was spiked now. She took a deep breath. "That sounds interesting."

Her father was quiet for a moment, and she knew he was smiling. "It is. The project is top secret and could take anywhere between a year and two years. You could live with Samira and me. I think you'd like her. She's clever, like you."

Cara rolled her eyes. "Samira? Isn't she your translator? Have you two moved in together now?"

"Yes. We've been seeing each other for a while. She'll be coming back to the UK with me after we finish the research." There was an awkward silence. "She's lovely, Cara. And we live in a nice compound. We'll have an office for you, and a driver who can take you anywhere you want, permitting that it's safe. I think it will be good for us both. I haven't seen you in such a long time, and I know that's entirely down to me. But we could catch up, spend some quality time together."

Cara closed her eyes. Maybe her father had a point. What else was she going to do? Being as far away as possible from both Dan and Billie seemed like the only option she had. "Sounds good, Dad. I'll see if there's any way I can get off the ship sooner."

"That's my girl." Her father cleared his throat, indicating he was done talking. "Let me know when and where you want to fly from, and I'll book you a ticket. And don't forget to pick up your phone when I call you. We need to get your paperwork sorted out. Bye now." With that, he hung up, leaving a monotone sound in Cara's ear.

50

"Are you avoiding me?" Billie blocked Cara in the narrow hallway leading to the elevators. "I haven't seen you since yesterday. What have you been up to?"

Cara gazed into the beautiful eyes that stared back at her. "It's bad, Billie," was all she could manage to say. "Dan knows."

"What?" Billie's eyes widened. "Why the hell did you tell him?"

"I didn't. Gwen did." Cara tried to get past, but Billie wouldn't let her. She steadied her hand against the wall.

"Wait. Gwen? Explain first, please. We need to talk about this."

Cara pushed past her. "I need to get to work."

"Bullshit. You're not even wearing your whites, so stop blanking me and get back to the cabin." She took Cara by the wrist and led them back, closing the door behind them. "Here, sit down." Billie took a seat next to Cara on the bed and put a hand on her knee. "Now tell me what happened."

Cara took a deep breath and tried not to cry again. "Gwen told Dan," she said. "She found him on social media and sent him a picture of us in the library... that night, when we kissed."

Billie closed her eyes and rubbed her temples. "That's ... I can't believe she saw us and kept it to herself all this time, only to use against me."

"Against you?" Cara frowned. "Against both of us, Billie. Dan's my closest friend. He's like family to me, and now he won't speak to me ever again. It's over." She sighed. "And you know what? I deserve it."

Billie put a hand on Cara's cheek to kiss her, but she turned away. "I can't, Billie. Not right now." There was pain in her voice. "It doesn't feel right anymore. I can't be around you. Even now, I feel like a terrible person for even talking to you. I hate myself."

Billie's eyes narrowed. "Don't say that. We can..."

"No, it's true," Cara interrupted her. "I can't be here anymore."

She let herself fall to the side and propped her head on the pillow. "I spoke to my father last night. I told him about losing my job, about Dan taking me in. And I also told him about working on this ship, about you and about what happened between us. I even told him I'd have nowhere to go once we get back to the UK. I was so upset after Dan called me, it just rolled off my tongue. All of it."

Billie nodded. "What did he say?"

"He offered me a job as his research assistant," Cara said, wiping away a tear. "He said I could live with him and his girlfriend in Saudi Arabia if I wanted to get away from everything. I've thought about it, and I want to go. It would be a great stepping stone into investigative journalism. It's going to be for one, maybe two years." She stared straight ahead, avoiding Billie's gaze. "I'm leaving in a month, when my contract ends. Sooner, if they'll let me take my holidays."

She swallowed hard. "It would be silly of me to turn it down."

"But I thought you weren't interested in doing that anymore. You told me yourself; you only studied journalism to impress your parents."

Billie squeezed her leg. There was sadness in her voice. "Can't you see what you're doing here? You're running away as soon as things get tough. You love cooking. And you're good at it, not to mention how happy you've been since you've started here. Doesn't that mean anything? Or are you just taking this job as an excuse to get away from me? It's not going to change what we did, Cara. Or what we have. Just because Dan's found out doesn't mean you should leave me. It's not going to solve anything."

Cara finally looked up. She saw the panic in Billie's eyes and all she wanted to do was take her into her arms and comfort her. But she couldn't do it. "I won't do this to Dan. I mean, I won't continue to do this to him. I can't, Billie. It feels wrong. Maybe if I stay away from you, he'll forgive me one day. Maybe when I'm back in two years' time..."

"That's ridiculous, Cara!" Billie sounded angry. "What about us? We've got something special here; you can't deny that! You told me yourself that you're happier than you've ever been. And you're willing to throw it all away because of a fight and a job somewhere in the desert?"

Cara closed her eyes. She felt sick with guilt over both Dan and Billie, trapped between two evils. There was no easy way out. The pain of leaving Billie and the thought of hurting her choked her up. She couldn't look at Billie, couldn't bear to see the pain in her eyes, so she stood up, opened her closet and shoved her clothes into her suitcase.

"It's not just any job. It's an incredible opportunity. I'll get to work on something big, something that matters."

Billie's eyes widened. "Oh, and this doesn't matter? I gave myself to you, Cara. I gave you all of me. How can you just walk away like it all meant nothing?"

Cara swallowed her tears. "It was never going to be forever. We both agreed on that."

"Right." Billie slammed the suitcase out of her hand. "Well forgive me for being so stupid to think that there might be a chance after all."

Cara cried silently while Billie's words tortured her. There was nothing she could say to make it better. "I'll ask Arnie to trade rooms with me. I'm sure he'll be more than happy to stay here with you. It will be easier for both of us if we don't see each other. I'll be gone as soon as I can."

Billie shot her a furious look. "Great. Just run away when things get tough. I was clearly mistaken about you." She turned to the door and left, slamming it behind her.

51

Billie looked around the room. Cara's things were all gone now. Her shoes and her chef's whites, her magazines, and her laptop. Her hair straightener and her basic collection of toiletries. Even her rubbish in the bin had been replaced by a clean bin bag.

Instead, the room was littered with Arnie's clothes. He had gladly accepted the room swap, and didn't hesitate to leave his mark right away. A plastic bag with empty beer bottles spread a sour aroma through the stuffy cabin, and she'd found dirty underwear in every corner. Then there was the water. Her bed was always wet. After every shower, Arnie repeatedly shook out his hair like a dog, until it was dry. It was a tick, he said. Something he couldn't change if he tried. He would often lay down on her bed, sweaty after a long day's work, and fall asleep. Billie hated the marks he left on her mattress every time he got back up.

But Arnie was sweet, and he meant well. The worst thing was his best intentions. A joke here, a joke there... a slap on the bum, a late-night cocktail. He was a people pleaser. Every night, he tried to cheer her up. And every night he failed. Billie had been miserable since Cara moved out of the room. Sure, she could put on a smile at work. She could pretend to be cheerful and cheeky, and everything the guests and her team needed her to be. It drained her energy though, and at night, she was so exhausted that she didn't want to speak to anyone.

Billie had looked for Cara. Outside the kitchen, in between shifts, in the library, and in the communal living room. Ibrahim told her Cara had taken on double shifts, so she was always working. There was no point in stalking her. Cara would come to her when she was ready. Billie sighed and sat down on her bed. She was angry, but it was always the sadness that won. She felt Cara's absence as keenly as she had felt her presence. It was almost a physical thing. The loss of Cara stung her, made her feel sick and incomplete. It was a pain she was unfamiliar with.

Cara's shampoo was still in the bathroom, the only thing she had left. Billie had washed her hair with it every day. She had also taken Cara's pillow from her old bed, and used it as her own, burying her face in it at night. Maybe Cara just needed some time. She was upset because of Dan, and that was only natural. *I'll give her another week to let things cool off. She can't ignore me forever?* But it had already been a week, and life without Cara had proven to be miserable. Billie cradled herself in her bed and cried quietly.

52

"Get your ass out of my face, Frank." Sujo poked Frank's behind with a pen. Frank was getting dressed in front of the bottom bunk, where Sujo had set up camp. There was a sign saying 'Sujo's room. Keep out', and the wall next to his bed was littered with pictures of nude ladies and his family dog.

"Stop that, you little shit. Unless you want to wear my underwear on your face." There was a chuckle from the other bottom bunk, where Darren was residing. The front was covered by a bedsheet, tucked underneath the mattress on the top bunk.

"What are you laughing about?" Frank pulled the bedsheet away, exposing Darren with his iPad. "Are you looking at porn again? Jesus dude, you need to get laid."

Darren gave him the finger. "I'm not looking at porn. I'm reading. Now put that sheet back, I need to concentrate."

"Yeah right. Concentrate on wanking, you mean." Frank and Sujo laughed.

Darren shot them a warning look. "Put it back!"

"Put it back or what?" Frank put on a clean shirt and searched for the hair gel in his toiletry bag. He used a lot of it.

"Or I'll fart." Darren scrunched his nose as he let out the longest and loudest fart Cara had ever heard.

She covered her face with her pillow and closed her eyes. *Oh, God. Is this happening?*

All three men burst into laughter, Sujo almost choking in the process. Darren, Frank, and Sujo were having a blast. Arnie's old roommates liked to drink, make fun of each other and fart, in no particular order. Frank was the self-appointed stud, now that Arnie was gone. When in the room, he was usually in front of the mirror admiring his tall frame, handsome features, and thick hair that he smothered in gel. Frank's thing was chasing women, and he wasn't unsuccessful in the field. Sujo was short but athletic, and of Indian heritage. He spent hours in the gym each day, and never let an opportunity pass to show off his six-pack. Darren was the chubby one in the room, but he didn't seem to care. He was confident and smart, although he didn't make a habit of using his brain very much. His hobbies were watching porn and drinking, and he wasn't afraid to share his passion for either of them.

Cara had been amazed by the infantile standard of their conversations from the moment she'd moved in. In any other situation, she would have laughed, and maybe even joined them in the banter. But she wasn't in the mood for any of it. She got up and jumped off the bed, searching for her hoodie.

"Where are you going?" Frank asked. "We've got rum. You can't say no to rum, Cara!" He pointed at the magnum bottle on his nightstand.

"No thanks, Frank. I'm good."

"Oh, come on. We're pre-drinking. There's a party on tonight. Someone's birthday. I think it's that chubby girl with the lazy eye. The one who works on the information desk." He turned to Darren. "What's her name again?"

"Patty," Darren said.

Sujo grinned. "Fatty. That's her name. I heard she's single, Cara." Again, there was laughter.

Cara rolled her eyes and zipped up her hoodie. "Look, I'm sorry but I'm just not feeling great, so don't count me in, okay?"

C ara checked the living room before she went upstairs, to the library. It was closed, so Billie wasn't there either. She had kept an eye out for her, because not seeing Billie had proven to be a lot harder than she thought it would be. She missed her every second of the day. The only way Cara had gotten through the past weeks on the ship was by working double shifts, exhausting herself so she could sleep at night. The guilt was the worst. Guilt towards both Dan and Billie. It never left the pit of her stomach, and it never left her mind. Cara wanted to talk to her, just one more time before she left. But Billie had been so furious that she didn't think she'd want to speak to her.

The front deck of the ship was quiet, apart from some fanatic, spinning around the running tracks. Cara walked over to the bench where she'd spent so many nights with Billie. So many wonderful moments. What have I done? Have I made the right decision? She slumped down and propped her feet up on the backrest of the bench in front of her. It was lonely out here now. The endless ocean and the starry sky that she had grown to love so much were no comfort. She felt empty, hollow. There was nothing there anymore, and it was all her own fault. The only two people she had ever loved were gone from her life. She had chased them both away.

53

"I'm sorry to hear your husband hurt himself, Mrs. Chapple, but I'm afraid it's not the animation team's fault, and the Pelican is not responsible for the damage to his teeth." Billie tried to be as professional as possible when she faced the giant redhead who had taken on an aggressive tone with her. "The sign by the pool clearly states that diving is strictly prohibited and..."

Her heart skipped a beat at the sudden sight of Cara. She hadn't seen her since their fight, but three weeks apart had made no improvement towards the constant emptiness she felt. And now it hurt seeing her again. Cara didn't look great. She was skinnier than before, and the blank stare on her face was emphasized by the dark circles under her eyes. She walked slowly, dragging her suitcase behind her towards the elevator. Her opponent had raised her voice now, but Billie wasn't listening anymore.

"Excuse me, Mrs. Chapple. I have an emergency. Please wait here; I'll be right back to continue our conversation." She rushed to get to Cara before the elevator doors opened.

"Cara! Wait!"

Cara turned, and Billie was shocked to see tears welling up in her eyes. "I'm so sorry," she stammered. "I saw you out there in the corridor, but I thought it might be better if I left quietly."

"Are you leaving?"

"Yeah." Cara nodded. "My father bought me a ticket from Casablanca. I guess I have everything I need right here, so I figured I wouldn't bother going home first." She sniffed, pointing to her suitcase.

Billie was unable to fight the tears when her eyes met Cara's. "I'm going to miss you," was all she could manage to say. She wanted to hug her, hold her, kiss her, beg her to stay. But she was nailed to the ground and couldn't seem to find the right words. And what could she say? Cara had made up her mind, and there was nothing she could do to change it.

Cara nodded slowly. "I'm going to miss you too, Billie." She hesitated before she got in the elevator. "Billie?"

"Yes?"

"I'm so sorry for everything. You deserve better than me."

Billie finally took a step forward and opened her mouth to speak but the doors closed. Cara was gone.

54

"Billie, are you okay?" Billie looked up at her mother. "I asked you if you were okay. You seemed to be drowning in your own thoughts."

Billie tried to produce a smile. "Oh, hi Mum. Sorry, still waking up." She looked down at the teal and orange coffee mug that she tortured herself with each morning. It was impractical, heavy, and far too big to take a decent sip out of. She needed both hands to hold it, but she used it anyway.

"It's almost midday," her mother continued. "Did you get up this late last week when I was at work?"

Billie shook her head. "No, never," she lied. In truth, she had been sleeping far more than she used to. It was the only distraction she had from thinking about Cara. She lifted the pint of coffee and took a sip, spilling it over her T-shirt. "Damn it." Each morning she wanted to smash it against the kitchen wall, and yet, she never did.

"I don't understand why you drink out of that mug. It's impractical. Have you had a shower yet? You look tired." She took a seat opposite Billie. "Billie, seriously, are you all right?"

"Enough with the questions, Mum! I'm okay. I'm just waking up, is that a crime?"

"Of course, it's not a crime, Billie. But you're thirty-two years old and living with us and…"

"I'm looking for a flat," Billie interrupted her, irritated by her mother's need to keep rubbing in her lifestyle. "I've been looking for places online. There are plenty of nice one-beds available. I just need to make some appointments and pick the best investment. I'll do it this week."

"Oh, well that's great, darling. I'll come with you. I'm sure there will be some nice places for sale around here. Oh, honey, I'm so glad you've finally come to your senses. We could help you out with your down payment if you need some extra cash?"

"I'm not looking around here, Mum. I want something close to the airport, so that I can rent it out to airline staff when I'm working. I've got the job on the new ship that does ten-month cruises. I'm Head of Entertainment. It's a big job; I'll have fifty people working for me."

"You have a new job?" Her mother sounded annoyed now. "And you're looking for an apartment? Why so secretive? Why didn't you tell me?"

Billie sighed. "Would it matter? You always disapprove of whatever I do. It's never good enough because it's not your way. You weren't happy for me when I got promoted to head of animation last year, which was a big deal for me, and you don't seem delighted now, so what's the point in telling you? Huh?" Billie was getting angry now. She was angry at the monstrosity of a coffee cup, angry with her mother's ignorance, but most of all, she was angry with herself, for letting Cara go without putting up a fight. "I'll tell you the truth Mum, but you're not going to like it." Billie straightened her back and faced her mother. "I've got a pretty good career going for myself, and this job is important to me. Most parents would be excited for their children, but you seem disappointed that I'm not working as a teacher and that I don't have a husband, two kids, and a dog. Well, guess what? I'm never going to have that." She paused. "I'm never going to have what you and dad have because I don't want it. And that's not because I don't admire your relationship and your love for each other. In fact, I do, and I'm grateful to you both for being such great parents. You gave us a lovely childhood, and that's more than most people can say. But that doesn't mean you have the right to expect me to follow in your footsteps."

"I never said I expected you to..." Her mother tried to get a word in, but Billie continued.

"Wait, Mum. Let me finish. Raising a family has made you and dad happy, and I respect you for that. But I don't even want to think about that right now. In fact, I'm struggling to get over someone, so getting into another relationship is the last thing on my mind."

Her mother's eyes widened. "I didn't know you were in a relationship either. How do you expect me to understand you if you don't talk to me?"

"Cara," Billie said. "Her name is Cara, and I love her, but she left me, and I don't think I'll ever see her again." Billie was unable to stop her rant. "She's living in Saudi Arabia somewhere and I have no idea how to find her, and if you think I didn't tell you because I was ashamed, you're wrong. I didn't tell you because it hurts just saying her name out loud. I don't care what you think, or Dad for that matter. I love her."

Billie was crying now. "And this is my only reminder of her." She held up her mug as the tears were streaming down her face. She felt like she was suffocating and gasped for air, shaking until her mother's arms were around her, holding her tight. Billie let go and stopped fighting her emotions. She didn't care if she looked ridiculous, or that she was too old to be crying in her mother's arms. Her mother didn't speak, and Billie was grateful for that. She hadn't been held like this for many years. She needed it.

55

"Hey, little angel. Nice to see you again." Big eyes stared up at Billie. The baby in her arms grabbed her nose and produced a comical grin. Billie laughed. "Oh Helen, she's adorable. I feel like I've missed so much in the past months. I mean, look at her. She's already got your sarcastic smile."

Helen chuckled as she poured Billie and herself a glass of red wine. "You didn't miss much, except for endless crying, sleepless nights and dirty nappies. I'm not going to lie, I found it hard at first, but it's getting more fun now. She interacts with people, and she's starting to become this little lady with a real personality."

Billie pulled a face at the baby, who burst into hysterical laughter. "She's great." She turned to her sister. "You look good too, Helen. I can't believe it's only been five months since you gave birth. You're so slim."

Helen rolled her eyes. "I'm dragging a small person around all day. It's basically like working out full time. I don't get any time for myself though. I can't remember the last time I went to the hairdresser." She sighed. "I'm so glad you're back, Billie. I was hoping you could babysit for me now and then, so I can go shopping, or meet up with friends. Don't get me wrong, I'm happy. I wouldn't miss her for the world, but being a single mum is much harder than I thought it would be. Mum and Dad work full-time, and it's not like my friends are dying to hang out with Daisy and me."

Billie took Helen's hand while she cradled little Daisy in the crook of her arm. "Anytime, sis. I'd be happy to help out." She shook the rattle she had bought in Vietnam, looking down at Daisy. "I've got half a year off, and it's not like I've got better things to do. You and I are going to have a lot of fun together, darling. We'll be up to no good."

Helen shook her head and popped an olive into her mouth. "Isn't it hard, living like this? I mean, you're not going to be here long enough to keep an interesting job. And what if you meet someone, like last time. His name was Dan, right? What happened to him anyway? Is he still around?" Billie shook her head, trying to force the vision of Cara away from her mind, but Helen was on a roll. "How can you stand leaving people behind all the time? As soon as it turns serious, you're gone."

"Helen please, stop it. You're doing it again." Billie downed her wine and helped herself to more from the bottle on the table. "I've always been clear to everybody about the fact that I work at sea. It's no secret, and Dan knew that too." She sighed. "Listen, Helen. I know this is more of a personal problem of yours. You feel like I'm abandoning you, or running away, but you have to understand that my life is out there. This is just a holiday, not the other way around."

Helen nodded. "Okay, I get that. I just want my big sister to be happy. And if that's what makes you happy, then I'll try to understand. But you've got this sadness in your eyes, and I worry that you're lonely or..."

"I met someone," Billie interrupted her. "I fell in love, and I mean, really fell in love, but it didn't work out. I'll need some time to get over her."

"Her?" Helen frowned in confusion. "I don't understand."

Billie closed her eyes. "Cara." She heard herself say her name for the second time that day. "I told Mum about her this morning. I wasn't planning on it, but I might as well tell you too now. Her name is Cara. She's Dan's best friend."

"The one you lived with on the Pelican?" Helen took a large gulp of her wine. "I didn't know you were into women. You never told me."

"Does it matter?" Billie asked. "I've never met anyone who was important enough for me to bring home, whether it was a man or a woman. Until I met Cara, it wasn't a big deal that I was into women too. She's amazing, Helen. She's gorgeous and cool and funny. I miss her so much."

Helen nodded slowly. "Okay. I'm sorry, Billie. I didn't see that one coming. But I guess you're right; it doesn't matter. You with a woman though... I find it hard to imagine." She giggled. "Please forgive me; I didn't mean to laugh. I just need some time to get used to the idea." She leaned back on the sofa and pulled her feet underneath her. "So, Cara you said. The one I spoke to when you were in Cape Town?"

Billie nodded.

"She's Dan's best friend? And I guess that's where it went wrong?"

Billie tried to fight the tears stinging at the corners of her eyes again. It hurt, but she felt an overwhelming need to talk about Cara, now that she had started. She sometimes felt like she'd dreamt it all, and talking about Cara made it real. Their time together seemed like such a dream when she thought back to it. Such a beautiful dream.

"Yes. He found out about us and..." Billie hesitated. "It shouldn't have happened in the first place. We did something wrong, and we both hurt Dan's feelings. Now she's in the Middle East, working for her father as a research journalist. I don't think I'll ever see her again." Billie took another sip of her wine. "She's got a new phone number, and I don't have her address. They're in a compound somewhere outside Riyadh, working on a delicate case, so they have to be careful." She swallowed. "I just want to talk to her, hear her voice one more time. I need to know that I'm not crazy, that it wasn't just a one-sided thing." She looked down at Daisy, who was now sleeping tight, her tiny little eyelids fluttering.

"Have you talked to Dan since you came back?" Helen asked. "Maybe he's got her number."

"Dan's not picking up either." Billie shrugged. "And besides, he's cut her out of his life. Can't blame him, right? I've considered going to his house to apologize, but I'm scared to face him."

"Of course you are." Helen reached out to take Daisy from her. "But if you don't do it, you'll probably regret it. Before you know it, you'll be gone again. Then it will be too awkward and too late to get back in touch."

"I know." Billie looked up at her younger sister. "Are Mum and Dad coming over later?"

Helen nodded. "Yes, Mum's bringing dinner so don't you dare take off now. They can't wait to have a family meal."

"You mean they can't wait to criticize my life again?"

Helen laughed. "Yes, that too. But if it's any comfort, me becoming a single mum didn't check the boxes on their perfect family list either, so I'm sort of glad it's your turn again. I've had enough grief while you were away."

56

"Welcome to your new home, Cara." Her father stopped the car in front of the terracotta wall that surrounded the compound. There was a generous amount of barbed wire, and an electric fence fixed on the top. The armed guards waved at him from behind the security gate, before opening it. One of them inspected Cara's paperwork while they waited in the car.

"Welcome, Miss Matthews." He smiled as he handed the file back to her. "Enjoy your stay in Riyadh."

"Why are we outside the city?" Cara asked once they were past the gates. "And why do we need security?"

"It's an expatriate compound," her father said, absently. "The religious police aren't allowed to enter here. It means men and women can mix freely and you won't have to cover up inside these walls. Due to the nature of our work, my publisher thought it would be best if we stayed here. They're helping me out with the rent." He parked the car and nodded towards the condos with private gardens and balconies. The complex looked nice, with its spacious recreational areas that surrounded the complex. There were a ping-pong table and a basketball court, and Cara could just make out the edge of a pool behind a neatly trimmed hedge. "It's mainly embassy staff that live here, but we also get some politicians staying, from time to time." He winked. "And sometimes they bring wine."

Cara arched an eyebrow. "It must be hard for you not to have your whiskey before bed."

Her father laughed. "Yes, well, what can I say? You make good with what you have."

Cara got out of the car to get her suitcase. The sudden dry heat hit her after being in the air-conditioned SUV, and sweat started trickling down her back. "Can I leave the compound?" she asked.

"Only with Samira or with me." Her father took her suitcase and headed towards an entrance at the left side of the building, shaded by palm trees. "You're a single woman, so it's best if you're accompanied by another woman or a family member. But don't worry. The locals are friendly and polite, and I think you'll like the restaurants and markets here. The food is very good. I don't go out very much, though. I'm working most of the time." He laughed. "You know me, always working. But Samira will be more than happy to take you anywhere you want. You'll need to cover up, of course, and I suppose I don't need to remind you that you don't talk about your sexual orientation here. Not even with my staff. Understood?"

"Got it." Cara looked around the deserted complex one more time, and back at the fence that had closed behind them.

"It gets busier in the evening. Everyone's at work now, but there will be plenty of people to talk to after six o'clock," her father said as if reading her concern.

"Ah! You must be Cara."

A woman who didn't look that much older than herself greeted them at the door. She had long black hair that reached all the way down to her hips, full, dark eyelashes and well-shaped eyebrows. Her figure was voluptuous and her face open and friendly.

"Hi, I'm Samira. Please come in; it's too hot outside." She rushed Cara into the hallway and led her towards the kitchen. "It's so nice to finally meet you. Sit down, can I get you a drink? You must be tired from your journey."

Cara sat down at the kitchen table, that could easily seat a party of ten. The kitchen was built in traditional Arabic style, and had a cosy feel to it, with patterned tiles on the floor and Arabian lanterns that spread an array of little stars across the ceiling. Jars with brown, white, orange and red spices covered the shelves above the worktop, and a giant fruit bowl held oranges and pomegranates next to a juicer.

"Thank you. It's nice to meet you too, Samira."

Samira smiled and put a tray with dates and Turkish delight in front of her, alongside a set of small glasses and a pot of fresh mint tea. "We'll have some food later, but first things first. And tea always comes first here."

Two men entered the kitchen and joined them at the table. The tallest one, who couldn't look more like a journalist if he tried, held out his hand first.

"Hey, I'm Rick. Your father's research assistant. Welcome to the team." Rick was in his late thirties, Cara guessed, but his messy non-defined haircut and round glasses, resting on a prominent nose, made him look older. He was tall, skinny and pale, and seemed like the serious type. Rick turned to his companion. "And this is Ali, one of our translators. He conducts most of the interviews with the locals."

"Nice to meet you." Ali shook her hand and smiled. He

was well built, groomed and handsome, almost feminine in a way.

"Ali and I studied together in London," Samira explained. "He's a good friend, and I trust him."

"Lovely to meet you both." Cara looked from Rick to Ali and back. "Seems like you have a great team here, Dad. I'm excited to join."

"Yes, I do indeed," Cara's father said. "It's been quite full-on the past couple of months, but these guys make life a lot easier." He sat down next to Cara. "I'm going to indulge in one of my rare tea breaks. And with the formalities out of the way, if you're not too tired, we might as well start the briefing straight away."

57

"Billie?"

Billie looked down to meet Dan's curious stare. She was sitting on the steps leading up to his front door, playing a game on her phone. "Oh, hi." She stood up to greet him, unsure whether to shake his hand or to hug him. "You weren't home, so I thought I'd wait here for a bit." To her surprise, Dan hugged her.

"It's nice to see you again." Dan shot her an uncertain smile, clearly not entirely comfortable with the surprise visit. He gestured to the door. "Do you want to come up?"

"If you don't mind." Billie waited for him to unlock the door. Dan looked good. He had shaved his beard off, and it suited him. He was dressed in clean jeans and a T-shirt and had filled out a bit, rather from the gym than from food, she guessed.

"Wow, what happened here?" Billie said as she entered his apartment. It was clean, and the walls had been recently painted, making the place look much brighter. There were even flowers on the kitchen table.

LISE GOLD

Dan laughed. "It's not me. It's my new roommate. She's amazing. If I had known there were people like her in this world, I would have kicked Cara out the moment she arrived and replaced her with someone who had OCD."

Billie flinched at the sound of Cara's name. She knew they would have to talk about her at some point, but she hadn't imagined it would be so hard. "Well, it looks great," she said, trying to ease the conversation with some small talk. "How are you?"

Dan grabbed two beers from the fridge and sat down at the kitchen table. He opened one and handed it to Billie. "I'm good, believe it or not. I've been able to pay the rent, I've started working out, and I've booked a couple of shows. One of them is even sponsored."

"That's great news, Dan. You deserve it."

Dan shrugged. "I don't know. Maybe I've just been lucky, but it's a start. I'll be spending a week in a gallery in Antwerp next month, and I'm waiting to hear back about a show in Berlin."

He opened his own bottle and took a long drink. "Billie, I'm sorry I've been ignoring you. I was angry, and I was trying to forget about the whole mess."

Billie held up a hand. "It's my fault. I shouldn't have shown up unannounced. Do you want me to leave?"

Dan shook his head. "No, please stay. Now that you're here, we might as well talk." He smiled at her.

"As much as I've tried, it's not nice to hold a grudge, so let me break the ice. I'm seeing someone. My roommate, actually. So, I guess that means we're living together. Her name is Dynamo."

"How sweet," Billie said, trying to suppress a nervous chuckle at the unusual name. "Dynamo. That's an interesting name. I'm glad to hear you've moved on."

Dan grinned and took a sip from his beer. "And you, Billie? How are you?"

Billie avoided his gaze while she nervously played with the loose corner of the label on her beer bottle. "I'm okay. I wanted to talk to you. I mean, I've wanted to talk to you for a while. So, first of all, thank you for letting me in." She hesitated. "I need to apologize to you. For everything that happened, with Cara. It wasn't planned. You need to know that. But it wasn't nothing either."

Dan frowned. "What do you mean?"

Billie shrugged. "I'm not sure how to explain it. It wasn't like Cara seduced me, and it wasn't me looking for a fling either. We became friends, and then this thing started between us, and it grew stronger and stronger with every day that passed. We tried to ignore it, Dan. You have to believe me when I say that we really tried to ignore the pull we both felt. For you." She sighed. "In the end, it was Cara who left me, because losing you was one of the hardest things she'd ever had to deal with. She told me you were the only real family she had, and that you were the most important person in her life."

Dan leaned back in his chair. "She said that?"

Billie swallowed hard. Her throat felt tight, and her voice was trembling. She took a deep breath and tried to stop the tears from falling, but it was too hard to talk about Cara with Dan. "I genuinely believe there is nothing she regrets more than what happened between us."

Dan was silent. He took another drink from his beer and produced a pack of cigarettes from his back pocket, that he held out for Billie. When she declined, he lit one for himself and took a long drag.

"Please say something, Dan. Or at least be angry with me. Anything."

Dan stood up and handed Billie a piece of kitchen roll. She wiped her tears, but there seemed to be no end to them. She had tried so hard not to think about Cara, but all the pain had resurfaced now, and she felt just as heartbroken as the day they'd parted.

"I assume those tears are not for me," Dan finally said.

Billie shook her head. "No, they're not."

"And you're telling me that what you and Cara had was genuine."

"Yes." Billie took a deep breath. "Honestly, Dan. Cara means everything to me. I'm not telling you this to rub it in your face. I'm telling you this because I want to be completely honest with you, so that maybe you can understand why things happened the way they did. I love her."

Dan sighed. The disbelief on his face slowly made place for a more neutral gaze. "Right. Well, thank you for telling me."

Billie waited for him to continue but Dan stared down at the bottle in his hand, opting out of the conversation.

"Well, I think I'd better go now," Billie said, straightening her coat. "Thank you for listening to me. You seem happy. I'm glad. And for what it's worth, I really am sorry, Dan. You're a wonderful person, and Dynamo is lucky to have you." She walked towards the hallway, ready to let herself out.

"Billie?"

"Yes?" Billie turned to meet Dan's kind eyes.

"Thank you. It was nice to see you again, despite the circumstances." He stood up and walked towards her. "Listen, you know I don't like awkwardness. Dynamo and I are going for a drink tonight. Just at the local, with some friends. You're welcome to join us if you're around. I think you'd like her."

Billie smiled at his generous offer. "That would be nice. I'd love to, Dan."

58

"The boiler is only two years old, and the underfloor heating still has a ten-year guarantee on it." The real estate agent's hands were flapping around in excitement as he pointed out the perks of the one-bedroom apartment in Luton.

"Right." Billie knocked on the boiler for no particular reason.

Aaron McRay was in his late twenties, she guessed, and eager to grow his career and his bank account. His suit was too big for his skinny frame, and the pink tie wasn't doing his blotchy, pale face any favours, but it was obviously a strategic choice to make him look cheeky and approachable.

"And," he continued, "the monthly service costs are remarkably low for a London apartment. It also comes with a private parking spot, just around the corner from the entrance. It's only a ten-minute drive to the airport from here, so it would be ideal for renting out, if that's something you were considering."

Billie regarded the flat with as much interest as she could muster. The location was far from exciting, but it was what she could afford. She couldn't imagine herself living here, but then she couldn't imagine herself anywhere else either. And it would only be for two months a year. How bad could it be? As long as it gave her a little bit of income, and a place away from the constant well-intentioned nagging of her mother, it was good enough for her.

"Where's the balcony?" she asked. "The ad said there was a balcony."

The agent beckoned Billie to follow him. "There's one off the bedroom, facing the back." He opened the bedroom door and crossed the room to open the curtains, exposing a balcony that was narrow, but still big enough to hold a table and two small chairs.

Billie tried to picture herself having coffee there in the morning, but the uninspiring view made it hard. There was the motorway, and a petrol station, and of course the other flats, that blocked most of the view. Behind it all was the landing strip of Luton airport. She could hear the planes circling over the block of apartments, waiting to land. Billie opened the door and stepped outside.

She couldn't help but wonder what Cara would think of it. The memories of their morning in Cape Town, on that quaint little balcony in the sun, came back in a flash. She thought about that morning a lot. Don't be silly. Cara will never be here. She shook it off as she had every time Cara entered her mind and tried to focus on the task at hand. Which was buying an apartment, after all, and she couldn't afford to be distracted.

Billie turned around and walked through the bedroom. It was spacious, with built-in storage. The wooden king-size bed was placed in the middle, with matching nightstands on either side. Behind it, the wall was painted an awkward shade of green that reminded her of the new Pelican shirts. She chuckled.

Aaron jumped in right away. "Not to your taste, this colour? It will only take a couple of hours to fix it. I can even ask the owner to…"

"No, it's fine." Billie shook her head. "It's a wall, it's not a big deal. Just a curious choice, that's all."

The noise from the planes penetrated the double glazing of the balcony doors, but she was used to noise. She inspected the bathroom without a clue as to what she was doing. *I should have brought my father.* Aaron seemed amused when she lifted the cistern cover off the toilet and looked inside as if expecting to find some sort of catastrophe to call him out on. Mildly embarrassed, she followed him back to the open kitchen and living room. Apart from the bedroom wall, the decoration was to her taste. It was clear that whoever lived here, was proud of the place. The floor was a nicer kind of laminate, and the dark grey couch sat on a fluffy, white rug. Two grey leather chairs faced the sofa, with a simple wooden table in between them. The curtains were white, with a Japanese, light grey print, and the walls were painted white, decorated with monochrome paintings that brought a sense of calm to the room. All in all, it looked pretty decent.

"Would the seller be open to leaving all the furniture?" she asked. "I mean everything, including the stuff on the walls and the lamps. I'd be happy to pay for it."

"Okay… sure." The agent looked surprised. "I could certainly ask. We don't get asked that question very often, so I haven't discussed it with her. It's about the only part that people tend to enjoy about buying a property – making it their own."

Billie shrugged. "I'm just looking for ease. I won't be here much myself. And there is a storage room downstairs, right?"

"That's right." Aaron searched for information in his pile of paperwork.

"It's quite a substantial space. All the apartments have one; most people use it to store their bikes. Would you like to see it? Let me just check how big it is..."

"No, it's okay. As long as there's a secure place to keep my paperwork and other private things, I'm good." Billie looked around the kitchen and living room one more time. There wasn't much time to think it over. Apartments like this one usually went in a matter of days. "Well, it looks fine to me. I'm happy to make an offer, providing they leave everything here. That will save me quite some hassle."

The agent stared at Billie as if she had just reinvented the purchasing process. "You want to make an offer right now?" he asked.

"Yes." Billie leaned back against the doorframe and crossed her arms. "Why, should I come back tomorrow to look at it again? Because it's not going to make me love it either way." She could tell by the look on his face that Aaron was confused by her. She looked like a homemaker, in her skirt and twinset. The cosy, broody type. The type that cared about the place she lived in.

"All righty then." The corners of Aaron's mouth tugged upwards, forming a tiny smile. Billie knew what he was thinking. Bingo. Jackpot. Bonus. "Let's sit down, and I'll talk you through the process."

59

"Cara, I'm going into the kitchen, we have guests tonight. Would you like to help me prepare some food?" Samira stuck her head around the door to Cara's spacious office.

The rugs on the floor were covered in newspaper articles, pictures, maps, government reports, and a timeline she'd put together of key events before the disappearances of both expats and locals, whom her father believed to have been killed. Most information had already been there, provided by her father's contacts in the city, but she had managed to find some missing links by searching through the newspapers from the past four years. That alone had taken her a full month, even with Samira's help. Fact-checking turned out to be a tedious job, far from the adventurous detective work she'd imagined she'd be doing.

Cara jumped up at Samira's request. "Oh yes, please. I would love that."

Against all expectations, Samira had become a great friend. Cara enjoyed spending time with her, mostly in the kitchen. She was getting pretty good at preparing a Middle

Eastern feast, and loved making everything from scratch, especially grinding down the spices and mixing them until they formed a perfectly balanced base. By now, she was able to taste the raw base and assess whether it was right.

Cara grabbed her leather notebook from her desk and followed Samira down the stairs. The notebook was almost full now. With all the new dishes she had learned, there were only a couple of pages left in her food bible, and Cara didn't like that one bit. It hurt each time she looked at the leather binder, but the pain felt good because it reminded her of Billie. Initially, she had imagined the notebook to be therapeutic, while she tried to move on with each page as time passed. She had hoped to forget about Billie, but now that she was near the last page, the pain of not being near her still weighed as heavy on her heart as it had the day she left the Pelican. Samira had offered to buy her a new one, but Cara had declined. Instead, she had started to write smaller and smaller, and now it was hard to read her latest notes and recipes.

"How are you? Are you feeling a little bit happier?" Samira asked, handing her a whole chicken to dissect.

"Yeah, I'm okay." Cara broke the main joints, then picked up a cleaver and cut through the carcass with force, careful not to splinter any bones. Samira and Cara worked seamlessly together in the kitchen, usually without speaking much. But apparently, Samira wanted to talk today.

"It's different here, that's for sure," Cara said, concentrating on her task. "And I have to admit, Riyadh was daunting when I arrived. To me, it's like being on a different planet. So red and dry and warm. No nightlife, at least not around here, no alcohol, and the fact that I can't go most places by myself is still a foreign concept to me. But I think I'll get used to it eventually." She tore the skin off the pieces of chicken and handed them back to Samira. "I felt confined at first. I guess I still feel confined. But that's okay, it's an amazing opportunity, and it's not forever." She looked up at Samira. "I'm sorry, I didn't mean to sound negative about your country. It's not that I don't like it, it's just that I don't feel like I fit."

Samira smiled. "Don't worry, Cara. I feel the same way sometimes. It was hard for me to come back here, after studying in London. When I met your father, it was as if I had a little piece of that time in England back." She handed Cara a bag of onions and a clean chopping board. "Has he told you I'll be coming back with him when this project finishes?"

Cara nodded. "Yes. He told me it would be too dangerous for you both to stay here when the book comes out" She hesitated. "And that you don't have any family left to worry about."

"That's right." Samira had a sad look in her eyes. "I broke off all contact with them after they tried to force me into an arranged marriage. The man in question wanted me to give up my job, and I had no intention of throwing away my career and my life to be a housewife. Besides that, I'd been living in the UK, and that changed me. I had boyfriends there, and I couldn't grasp the concept of marrying someone I didn't love." She laughed. "It's kind of crazy that I'm still here, isn't it? But regardless of what's happened here, I love my country, and I've learned to respect everyone's choices. I'm lucky that I've got my job as a correspondent, and my research here with your father."

"So how do you feel about moving to the UK?" Cara asked.

Samira shrugged. "I'm not sure. My life is here. My work, and my friends. In England, I'll have to start from scratch, figure out who I am all over again. It's been a long time since I was last there, and I haven't stayed in contact with anyone I met back then, except for Achmed."

"I'm sorry to hear that." Cara said. "But you're doing good work. I hope I can help you settle back in, the way you've helped me here."

"Thank you," Samira said, smiling. "That's very kind of you. And your father... well, I love him. We're the same, in a way. We both live for our job, and we both have a drive to find the truth. The only difference between us is that I can switch off when I cook, and he never switches off." They both laughed.

"And you?" Samira asked. "Your father told me you had..." She paused. "Girlfriends before?"

Cara looked up in surprise. "He told you that?"

Samira nodded, casting her an apologetic look. "Should he not have?"

"No, it's fine. I just assumed that..."

"Assumed that I would have a problem with it?" Samira finished Cara's sentence. "No, of course I don't. Did you really think I'd be fighting oppression in my own country, and have a problem with people being gay?"

Cara giggled. "No, I suppose not." She pointed at the shelf next to Samira. "Could you hand me that bowl please?"

Samira reached up to the top shelf, her black hair flowing behind her, all the way down to her curvy hips. Cara understood what her father saw in Samira, but she didn't quite get it the other way around. Her father was fifteen years older and quiet, always absorbed in his work. Whenever he found a new challenge, he left and started over again as if it was nothing. She never blamed her mother for being bitter about that.

"What happened at sea?" Samira asked, handing Cara the bowl. The question came out of nowhere. "You fell in love, right?"

As always, Cara felt a pang of guilt in her gut, thinking of Billie. She still missed her, every single day. Cara was the one who had left. She was the one who had chosen to run. And for what? Dan still wouldn't speak to her.

"Her name is Billie," she finally said. "She was my best friend's girlfriend. What we did was wrong, and I really hurt my friend. That's why I'm trying to stay as far away from them both as I can."

"Is that why you came here?" Samira was clever indeed. Her father hadn't lied about that.

"No, of course not," Cara said hastily. "It was the job, mainly. It's the opportunity of a lifetime, right? I mean, I've never had an interesting job in journalism. Not like this. It's an amazing chance to grow my career when I get back."

"But you still prefer cooking?" Samira held up a pomegranate. "I can tell by the way you treat ingredients and by the way your face lights up when I ask you to help me. You knew after only one demonstration how to make basic Middle Eastern dishes, which means you have great flavour memory. That's what we call it here. And look at how calm you are, standing here with the knife in your hand. It's like your facade drops, and you relax into this trance-like state."

When Cara didn't reply, Samira put her knife down and turned to her, leaning against the sink. "You're a great researcher, Cara. And I have no doubt you'll be an amazing journalist. You've found information that we all missed, and you've asked questions we haven't thought about asking. But you're also great at cooking. And if that's where your passion lies, there's no shame in wanting something else. You don't have to do this just because your father does it."

Cara stopped what she was doing and sighed. How could Samira possibly be so intuitive, and so right? She missed the pressure of the kitchen, and the sense of accomplishment at the end of a service. She missed fine plating and the banter amongst staff. Hell, she even missed having a drill sergeant chef shouting at her and telling her what to do.

"I suppose so," she said, putting down her knife too. "But I think my father would have a heart attack if I told him I want to be a chef. He doesn't seem to grasp anything outside his own latest projects or obsessions."

"Your father's lack of understanding isn't your problem. It's his," Samira said quietly. "You need to do what feels right to you. Stop leading with your head and go with your gut, it's the most important lesson I've ever learned. That feeling deep down in your core, when you know everything is exactly the way it's supposed to be. It's so much more powerful than having your thoughts in order and doing what you're supposed to do."

Cara nodded and put on a brave smile. "Thank you, Samira. It's good to be reminded of that sometimes. And you're probably right, but I've got nothing to go back to anymore. So, for now I'm good here. As long as you take me to the market now and then and teach me to cook all these great dishes, I'll be fine."

60

"Cara?" Cara's heart nearly stopped when she heard Dan's voice on the phone. "Hey, it's Dan. Can you talk?"

She smiled and got up from the Persian rug she was sitting on, surrounded by notes and piles of articles. Cara held on to her stomach. It felt warm and fuzzy. "Dan, it's so good to hear your voice. How are you? I've tried calling you so many times."

"I'm okay," Dan said. "I... I thought it was about time that I called you back, after over two hundred missed calls and voicemails."

Cara sighed in relief. "Thank you for that." She paused, suddenly unsure of what to say. She had rehearsed the apology over and over in her head, but Dan calling her out of the blue had caught her off guard. "Are you calling to tell me I have to pick up the rest of my stuff, or are you finally going to shout at me and give me a chance to apologize?"

"Neither." Dan's voice sounded neutral, but Cara could have sworn she detected a cheerful undertone. "Anyway, your clothes are gone." He laughed. "I burned them on stage during a performance a couple of months ago. I had a picture of you on a big screen in the background. You know, the one that you hate more than anything, and that I promised never to show to anyone."

"The one where I fell asleep eating a burger? Oh God..."

"Yeah, that one. My piece was called 'Cara, Cara, Burn the Bitch.'"

Cara giggled and shook her head. "Okay. That's fair enough, I suppose."

Dan laughed too. "But your hairdryer and other electrical appliances are still here. The premises wouldn't let me burn them due to health and safety regulations, so if you want them, I can send them over. You're in Saudi Arabia, right? How's life there?"

"How did you know I was here?" Cara walked over to the window, almost expecting to see him.

"I have my sources," Dan said in a smug voice.

"You mean you asked my mother?" Cara chuckled.

"Yeah. And that too." There was an awkward silence. Dan cleared his throat. "So tell me, what's it like, living in a desert?"

"Well, we're not really in the desert. Were in Riyadh. But I can see the edge of the desert from my window. It's dry. And warm. There are no camels in the backyard, in case you were wondering. In fact, I haven't seen a single one since I arrived."

She looked out over the dusty landscape behind the derelict buildings on the outskirts of the city. She still wasn't used to the barbed wire that ran along the top of the compound walls and the guards at the gates, carrying machine guns. It was a stark contrast to life at sea. "I'm locked up here. That's the thing. I can't just come and go as I please, but I guess it's about the job, right? I'm working for my father as a research assistant. I assume you've heard that too?"

"I have. But that's about it. Your mother isn't exactly the chatty type." He paused. "I hope you're careful out there. Is it weird living with your father?"

"It's okay." Cara looked at the Post-it Notes he had left on the documents. There were at least fifty of them, and most of them said 'double check.' "We have dinner together when we have guests over. Other than that, he's usually in his office, upstairs. I spend more time with his girlfriend, Samira. She's nice, and she's become a good friend. I wouldn't know what I would do without her." Cara swallowed hard. "I miss you, Dan. I miss talking to you. And I wish I could make it all undone. It was..."

"No more apologies," Dan said. "I've kept them on my voicemail, and I've played them over loudspeakers during my performance, so I've heard them all. It was thirty-five minutes' worth of crying and apology. Did you know that? It lasted longer than it took to burn your clothes, so I just stood there like an idiot for the last ten minutes, with about a hundred people staring at the ashes, waiting for me to do something."

Cara cringed at the thought of strangers listening to her personal messages, but she didn't protest. "That must have been some performance," she said. "Not sure if I would have wanted to be there, but still. A hundred people. That's the biggest turnout you've ever had, right?"

"Yeah, it was good." Dan sighed. "Got me a space at a gallery in Antwerp, and a show in Berlin later on this year. They're giving me a week to do whatever I want. I'm not sure what I'm going to do yet."

"That's fantastic, Dan. I'm so proud of you. This could be your big break." Cara laughed. "Any chance I could come with you? You could call it 'Making peace with Cara'. We could do this John Lennon and Yoko Ono thing where we…"

"No need," Dan interrupted her. "If you want to make it up to me, come to my birthday dinner in two weeks. I'm turning thirty-five, and I thought you could do the catering. Since you're such a great cook now." He paused. "If you can get some time off…"

Cara felt tears welling up. It was so much more than she could ever have hoped for. She sniffed, unable to keep a steady voice. "Oh my God, Dan, really? Of course, I'll come! Thank you." She sighed. "You have no idea how happy that makes me. I won't disappoint you, I promise."

Dan laughed. "Stop crying. Just be here. I've got about fifteen people coming, and I want three courses. That's the deal."

Cara smiled and kissed the loudspeaker on her phone. "I'll give you five courses. Thank you."

61

"Let's get our facts straight, guys. It seems like we're on to a breakthrough." Cara's father was pacing up and down the kitchen. Cara, Samira, Achmed, and Rick were sitting around the kitchen table, trying to digest the latest intel they had been given.

"All events and evidence so far point towards Raker, the oil company that the two missing expats worked for. What do we know?" He started writing on a whiteboard that was resting on an easel.

"We know that two Raker employees disappeared. We know they were asking questions about safety procedures on the oil rigs. We know that a journalist disappeared. We know the journalist was investigating the disappearance of the employees. We know the journalist was last seen at the Raker head office in Riyadh. We have two anonymous eyewitnesses who can confirm that. We also know that there's no video surveillance from that day. Raker claims their cameras were out of service. We know the journalist was on to something, but we don't know the details." He counted the facts on his fingers, his eyes wild with excitement. "Is this enough to steer the investigation towards Raker?"

Samira nodded. "I believe we have valid grounds to start from."

She looked at Achmed. "I agree. Let's do it."

Cara's father looked at Cara and Rick. They both nodded.

"We now have the full list of employees that were there on the day the journalist disappeared," Cara said. "We've spent the past two weeks collecting their addresses. It would be a good starting point."

Her father smiled. "Excellent. Let's start with that." He sat down at the table, nervously patting his fingers on the surface. "Samira and Achmed, you two should interview them. I think the locals will feel more comfortable if you do it. Go together though. Always. Cara and Rick, try to get hold of the family members of the missing expats again. We also have a list of friends they spent time with here. Ask them if they've ever let any negative remarks drop regarding Raker." He sighed. "I'll write up a proposal for the publisher. It's not what we expected, but I think they will be thrilled to hear we've got good grounds to stand on." He raised his teacup towards the group. "I know it's not Champagne, but right now, it makes me just as happy."

"How do you feel about going after Raker?" Cara asked, when she was alone with Samira, buying groceries at the market. "You must be relieved it's not your own government you'll be accusing of conspiracy and murder?"

Samira picked a couple of oranges and handed them to the salesman. "Nothing is ever that simple here. Most things are connected somehow, especially when a lot of money is involved."

Cara nodded. "Of course. I know that. But still, you won't have to feel like you're betraying your country."

"Yes." Samira sighed. "I'm not going to deny that I'm relieved. It will make things a lot easier for me. I'll be able to come back to visit friends here, and that's more than I could have hoped for. I could even move back after the whole scandal has blown over. Not that I'm planning on it. I've already made up my mind about moving to London with your father." She smiled, picking out the ripest figs from the same fruit stall. "I love him, and I think we make a good team together. But you know what, Cara? The truth shouldn't be convenient. Not to me, not to anyone. That's how injustice happens, and I've seen too much of that in my lifetime. The truth is just the truth, and we can only hope to find it. It's my job, however big the sacrifice."

"Spoken like a true journalist," Cara said. "I admire you, Samira. The way you've put everything on hold for this project, the way you've put up with my father and his endless obsession and dedication to his job."

"Isn't that what you're doing?" Samira asked.

"It's not the same." Cara followed her to the next market stall, dragging the grocery trolley behind her. "I can't do this forever, not the way you do. I mean, I'm so proud to be a part of Dad's team, but I don't think I want to be a journalist for the rest of my life. I've had a lot of time to think about it." She chuckled and gestured to her surroundings. "It's not like I've got much else to do around here. I want to live a little. Don't you ever feel like that?"

"Living is different for everyone," Samira said. "It's about doing what you love, what makes you feel good." She pulled back her headscarf and glanced at Cara. "What makes you feel good, Cara? Because if you can answer that question, you're already halfway there."

Cara produced a sad smile, thinking of Billie. "I know what makes me feel good," she said. "But we can't always have what we want, can we?"

"Your special friend?" Samira asked, keeping her voice down.

Cara nodded. She still missed Billie every day. She missed her smile and her laugh. She missed talking to her, being close to her. She missed her touch. At night, in bed, Cara wondered if Billie had moved on. If she was seeing someone new. Billie deserved to be happy, but the idea of her being close to someone else was almost unbearable.

Cara hovered over the buckets of spices and closed her eyes as she inhaled. "Hey, can we get some of this saffron? I want to take some home with me."

"Sure." Samira talked to the salesman and handed Cara a generous amount of saffron in a sealed bag. "When are you going home? Are you seeing family?"

"I guess you could say that." Cara turned to Samira and pulled her headscarf further over her forehead, shielding her eyes from the sun. "Dan called me." She smiled at the thought of seeing him again. "He invited me for his birthday."

"Oh Cara, that's wonderful." Samira took her arm and squeezed it. "Why didn't you tell me sooner? You must be over the moon."

She pulled Cara along towards the next stall. "Does that change things with your... friend, Billie?"

Cara shrugged. "I doubt it. I mean, I was the one who left. She probably moved on a long time ago."

"What if she hasn't?" Samira looked at her intently.

"I don't know. I'm finally back in touch with Dan, and I don't want to do anything to ruin it again. Contacting Billie wouldn't be a smart thing to do, if I want things to be the same again between Dan and me."

Cara pointed at a crate of large, ripe tomatoes, and held up four fingers to the salesman, who bagged them for her. "It doesn't mean I don't miss Billie, though. I think about her all the time." She let out a deep sigh. "I'm trying so hard to let go, Samira. I really am. But there's this empty space inside me that I can't seem to fill unless I'm thinking of her. And that's the only way for me to feel complete, however briefly."

Samira lowered her voice while she paid for the tomatoes. "You love her, don't you?"

"Yes, I do." There it was. She'd said it out loud.

"Then talk to Dan," Samira said. "Not right away, but when things have settled down. Tell him how you feel about Billie. Ask for his blessing and call her."

Cara shrugged. "But what if Dan gets angry? Or what if Billie wants nothing to do with me, after I left the way I did?" She paused. "What if she's seeing someone else?"

Samira shook her head and hooked her arm into Cara's. "Then you let her go. But not before you've put up a fight. If you're meant to be, the universe will find a way to bring you back together. And in the meantime, there's no harm in giving destiny a little hand."

Cara couldn't help but smile at that. Samira had such a refreshing view of life. "Okay, you're right. I should talk to Dan." She squeezed Samira's arm. "But first, I intend to give him the best birthday he's ever had. He asked me to cook dinner for him and his friends."

"Perfect." Samira steered them towards a row of bakeries behind the market stalls.

"In that case, you'll need more than just saffron. Come

on. Let's get you some delicacies to take home. And after that, you and I are going to treat ourselves to lunch."

62

"Are you sure this is a good idea?" Helen looked up from the kitchen table where she was changing Daisy's diaper.

Billie inspected herself in the reflection of the window. Her hair was draped around her shoulders, loose curls bouncing as she moved. "Why wouldn't it be?"

"Well, an ex is an ex for a reason, right? Isn't it awkward?"

Billie rolled her eyes. "Come on, Helen. I'm just trying to do the right thing here. Besides, I think it's nice of Dan to invite me to his birthday." She straightened the hem of her black dress, before slipping into her heels. "I'd like for us to be friends again. I had a great time with him and his girl-friend, and believe it or not, it feels like we can finally leave the past behind and move on."

Helen didn't seem convinced. "I don't get this whole 'friends with your exes' thing, but who am I to speak, right?" She shot Billie a sceptical look, gesturing to little Daisy.

"Not every ex is an asshole, Helen. In our case, the

asshole would be me anyway." Billie turned around, facing Helen. "How do I look?"

"You look beautiful," Helen said. "You always do." She grimaced as she threw Daisy's dirty diaper in the bin, before sitting down on the couch with her. "Why are you so dressed up anyway? Do you think there's a chance Cara might be there?"

Billie's heart rate shot up at the mention of Cara's name. "Of course not," she said. "Cara lives on the other side of the world, and Dan's not even speaking to her."

She took her phone out of her pocket and held it up for her sister to see. "But I did manage to get her number. I called her mum at the British Embassy in Abu Dhabi. I remembered Cara telling me she worked there."

"Jesus, Billie." Helen rolled her eyes. "You called her mother?"

Billie nodded. "Yeah, she was nice." She looked from her phone screen to Helen and back. "I've had her number for a week now, and I've been meaning to call her, but I'm terrified." She stared down at the number and sighed. "What if she doesn't want to speak to me? She's probably moved on, and I don't want to mess up her new life."

Helen chuckled. "Come on, Billie. I'm sure she'll want to speak to you. And even if she doesn't, it might finally give you some closure. It's actually painful, how much you talk about her. In fact, I think you mention her name more than I mention Daisy's. And I've been told people are getting bored of my baby-talk."

Billie couldn't help but laugh. "Am I really that bad?" She pursed her lips, retrieving the number. Then she groaned and put the phone back on the table. "I can't do it."

Helen looked at her with annoyance, and stood up to put the now sleeping Daisy in her cot. On her way, she took

Billie's phone from the table and threw it in her lap. "For God's sake, Billie. Get in touch with that bloody woman already. I don't know what she's done to you, but you're literally pining for her, like in those old romance novels we had to read in college."

Billie laughed. "Okay, okay. I'll call her." She took a deep breath. "But not now. I'll call her in my own time."

"Good. Case closed." Helen sat back down and nodded towards the bottle of Champagne in the cooler on the kitchen counter, holding out her empty glass. "Pour me another one, will you? We need to celebrate before you go out. It's not every day you buy a house, after all."

Billie smiled and refilled both their glasses. The alcohol had started to loosen her up, and the nerves she'd felt about having dinner with a group of people she'd never met were slowly melting away. "You're right," she said with a smile. "Cheers to me and my new apartment."

63

Here she was again, in the place where her short-lived cooking career had begun. Cara smiled at the irony of the situation. She set up an extra folding table to hold all the serving plates in Dan's kitchen. People had started to arrive, so she poured prosecco into glasses and dropped a raspberry into each one. Then she turned on the deep fat fryer, put water on the boil in two deep pans and unpacked another three frying pans from the box she'd packed. There weren't nearly enough utensils to cook for a large group of people, so she had brought those along too. Everything was prepared. The starters were in the fridge, the bread was in the oven, the soup was simmering on the stove, and the swordfish was marinated, ready to be seared. She would finish off the saffron risotto, and the gnocchi with wild mushrooms and truffle, just before serving.

Cara took a peek into the living room. It looked great, just like an Italian pop-up restaurant. Cara and Dan had moved all the furniture upstairs the night before and decorated the tables, borrowed from neighbours and friends. They were covered with red and white checked tablecloths, candles in empty wine bottles, and ivy that Dan had stolen from a fence they'd passed on the way back from the market. They had even decorated the ceiling with ivy and fairy lights, creating an intimate atmosphere in the usually uninviting space. The life-sized pony with the creepy grin stood next to the living room door, welcoming the guests. Everything had been just like it used to be between Dan and Cara, and as far as she could tell, there was no bad blood.

"Have you got more aspirin?" Dan asked, leaning against the wall. He rubbed his temples. "I'm still not over those three bottles of wine we had last night."

Cara threw him a box and poured a glass of water. "You'll feel even worse tomorrow, but it will be worth it, birthday boy."

"Thanks." He grinned and gestured to the living room. "I think I'll keep the restaurant. I like it. Maybe I'll teach myself how to cook, make a bit of money on the side. I can be a good host too, you know. I even took the time to do a table plan while you were sleeping this morning, and I made name cards. I think you'll find the set-up interesting."

Cara laughed. "That's impressive. Take these, good host," she said, handing him the tray with Champagne flutes. "And try not to break them."

"Wow. Fancy." Dan arched a teasing eyebrow. "I take it your dad pays you well, then? Are you really going to stay there for another year?"

The doorbell rang, and Dan ran off before Cara had the chance to answer. "That's my date," he shouted. "Be nice to her." He came back and stuck his head around the corner. "Oh, and try not to sleep with her, will you?"

Cara rolled her eyes. "Haha. Very funny. Stop rubbing it in, Dan."

Cara smiled at the laughter coming from the living area.

The first people had just arrived, and there seemed to be a good vibe tonight. She only knew a couple of Dan's friends. He wasn't a very sociable person, but his fellow artists from a group he had joined, called 'The Crew,' seemed like a lovely bunch.

"Hey. You must be Cara." Dan's new girlfriend, an extravagant-looking lady in a leopard printed leotard with bright pink hair, held out her hand to greet Cara.

"Hey." Cara shook her hand, surprised by her appearance. She was at least fifteen years older than Dan was, but she had a youthful enthusiasm about her that was both refreshing and captivating. "Great to meet you, Dynamo. I've heard a lot about you." Dynamo took a glass and helped herself to Champagne.

"Likewise. I'm sorry I couldn't help you guys last night. I was at my mother's in Scotland." She gazed over the pans on the kitchen table. "But I see you've managed just fine." She stuck a finger in the mushroom truffle paste and put it in her mouth. "Mmm, this is good. Can't wait to taste everything. Do you want some help?"

Cara shrugged. "Sure. If you don't mind. I've been dying to meet you. We can get to know each other while you help me out."

Dynamo smiled, her red lips almost stretching from ear to ear. She pointed to Cara's chef's jacket. "Have you got another one of those?" She giggled. "I've always wanted to wear one. There's just something about uniforms, don't you think?"

Cara laughed. "Yeah, there's another one in the box. Help yourself."

After Dynamo had studied her reflection in the kitchen window and decided to wear the chef's jacket closed with her belt over it, they went to work, dividing the antipasti over long serving trays. Dynamo worked fast and methodical and chatted away while they worked.

"I'm just going to check if they need more drinks in there," Cara said, reaching for the crate with wine bottles. "I'll be right back."

"No!" Dynamo shook her head and picked up two bottles of white wine. "I'll do it. Why don't you just concentrate on the food, huh?"

"Okay." Cara chuckled at her persistence. "I'll bring the bread out then."

Dynamo jumped back again. "No, leave it. Dan wants to wait till everyone's here."

Cara frowned. "But everyone is here. And besides, it's only bread. Since when does Dan care about timing?"

Dynamo shot her a warning look. "Just trust me, okay? It's Dan's night, and it's important to him that everything runs smoothly."

Cara rolled her eyes, but she managed to keep her opinions to herself. "Okay, Dynamo. You're the lady of the house." *Control freak.*

Half an hour later, she was still lingering in the kitchen, sipping on a gin and tonic. She was annoyed with Dynamo's insistence to wait with the food, and if she weren't Dan's girlfriend, she would have shoved the bread up her ass.

64

"Hey, Dan. Congratulations." Billie kissed Dan on both cheeks and looked around the table. The party seemed to be in full swing already. "I'm sorry, am I late? I thought you said eight o'clock."

Dan shook his head. "I might have changed the time and forgotten to let you know. My bad." He gave her an apologetic look. "Birthday stress, nothing personal. I don't normally host parties and..."

"No, don't apologize," Billie said. "It's your night. Please, just enjoy it." She looked over at the empty seat next to Dynamo, who was waving at her. "Do you mind if I go and sit next to your girlfriend?"

"Please do." Dan gestured towards the table. "Help yourself to a drink. The starters will be out soon; I'll just go and check in the kitchen."

"Come over here, girl. Let me pour you some Champagne." Dynamo, who had gone all out for the night looking every bit the artist that she was, pulled out a chair. Billie sat down, grateful to have a somewhat familiar face to talk to.

"Wow, did you do all this?" she asked, looking around the room. "It doesn't seem like Dan, to go to all this trouble."

Dynamo winked and handed her a glass. "I helped. But Dan did most of it with a friend. They were up all night. It looks good, don't you think?" She shifted in her chair and looked Billie up and down. "Speaking of which, you look nice too, Billie. Good choice of dress for tonight."

"Thanks." Billie smiled. "Although I'm afraid I'll fade into the background next to you. I love your outfit." She let her fingers run over the velvet fabric of Dynamo's leotard.

"I made it myself," Dynamo said with a proud smile. "So, how are things with you? Anything exciting happening? How's your love life?"

Billie shifted in her chair. She still wasn't comfortable with the topic. "Non-existent." She shrugged. "It's no different from three weeks ago when we spoke in the pub, and I'm not looking either." This was a weird conversation to be having. Especially with Dan's new girlfriend, who was dressed like an eighties pop star.

"Good. That's good," Dynamo said.

Good? Billie downed her drink in one go, almost choking on the raspberry. "Listen, Dynamo." She was starting to feel less and less comfortable as their conversation carried on. "I don't know what you think I'm doing here, but if you have this idea that I'm after Dan, you're wrong. And if you'd rather not have me here, I can go..."

"Nonsense." Dynamo held Billie down by the shoulder, making sure there was no way she could escape. "I didn't mean to make you feel uncomfortable. Just making small talk, that's all." She picked up the bottle and refilled Billie's glass. "I know you're not after Dan, and even if you were, I'm very comfortable in my relationship with him, so that's not something I worry about. We love each other, Dan and I.

We're spiritually connected." She put a hand on her heart and batted her long, fake, diamante studded eyelashes.

"I know that," Billie said, unsure of what spiritually connected meant. She accepted the full glass with an unsteady hand. "And I'm happy for you both. Really, I am."

"Good." Dynamo held up her glass. "Then let's raise a toast. To love. The only thing worth living for."

65

"Okay, you can bring in the food in ten minutes." Dynamo smiled through gritted teeth. "Sorry that it took so long."

Cara frowned, resting a hand on her hip. "Are you sure I'm allowed out of the kitchen now, your ladyship?"

"Come on, Cara. Don't be mad." Dynamo pointed to the trays. "I just need to say hello to someone, but I can come back later to help you with those."

"No, I'm good, thanks." Cara shook her head. "Why don't you sit down with Dan and enjoy dinner? I'll take care of the rest." Cara was just about done with Dynamo's interference by now. *Let it go. You have to try to get along with her. Don't ruin it with Dan again.*

Finally, she walked into the living room with three trays, balancing one on her arm. It wasn't an easy task, but she'd had enough practice to manage.

"Please, can we have applause for Chef Cara, people!" Dan shouted.

His friends clapped and cheered. Cara smiled at the crowd, when her eye caught a glimpse of a blonde woman, sitting next to Dynamo. Her mouth fell open when the woman turned her way, seemingly just as surprised as she was. Cara looked down at the trays she was carrying. They threatened to fall on the floor. One of Dan's friends stood up and took them off her, but she didn't even notice her empty hands and the fact that she was still standing in front of the table with her arms spread out.

"What?" Her mouth moved as she tried to speak, but no sound came out. There, at the table, was Billie. Billie smiled at Cara, nervously fiddling with the stem of her glass. She was even more beautiful than Cara remembered. Her blonde hair fell over her shoulders in wavy locks, framing her high cheekbones. She was wearing a sleeveless black dress, belted around the waist, showing off her toned arms and shoulders.

Cara couldn't breathe. She was trying to decide whether to run to Billie or run away, when Dan stood up and took her hand.

"I've put you next to Billie, if that's okay. I believe you two have met before," he joked, leading her towards her seat. Then Dan turned back to the conversation with his friend, ignoring Cara's panic. The party threw themselves onto the starters, and nobody seemed to notice the tension between the two women.

Billie finally patted the seat next to her. "Hey," she said softly. "Sit down; I won't bite."

Cara couldn't speak, so she only nodded. Her heart was pounding, and all reason had abandoned her. She was lost for words. "Billie," she whispered, sitting down beside her.

Billie put a hand on her knee. Her cheeks were bright red, her eyes wide. "I didn't mean to startle you. I'm just as surprised as you are." She gestured to Dan. "He invited me over tonight. I thought it would be a good way to make amends." She giggled nervously. "I suppose Dan had other plans."

Cara glanced over at Dan, who winked at her before refilling his guests' glasses. She opened her mouth to speak but got distracted by Billie's blue eyes. It had been a long time since she had indulged in them. They were focused on her, waiting for her to say something.

"I..." Cara lifted her glass with trembling hands and took a long drink of her wine. She could feel her eyes stinging and tried her hardest not to burst into tears at the table. Dan's sweet and selfless act and Billie's unexpected presence was almost too much to take in. "I've missed you," she whispered. "Oh God. I've missed you so much, Billie."

Relief spread over Billie's face, resulting in a huge smile. A tear trickled down her cheek. "I've missed you too, Cara. It's been hard without you. I've thought about you every single day since you left."

Billie paused. "Listen, I know you've moved away, and you've probably moved on too. But even if I just get to see you tonight, that's enough for me. We never said goodbye, and I never got the chance to..." She took a deep breath and lowered her voice. "Well... I never got the chance to tell you that I loved you. I still do, Cara. If that scares you, I apologize. I just want you to know. It's important to me that you know."

Cara's hand reached out for Billie's under the table, and she blinked away the tears. The touch of Billie's hand was warm and soft, just like she remembered. She squeezed it gently. "I love you too." Her voice was shaky.

She lowered her gaze to Billie's mouth. It was the most beautiful mouth she had ever kissed. The naturally plump and peach coloured lips drew her towards them, and there was nothing she could do to stop herself. Billie leaned in too, and they kissed, their lips barely touching. They both shivered at the contact. A jolt of electricity spread throughout Cara's body, and she had to stop herself from taking it any further. Her hand was still holding Billie's. Her other hand gravitated towards Billie's face, cupping her cheek, and she could feel Billie's mouth pulling into a smile against hers.

When Cara pulled back, there was silence at the table. Thirteen pairs of eyes stared at them with intense curiosity. Cara and Billie looked at each other and then at the other dinner guests, letting out a nervous giggle. "I'm sorry," Cara mumbled, her face flushed. "I didn't mean to do that at the table." She tried to steady her breathing while she unbuttoned the black chef's jacket. Finally collecting herself, she let out a deep sigh and smiled, unsure of what to do next.

Dan stood up and came to the rescue. He was grinning from ear to ear. "Billie, why don't you help Cara with the food tonight? She looks like she could do with some help." He laughed and turned to his friends. "Excuse me, lovely bunch. I'll go and get some more wine."

Billie smiled in relief. "Come on, let's go into the kitchen," she said, taking Cara's hand as she stood up.

Cara followed her, barely able to walk. "I can't believe you're here," she whispered, as soon as they'd turned the corner.

"And I can't believe you came," Billie said, reaching for the collar of Cara's jacket. She seemed shy, and that was a first. "I've thought about you every single day and I..."

"I'm so sorry I left you," Cara interrupted her. "I thought I was doing the right thing, but you were right. I was running away, and it was stupid." She looked down at Billie and put her arms around her, pulling her into a tight embrace. "I was running away from the best thing that ever happened to me, and I've never regretted anything more. You're..." She closed her eyes, inhaling the scent of Billie's shampoo. "...You're here. God, I've missed you so much."

Billie looked up at her through hazy eyes. "Show me how much you've missed me."

Cara smiled. She pushed Billie against the wall and kissed her hard. For a moment, she wasn't sure if she would survive the impact their kiss had on her. Her stomach was doing summersaults, her legs were going limp, and she felt dizzy with desire and an urgent need for more. Billie moaned when their tongues met. She closed her eyes and sank deep into the kiss. Cara had her hands in Billie's hair. She felt the soft locks run through her fingers before she moved them down to Billie's neck, taking a possessive hold of her. Billie moved a hand underneath Cara's shirt and moaned when they deepened their kiss.

"Maybe we should wait," Cara mumbled, shivering at the sensation of Billie's nails, scraping down her back. "Someone might come in."

Billie dropped her hands and nodded, breathing fast. "You're right." She looked around the kitchen, flustered. "Anyway, aren't you supposed to cook?"

Cara chuckled and kissed her again. "Yes. I almost forgot about that," she whispered against Billie's mouth. "Will you stay here and help me?"

When everyone dug into the main course that night, Cara stood up and cleared her throat. Dan shook his head, trying to stop her, but Cara had made up her mind. She was going to thank him, whether he wanted her to or not.

"I'd like to propose a toast," she said. "To Dan, our birthday boy and my very best friend. Dan, I love you."

Dan's expression softened. "I love you too, Cara," He said in a thin voice.

Tears trickled down from the corners of Cara's eyes. She wiped them away with the sleeve of her jacket and composed herself before she looked around the table. "I know tonight is not about me, so I'm not going to bore you all with our painful history. Some of you might have an idea of what happened if you've been to see Dan's last performance." She couldn't help but chuckle at the laughter coming from several of Dan's friends.

"But what Dan did for me tonight..." She hesitated and looked at Dan. "What you did for us tonight, for Billie and me, was the most selfless thing anyone could ever do." She swallowed hard. "I don't deserve to be your best friend. I don't even deserve to be your friend. But I need you to know that I love you like family and that I hope to be in your life forever."

She raised her glass higher. "Dan, this is to you, and to another great year ahead, with your amazing girlfriend Dynamo." Cara turned her attention to Dynamo. "I'm glad to know you were playing me in there." She pointed to the kitchen. "Because I almost killed you tonight." Dynamo laughed and winked at her, and Cara paused to look at Dan. "May this year be filled with love and kindness and all that you wish for. I know I will do everything in my power to make it happen for you."

"To Dan," The crowd cheered.

Dan himself was in tears now. He walked over to Cara and hugged her. "Look what you made me do, Cara. Now I'm crying in front of my friends." He pulled her closer and gave her a quick squeeze before he let go. They both laughed. "It's good to have you around again," he said. Then he looked at Billie. "And you, Billie. Now get the hell back into the kitchen because I want my birthday dessert."

66

"Are you staying the night?" Cara whispered, even though she didn't have to worry about keeping their conversation private. The last people left at the table were drunk and rowdy. Some of Dan's friends were singing along to the music; others were engrossed in deep conversation. Dan was grinning and looked like he couldn't have been happier if he'd won the lottery. Dynamo was sitting on his lap, stroking his hair.

"If you want me to." Billie blushed. "Are you sleeping in your old room?"

Cara nodded and shot Billie a flirty smile. "Come on. They won't even notice that we're gone." She took Billie's hand and led her up the stairs towards the door with graffiti sprayed over it. 'This is not a toilet!'

"Do you remember the first time I walked in here?" Billie pushed open the door and chuckled. "You were rude."

Cara laughed. "Yeah. I guess I was. But you were intrusive." She locked the door behind them and switched on the light on her nightstand, leaving them in comfortable silence, with only the faint music from downstairs playing in the background.

"Your room has changed," Billie remarked with an amused smirk.

The walls had been painted off-white, and there was a brand-new carpet on the floor. A new white wardrobe and a matching chest of drawers were placed against the side wall, the latter underneath two hideous paintings of horses. The bedsheets and pillowcases had horses printed on them too, matching the pillow on a chair next to the door. All in all, it looked like a nineties teenage girl's bedroom. They both laughed.

"Who would have thought we'd end up like this, huh?" Cara took a step forward, closing the distance between them.

"Not me." Billie sighed, looking up at Cara. There was a faint smile tugging at the corners of her mouth. "But now, I can't imagine it being any other way." She unfastened her belt, reached behind her and unzipped her dress without taking her eyes off Cara.

Cara reached out to touch Billie's face. She let her hands linger on her cheeks, then traced her neck down to her shoulders, sliding the straps down her arms. Her heart was pounding in her throat when the dress fell on the floor. Billie was wearing a full lace, nude-coloured lingerie set that hugged her in all the right places. Her tan hadn't faded yet, and she still had the pale tan lines from the Pelican swimsuit she'd been wearing all season.

"You must be the most beautiful woman in the world," Cara whispered.

Billie smiled as she took off Cara's chefs' jacket, leaving her in a white T-shirt. "You're beautiful," she said, running a hand through Cara's hair. "Take them off." She nodded towards Cara's clothes.

Cara's hands were trembling when she took off her T-shirt, her sports bra, and her jeans. She shivered at her sudden nakedness. "I'm cold." She bit her lip and took Billie's hand, leading her to the bed. "I'm afraid you might have to warm me up."

Billie giggled. She pushed Cara down on the mattress and lowered herself on top of her. They both sighed at the first contact when their bodies came together. Billie gave Cara a teasing smile as she traced a hand along the side of Cara's torso, resting her thumb in the dip of her hipbone. "I'd be more than happy to." She kissed Cara's temple and ear, and the hairline in her neck, making Cara's chest rise in anticipation. "Are you starting to feel warmer yet?" she whispered. She continued the trail of kisses down to Cara's breasts, taking a hard nipple into her mouth.

"Uhuh." Cara moaned while lowering a hand in between them. She reached between Billie's legs and stroked the soft skin of her inner thigh. She could feel Billie's muscles tense as she traced a finger up towards her panties. Billie let out a heated breath, gazing down at her with a look of desire and hunger in her eyes. Cara lifted the edge of Billie's panties and moved her hand underneath it, exploring her aroused centre.

"Oh God, yes!" Billie cried when Cara trailed a lazy finger over her clit, rubbing it softly. She moved her own hand in between them, inside Cara's boxers. Cara closed her eyes and let out a throaty groan when Billie teased her opening, drawing her own wetness up and around her clit. "You're so wet," Billie whispered, before sinking a finger deep inside of her.

Cara moaned, arching her back. She pulled Billie's face

closer by her hair, and watched her gasp in delight when she entered her too. "You feel so good," She said in a hoarse voice. Her hips moved to meet Billie's thrusts over, and over again until they were both close.

Billie circled her hips, slow and seductive. Their eyes locked when their breathing became more ragged and their movements faster. "Kiss me," Billie begged, lowering her face.

Cara took hold of her neck and pulled her against her mouth, fuelled by need. She felt Billie shaking when she kissed her deeply, and her own core tightened as a rush of heat spread through her lower body, making her toes curl. She pushed the palm of her hand up against Billie's centre. "Yes?" Cara whispered against her mouth.

Billie nodded. "Yes." She raised her head and exploded with a loud cry, moving into Cara with her full body weight.

Cara bucked underneath her and held on tight when they tensed up and rode out the release together. She should feel Billie's rapid heartbeat slowing down as they lay there in silence, holding each other. Billie's head was buried in Cara's neck, shivering when Cara stroked her back.

Billie lifted her head and sighed, looking blissfully happy. "I love you, Cara."

She smiled and tucked a lock of blonde hair behind Billie's ear. Her eyes were dimmed with tears, and her voice choked with emotion. "I love you too."

EPILOGUE

The Royal Palace was a brand-new ship. Almost twice as big as the Pelican, it was one of the largest cruise ships ever built, and that had attracted quite some press on the day of its first departure.

Cara inhaled the scent of new carpets and furniture as she and Billie followed Arnie through the spacious corridors over a red velvet walkway. The ship was still empty, of guests, silently waiting for its first world trip, but there were plenty of staff getting ready for the ship's maiden voyage. Immaculately dressed waiters were stacking up Champagne glasses on long tables by the six entrances, while the styling team took care of the lush flower arrangements.

Billie took Cara's hand and squeezed it. "Nervous about your first shift?" she asked.

Cara laughed. "Nervous would be an understatement. I mean, the pressure was on at the Pelican, but this is a whole different ballgame." She looked around, amazed by how much preparation went into the departure. "But we've practiced the menus for three full days, so I'm hoping I'll be fine."

"Well, you're a chef de partie now, so you'd better have your A-game on." Billie winked.

"Thanks for that. Not helping." Cara laughed. "How was your first team meeting?"

"It was overwhelming." Billie pointed towards the Grand Theatre. "There were sixty people in there, all waiting for me to speak. I could hardly get the words out." She shook her head. "My team leaders are great though, so I have no doubt it's all going to be fine."

They passed an Italian restaurant, an Asian buffet restaurant, and finally Tahdig, the Middle Eastern à la carte restaurant where Cara would be working. They both peeked around the corner. The tables were already set, and the cosy, intimate dining room looked immaculate. It smelt of oranges, and Cara could only imagine what it would look like full of people with all the candles lit and music playing in the background.

"You'll have to bring me leftovers after your shifts," Billie said. I can't wait to taste your magic."

"We can have late-night dinners together." Cara giggled. "Now that we have the smallest dining table in the world in our cabin."

Billie nodded. "I know. Can you believe it? A table and two chairs!" She held up her hands and looked upwards as if thanking the stars. "But my favourite thing in our new room is that tiny window that actually opens. Imagine. We'll have daylight and fresh air. How's that for luxury?" They both laughed.

"Hey, do you want to say hi to Arnie?" Billie asked. He's supposed to be on the front deck." She sighed. "I can't believe I'm saying this, but I've missed him."

They took the stairs up to the fifteenth floor, where they passed a swimwear store, a hair salon and a library.

"Are you going to miss Margret?" Cara asked. She looked into the modern room filled with books and magazines.

"Sure I will," Billie said. "I promised her I'd keep in contact though." She sighed as she looked around, still amazed by the grandness of the ship. "But apart from her and a couple of people I've worked with for years, I won't miss much. I mean, look at this." She gestured to their surroundings. "It's pretty amazing, right?"

As they came to the end of the corridor, the automatic doors opened, revealing the outer deck. They were welcomed by the main pool, surrounded by an oasis of green. The pool, which was built to look like a natural spring, had six side arms that covered the full width of the ship, with sun loungers and parasols on the islands in between. The majority of the plants and trees were real, giving off a tropical scent that seemed misplaced on the English coast. The bars and kiosks were scattered in between the green on the islands, blending into the theme with their straw roofs. Staff were running around, stocking fridges and placing towels on the sun loungers and bottles of water into the coolers next to them.

"It's just crazy," Cara said, gazing over the deck for the second time that day. "Did you get the full tour this morning?"

Billie nodded. "Yeah. It lasted two hours." She laughed. "I've got a feeling I might need a map for the first week or so."

"Yo! Billie-Boo! Cara!" Arnie waved from behind one of the tiki bars.

Cara and Billie ran towards him, crossing the network of bridges and islands. He picked them both up and squeezed them, almost bruising them in the process. "My two favourite lesbians in the whole world. It's so good to see you guys again," he said with a big smile on his face.

Billie rolled her eyes and laughed. "You mean the only lesbians you know?"

Arnie shrugged. "Okay then. My two favourite people in the world. How's that?" He reached behind the bar and handed them both a bottle of coconut water. "You should try this, it's so good, and I have an endless supply." Then he pulled himself up on the bar and sat wide-legged, facing them. "It's been too long, guys. Why didn't you call me?"

Billie leaned into him and patted his knee. "I'm sorry Arnie. We've been busy." She looked at Cara and winked.

"Busy with what?" Arnie arched an eyebrow. "Whatever it was, I doubt there were any clothes involved."

"Actually, we moved in together," Billie said, putting an arm around Cara. "I bought an apartment last year, and we've been decorating it. I didn't want to do anything about it at first, but Cara convinced me, so we've been painting, and we even put a new floor in so it will look nice for when we get back. In the meantime, we'll have a tenant in there."

Now it was Arnie's turn to laugh. "You two moved in together? You guys just got straight to the point, didn't you? No messing about."

Cara shrugged. "Yeah well, I needed a place to stay after we came back from Riyadh, and since we've practically been living together since we met..." She grinned. "Billie came with me to Riyadh. We spent two months there, while I finished off the research for my father."

Arnie looked from Billie to Cara and back, unable to hide his surprise. "So, you stayed with Cara and her dad?"

Billie nodded. "Uhuh. I didn't work though. Spent two wonderful months by the pool doing absolutely nothing, apart from the odd game of table tennis with the neighbours' kids. Oh, and I ate a lot. The food there is mouth-wateringly good." She patted her belly. "After that, we went back to the UK and moved into my apartment in Luton." She crossed her arms and smiled. "So what have you been up to, Arnie?"

Arnie shrugged and cast her an amused smirk. "I didn't move to the other side of the world, buy property or pour myself into a serious relationship, if that's what you're asking. But I did win a spaghetti-eating competition." He grinned, beaming with pride. "And that counts for something, right?"

"That is indeed quite an achievement," Cara said. "And I see you picked your bar staff wisely as always?" She nodded towards a girl who wore the same T-shirt as Arnie. She was dragging crates of beer behind her on a trolley. She was blonde and slim, with a generous cup size and big pouty lips.

Billie laughed. "Yup. That looks like Arnie's type, for sure."

Arnie jumped off the bar. "What can I say? I've got an eye for talent." He waved at the girl. "Hey, Angela. Let me do that for you." He turned around before he walked off. "I'm happy you both came to your senses. Let's catch up properly this week."

Cara took Billie's hand and grinned sheepishly when Billie's fingers entwined with hers. "I'm glad I came to my senses too," she said.

Billie turned to her and smiled. "Me too." She placed a kiss on Cara's temple. "Hey, do you want to see something cool?"

They took the stairs down to the third floor and turned a corner after they passed the information desk and the travel agents. "Where are we going?" Cara asked, following Billie through a narrow corridor.

Billie stopped in front of one of the doors and pointed to the sign. Cara read it out loud. "Billie Williams, Head of Entertainment." She gasped. "No way, you never told me you were getting an office."

"Maybe I wanted to impress you." Billie opened the door with a beaming smile. The modest space was styled in muted colours with modern furniture. There was a window behind the desk, facing the docks of Southampton. A small grey couch was placed against the back wall, underneath a row of hanging filing cabinets. In front of it was a swanky glass coffee table with a plant on top. There was also a minibar and a coffee machine.

"Fancy," Cara said, taking in the room.

"Welcome to my office." Billie walked over to her white desk and took a seat on top of it, crossing her bare legs. She was wearing a denim skirt, a white cotton shirt, and white trainers. All in all, she looked far from corporate.

Cara grinned as she let her eyes wander over Billie's legs. She closed the door behind them. "You look sexy as hell, sitting on that desk."

"Yeah?" Billie chuckled. "That's good because I think we're going to have a lot of fun on this desk."

Cara walked over to her and spread her legs apart, taking a stance in between them. She lifted Billie's chin, gazing into her eyes while tracing a finger down to Billie's throat towards her cleavage. "Let's not waste any time then."

AFTERWORD

I hope you've loved reading The Cruise as much as I've loved writing it. If you've enjoyed this book, would you consider rating it and reviewing it on www.amazon.com? Reviews are very important to authors and I'd be really grateful!

ACKNOWLEDGMENTS

A huge thank you to everyone who's given me insights on cruise life. I've loved all your stories and you made me want to join you on a cruise!

Also, thank you to my readers. Your support and enthusiasm will keep me going for many more books to follow. I love you all.

ABOUT THE AUTHOR

Lise Gold is an author of lesbian romance. Her romantic attitude, enthusiasm for travel and love for feel good stories form the heartland of her writing. Born in London to a Norwegian mother and English father, and growing up between the UK, Norway, Zambia and the Netherlands, she feels at home pretty much everywhere and has an unending curiosity for new destinations. She goes by 'write what you know' and is often found in exotic locations doing research or getting inspired for her next novel.

Working as a designer for fifteen years and singing semi-professionally, Lise has always been a creative at heart. Her novels are the result of a quest for a new passion after resigning from her design job in 2018.

When not writing from her kitchen table, Lise can be found cooking, at the gym or singing her heart out some-where, preferably country or blues. She lives in London with her dogs El Comandante and Bubba.

Sign up to her newsletter: www.lisegold.com

ALSO BY LISE GOLD

Lily's Fire

Beyond the Skyline

French Summer

Fireflies

Northern Lights

Southern Roots

Eastern Nights

Western Shores

Northern Vows

Living

The Scent of Rome

Blue

The Next Life

In The Mirror

Christmas In Heaven

Welcome to Paradise

After Sunset

Paradise Pride

Cupid Is A Cat

Members Only

Along The Mystic River

In Dreams

Chance Encounters

We only part to meet again.

— JOHN GAY